OTHERWORLD
CHALLENGER

JANE GODMAN

First Published in Great Britain 2016
By Mills & Boon, an imprint of HarperCollins*Publishers*
1 London Bridge Street, London, SE1 9GF

© 2015 Amanda Anders

ISBN: 978-0-263-92183-0

89-0916

Jane Godman writes in a variety of genres including paranormal, gothic and historical romance and erotic romantic suspense. She also enjoys the occasional foray into horror and thriller writing. Jane lives in England and loves to travel to European cities, which are steeped in history and romance—Venice, Dubrovnik and Vienna are among her favourites. A teacher, Jane is married to a lovely man and is mum to two grown-up children.

This book is dedicated to my family, who always support and encourage me… and never complain about the strange ideas I bounce off them!

Chapter 1

"I'll do it."

The words had the same effect on the assembled company as a volley of bullets fired into the ornate ceiling of the vast banquet hall. Every head turned in the direction of the man who had uttered them. Lounging back on two legs of his chair, his broad shoulders against the wall and his booted feet on the round meeting table, he returned their stares with his customary nonchalance and continued munching on an apple.

"You can't seriously be prepared to listen to *him*. He'd sell his grandmother to the imps if the price was right." The words burst from Vashti's lips before she could stop them.

"The Crown Princess Vashti is reminded of the Alliance's fundamental principle of respect for all species." The condemnatory voice of the clerk echoed around the room. "Moreover, all speakers must first be approved by Merlin Caledonius, Leader of the Council."

Vashti felt a blush of embarrassment turn the heat of rage already burning her cheeks a darker shade of red. It didn't help that *he* was openly smirking at her humiliation. "I withdraw my remark." She spoke the words stiffly.

"Thank you." Merlin Caledonius, or Cal as he preferred to be known, inclined his head in her direction before turning to address Jethro de Loix. "What will you do exactly?"

"Exactly what you want. Find the true King of the Faeries and bring him back here to challenge Moncoya for the crown."

A murmur of interest rippled around the table and Vashti smothered her derisive exclamation by turning it into a cough. Couldn't any of them see Jethro de Loix for the maverick he was? Even the way he was dressed flouted convention. Everyone else around the table respected the formality of the occasion. Not Jethro. His white-linen shirt was unbuttoned a little too far, the waistcoat he wore over it hung casually open. Those long, long legs were encased in a pair of well-worn black jeans and the battered boots that rested on the conference table looked like they had walked the length of Otherworld and back. Perhaps they had. With his overlong jet-black hair tied at the nape of his neck with a leather thong and his hawk-like profile he was too—her mind searched for a suitable adjective and could only come up with *swashbuckling*— for this solemn setting.

Jethro bit into the apple again, his teeth startlingly white against the red skin of the fruit.

Several hands were raised around the table and the clerk, a pompous little elf, noted their names in his record book. "Prince Tibor wishes to address the Council meeting."

The vampire prince rose, bowing his head slightly in Cal's direction. Vashti could never see Tibor without being struck by two things. His stunning physical beauty and the fact that she had never met anyone who looked less like a vampire. Stella, Cal's wife, had once remarked that he looked like a fashion model or a Scandinavian soccer player. Vashti, with her limited knowledge of the mortal realm, had no way of knowing what the comment meant, but she didn't think either option sounded vampire-like.

"Esteemed Council Leader, fellow Council members, our Alliance is a new and fragile one. We have taken the decision to offer our individual dynasties democracy. Our people will soon get to vote for who will lead them and represent them at this table in the future. It was a brave and noble act on our part." Heads nodded around the table. "We believe our dynasties will vote wisely…"

Do we? Vashti risked a glance around the table. Tibor might be secure in the vampire vote—his loyal followers were not about to overturn centuries of tradition—but there were others whose places at the table were not so secure. Anwyl, the wolf leader, fought a constant battle against Nevan, a ferociously ambitious alpha newcomer who sought to usurp his place as pack leader. And, of course, there was the reason they were all here today. The problem that united them all. *Daddy dearest.*

"…but there is one dynasty for which we all fear the outcome. If the faeries vote to confirm Moncoya's place as their leader, Otherworld will descend once more into chaos. My friends, I fear there will be no return to order next time."

"Garrick wishes to address the meeting."

The elf leader stood. "You paint a gloomy picture indeed, Prince. Yet did this Council not, at its first meeting, request that Merlin Caledonius issue a warrant for the arrest of Moncoya as a war criminal for acts of barbarity against his own people? There is still time to do that. Then, should he attempt to return and take his place as leader of the faeries, surely his reign would be short-lived? Not only would he face imprisonment, if he is found guilty it is likely he would be executed for his crimes. Even Moncoya's arrogance would not lead him to take such a step."

Cal cast an apologetic glance in Vashti's direction. He knew how hard it was for her to listen to accounts of her father's atrocities and maintain an outwardly impervious manner. "I am reluctant to take such a step at this stage. Although the battle for control of Otherworld drove Moncoya into hiding, it did not topple him from his throne. He is still the King of the Faeries and there are many who wish to see him return openly. If the faeries elect Moncoya as their leader, we will have to tread carefully. The fae population is one of the largest in Otherworld. We cannot risk alienating them by taking an inflammatory action against the leader they choose. *If* they choose him. Princess Vashti, perhaps you can aid this discussion by telling the Council the mood of your people?"

Cal had warned her in advance that he would ask her this question today. Rising, she was conscious of all eyes upon her. So why did the intense gaze of Jethro de Loix, who wasn't even part of this Council, bother her more than any other? "I wish I could give my fellow Alliance members a definitive answer to that question. Sadly, I cannot. If the faeries were asked to vote tomorrow, indications are there would be an even split with half voting for Moncoya—" she had schooled herself not to refer to him as "my father" in this setting "—and half evenly split between the other opposition parties."

Prince Tibor raised his hand. "The princess's words raise the real possibility of Moncoya taking his seat at this table in the near future."

The clerk gestured to Anwyl the Wolf. "I will not be part of an Alliance that includes Moncoya." Several heads around the table nodded in agreement.

So it begins. Moncoya's return would destroy all the good work they had done. Otherworld would descend once more into the constant battles that had threatened to tear it apart before the Alliance had been formed. Vashti met Cal's eyes briefly and she knew he was thinking the same thing. "Anwyl, the sentiments you express are the reason why it is so important for us to find the true heir to King Ivo, the faerie leader who was killed by Moncoya in the bloody coup through which he seized power. The current opposition parties, all well-meaning, do not offer the faerie race a viable alternative to Moncoya's strong rule. King Ivo was deeply loved by his people. If we can produce his heir, I believe that will sway their vote."

Anwyl, still on his feet, looked skeptical. "What proof do we have that this so-called heir even exists?"

"We have the word of the leader of the Dominion, the fourth choir of angels. We also know that the Goddesses of Fate summoned Princess Vashti's sister, Tanzi, to them at the palace of Gladsheim recently and spoke to her of the true heir. Our biggest problem lies in the fact that the identity of the heir has been so well hidden he himself is unaware of it. The goddesses told Tanzi that the answer lies on the Isle of Avalon."

Anwyl's noble features remained mistrustful. "The Goddesses of Fate delight in interfering."

The clerk cleared his throat in preparation for another

reminder about respect, but Cal spoke before he could intervene. "While that may be true, the goddesses are not able to lie. If we are to find the heir, someone must go to Avalon in search of him. It is a journey that is both perilous and unprecedented. We have only one offer to make the attempt. That offer has come from Jethro."

Everyone in the room knew Prince Tibor hated Jethro and had sworn to kill him for the perceived crime of stealing the vampire leader's human servant from him. Even so, the prince's words, when he turned to speak to the necromancer, were polite. "You would do this? Knowing the dangers, you would be prepared to go to Avalon in search of the faerie heir?"

Jethro's smile—the piratical one, the one Vashti loathed with every fiber of her being—dawned. "For the right price."

"And what is that price?" Cal's voice was razor-sharp. As the Council leader, he was scrupulously fair. He would offer no favors just because Jethro was a fellow necromancer and a close friend.

"One million mortal dollars."

The Council leaders were huddled in groups during lunch, but it was obvious there was only one topic of conversation. Would they be prepared to part with a million dollars to maintain their Alliance and rid Otherworld of Moncoya?

"Are you serious?" Cal asked Jethro as the two men took their plates of food out onto the terrace.

"I never joke about money."

"A million dollars is a hell of a lot of cash. It might not seem so much in the mortal realm these days, but to the Otherworld leaders, it represents the equivalent of a huge amount of money."

"It's a hell of a dangerous job." Jethro leaned against the stone balustrade and looked through the open full-length windows into the banquet hall. "I'll be turning down some much easier work to do this favor for you, Cal."

"I'm honored." Cal's voice dripped sarcasm.

Jethro turned back to face him, all trace of humor gone from his face. "My other work is hit-and-miss. This would be one big, guaranteed payday. I've been thinking for a while of giving up the mercenary lifestyle, but when the vampire prince has sworn to rip your throat out, you need a larger-than-average nest egg."

"I could try to intercede with Tibor on your behalf about this revenge thing he has going against you. I never could understand why his human servant switched allegiance and suddenly decided you were his master."

"No one could. Least of all me." Jethro felt his lips thin into a line at the memory. He glanced into the room. Tibor was talking to Vashti, leaning attentively toward her as the princess smiled up at him. Since Princess Tanzi had recently thrown the prince over, it looked like Tibor was about to make a move on her twin sister. Good luck to him. They were two of a kind. "But Dimitar left him and became my friend. That bastard killed him for that reason and no other. Now he wants to do the same to me. Let him try. Don't grovel to the blood-sucking son of a bitch on my behalf."

The good thing about Cal, Jethro decided, was he knew when to change the subject. It was the wisdom acquired through centuries of being the world's greatest sorcerer. When you were the man responsible for bringing King Arthur to the throne—the whole Camelot and Knights of the Round Table thing—you'd probably seen it all before. "Will you be going to the wedding?"

Jethro laughed. "I might have to. Just to prove to my-self that my old friend Lorcan Malone is going to get married at last. And to one of Moncoya's daughters." He looked back to where Vashti was standing alone now. Her physical beauty was undeniable…and breathtaking. That lily-pale, flawless complexion and short, light blond hair gave her a fragile appearance Jethro knew was deceptive. She was a lethal fighting machine, as vicious as Moncoya himself. And about as trustworthy. "Personally, I'll never understand the attraction."

"I've gotten to know Vashti since the battle that led to Moncoya's exile. Except in looks, she doesn't resemble Moncoya, and I have a great deal of respect for the de-votion she has shown to the faerie dynasty. It can't have been easy for her to have learned of Moncoya's crimes against his own people."

Jethro shrugged. It wasn't like Cal to be easily duped, but he wasn't going to waste time debating the matter. His only interest in Vashti lay in whether she could sway the other Council members against him. He knew she was about to give it her best shot. "Will they go for it?" He nodded toward the banquet hall where the dignitaries were resuming their places at the table.

Cal grinned. "You'll find out soon enough. Wait here. The clerk will call you in when we've reached a decision."

It was a long wait. Jethro paced the terrace outside the banquet hall a dozen times. What the hell was there to talk about? They were either going to pay him or they weren't. Obviously he hoped they would, but he wasn't going to lose sleep over it if the answer was no. He had a few al-ternative offers lined up, none of them particularly excit-ing. He didn't need the money for himself. He'd named the sum for the devilry of it, but now the challenge was out there and Jethro had never backed down from one of them. He needed this adrenaline rush...strange considering the entire vampire dynasty was looking to drain his blood. And there was the new threat of the mysterious but incredibly powerful sorcerer and trickster called Iago, who had sworn to kill Jethro, Cal, Lorcan and Stella.

I don't just need eyes in the back of my head, I need them on both sides, as well. Truth be told, I might already have more adrenaline than I can handle.

Jethro wondered if the Council was taking their time because they wanted to haggle over the price. He shook his head. If that was the case, they could find themselves another mercenary. *I'm not a cut-rate guy.*

The French doors opened and the little clerk appeared, interrupting his deliberations. "Merlin Caledonius requests your return to the Council table."

Jethro followed him inside and resumed his previous seat. A glance around the table told him nothing. The faces of the representatives were impassive.

Cal got straight to the point. "The Council has agreed in principle to your proposal to track down King Ivo's heir and bring him back here to stand against Moncoya. In return, the Council members have agreed to pay you the sum of one million mortal dollars."

Jethro cast a glance in Vashti's direction, expecting to see a sulky expression on those perfect features. Clearly she had lost in her attempt to thwart him. To his surprise, she returned his gaze steadily and with serenity. A faerie who was a good loser? He supposed there had to be a first time for everything. He turned his attention back to Cal, who was still speaking.

"We do, however, have one condition."

Jethro's brows snapped together. "A condition?"

Cal nodded. "If we are to invest such a huge sum in

this venture, we must be absolutely sure we have the right man at the end of it."

Jethro laughed as his understanding of the words dawned. "I see. You think I might lie low for a month and then present you with an impostor after claiming to have been on a long, tortuous journey?"

Garrick, ever the diplomat, coughed. "You can see how it might be a possibility."

Jethro grinned appreciatively. "It hadn't occurred to me, but it's a great idea. Who thought of it?" He raised a brow, looking directly at Vashti. She returned his gaze without flinching.

"I did." Her voice was icy.

"You're in the wrong job, Princess. With a mind as devious as that, you should be planning bank heists or conning old ladies out of their savings." He turned to Cal. "So what is your condition?"

"The Council wishes to send an observer to accompany you on your mission. Our representative will ensure that the person you bring back to us really is the heir to the faerie crown."

"Not a chance in hell." Jethro felt his facial muscles stiffen.

"Then we don't have a deal." The implacable note in Cal's voice left Jethro in no doubt. Negotiating about this condition of theirs wasn't going to be an option.

He decided to try anyway. "You couldn't send anyone with me who would have the physical strength to keep up with me on a mission of this sort. Worse than that, I'd end up as a nursemaid to your observer in the middle of a fight. And there will inevitably be fights...particularly if Moncoya finds out what I'm doing."

"We've thought of that. Our chosen observer will have

both the strength and skill to keep pace with you and to fight alongside you if necessary."

A million dollars. He could put up with a wolf or an elf on his heels for that sort of cash, couldn't he? Hell, he could probably even cope with a vampire. It would be an incentive to get the job done faster. "Okay, I'll accept your condition."

There was a collective sigh of relief around the table. Cal shuffled his papers, signaling the end of the meeting. "Very well. I will leave you to make the necessary arrangements with Princess Vashti."

"Princess Vashti?" What did she have to do with any of this?

The sidhe ring of fire in Vashti's eyes blazed bright, making the irises appear bluer and icier than ever. There was triumph in their depths; a fact that triggered an uneasy feeling deep in Jethro's chest. It was his early warning system, a signal that something wasn't right. His instincts were usually reliable and it seemed they hadn't failed him on this occasion.

Vashti smiled sweetly. "I am the Council's observer."

Chapter 2

"You could at least stop sulking long enough to pretend to be happy for your friend." Vashti's murmured words earned her a look of intense dislike from Jethro. She bit back a smile and turned to watch the ceremony.

Vashti still found it incredible that Tanzi—her sister had abandoned the title "princess"—was prepared to give up her royal lifestyle and live here on the remote Isle of Spae. She thought back to the days of Moncoya's rule, prior to the battle that had sent him into hiding. It was hard to believe only months had passed.

Before their father's exile, Vashti and Tanzi had lived a privileged lifestyle as befitted the daughters of the faerie king. Tanzi, in particular, had embraced her celebrity status. She had been Otherworld's darling fashion icon, unable to step foot outside her door without being photographed from every angle. Not a day had gone by without some speculation about her clothing, hairstyle or potential marriage partner. Vashti had received similar treatment, although in her case, because she didn't court attention, it had been to a lesser degree.

Of course, there had been another side to their lives. They were Moncoya's daughters, Moncoya's weapons. He had trained them to fight and trained them well. Enja, the mother they never knew—the mother Moncoya had murdered when she'd tried to leave him—had been a Valkyrie. Moncoya's obsession with warrior women had led him to have his daughters trained by Valkyrie fighters. Vashti and Tanzi were deadly killing machines and Moncoya had used them to intimidate his enemies. *We knew no better.* Then.

Even though they were twins, they had not been close as they grew up. Looking back, Vashti believed now that Moncoya had deliberately discouraged them from caring too deeply for each other. Divide and rule. That had been his policy toward his daughters as well as his enemies. He had instilled in them a belief that they were above mortal emotion. It was only when he had recently tried to force Tanzi into marriage with the devil that she began to question her own ability to feel. Lorcan Malone, the man she had run to, to escape her father's plans, had taught her how to love.

"If I can do it, so can you," Tanzi reasoned.

Vashti remained unconvinced. But one good thing had come out of that whole escapade. They had finally discovered the closeness other siblings shared. Even more than that. They had found they were able to communicate telepathically in the way that was unique to faerie twins.

Vashti was struggling to reconcile *this* Tanzi with the one she had grown up with. Her sister stood at the water's edge, her hand clasped in Lorcan's, while Ailie, the island elder, spoke the words of the simple ceremony. Tanzi's feet were bare and she wore a plain, white shift dress. Fresh flowers had been woven into the bright gold curls of her hair. Lorcan wore rolled-up jeans and a fisherman's sweater, and his feet were also bare. The waves lapped at their toes as they spoke their vows. Even Vashti, who found the emotions of others so difficult to read, could sense their love for each other. Next to Vashti, Stella, Cal's wife, sobbed constantly into her handkerchief, much to the amusement of her husband, who cradled her head against his chest.

"That was the most beautiful thing I've ever seen," Stella said when the ceremony ended.

"But it made you cry." Confused, Vashti fell into step beside her.

The villagers hoisted Tanzi and Lorcan onto their shoulders and carried them in a parade along the path back to the town square where a celebration feast was to be held. The guests followed the laughing, chattering group at a more sedate pace.

Stella caught hold of Vashti's hand. "These are happy tears. Do you remember when we first met?"

"Yes. I wanted to kill you."

Stella laughed. "I can always count on you to be brutally honest. We've come a long way." Stella nodded to where Lorcan and Tanzi reached across from their respective perches on the villagers' shoulders and, laughing, managed to grasp each other's hand. "I want what Tanzi has for you, Vashti. I want you to feel it all, too. One day, I want to cry at your wedding."

Vashti felt a frown furrow her brow. "You have some strange ambitions, Stella."

Stella patted the slight swell of her stomach. "It must be the pregnancy hormones. Will you promise me something?"

"If I can." Vashti was wary of promises. They usually imposed restraints she inevitably ended up breaking.

Stella glanced at the commanding rear view of Jethro, and Vashti followed her gaze. He walked alone, slightly to one side of the crowd. It seemed to be a metaphor for his life. He was known throughout Otherworld as a loner. The mysterious human necromancer whose loyalty was for sale to the highest bidder.

Her eyes took in the broad shoulders, set in a rigid line, then dipped lower to his trim waist. Something about the way those faded jeans clung to his shapely buttocks as he walked made Vashti's mouth go dry. It was a new sensation and one that brought a rush of blood to her face. She hoped Stella hadn't noticed it.

Jethro de Loix probably took it for granted that every woman was watching him. It wasn't just the perfect body that drew her eye. His face was too handsome for his own good. Luckily, he didn't have the sort of looks Vashti admired. He was way too overtly rugged and sure of his own masculinity. Vashti preferred a bit of finesse. *I mean, seriously, when was the last time he used a razor?* Not for a few days, judging by all that designer stubble. Nevertheless, up close, it was hard to stop watching him. He was like a work of art. As if a masterful hand had decided to create a perfect image of manliness and, once finished, had stepped back as if to say, "Soak it up, guys. This can't be beaten."

"Be careful on this mission. Jethro won't back down from a challenge."

The smile that touched Vashti's lips was grim. "Good, because nor will I."

The Spae knew how to celebrate. There was delicious food, home-brewed beer, singing and dancing, with the wedding festivities continuing long into the night. Vashti's initial attempts to avoid being flung wildly around in intricate whirling dances she didn't understand had proved futile and her hand was claimed repeatedly by the younger men of the village. After her annoyance gave way to resignation, she started to find the experience quite exhilarating. But that might have something to do with the effects of the beer.

"Aren't you the belle of the ball?" Lorcan, intervening before she could be thrown from one partner to another—the prevailing etiquette on the village green that served as a dance floor—caught hold of her hands. "I thought it was time we danced together. After all, we're family now."

The words jolted Vashti. For a long time her family had consisted of Tanzi and Moncoya. Recently her feelings toward both had undergone a dramatic change. Now she had a brother-in-law and Tanzi was pregnant, so she would soon have a nephew. She should probably try to say something welcoming to Lorcan. Her brow furrowed with the effort of trying to come up with the right words.

"You look quite ferocious. Have I done something to upset you? Other than marry your sister?" Lorcan slowed the steps of the dance so they could converse.

Vashti shook her head. "I'm glad she has found someone to love." She took a deep breath. May as well get the apology out of the way. "And I think you will care for her." She hoped he realized that was as close as she got to groveling.

He grinned. "I certainly intend to. Can we declare a truce between us? For Tanzi's sake?"

It was easy to see why Tanzi had fallen for him. That smile was breathtaking and his charm was legendary. The surprise was that Lorcan was prepared to settle down with one woman. Until now the rumor had been that he was impossible to tame. Aware there was a suspicion of curtness about her nod, Vashti tried to be conciliatory. She should try to put the past behind her. The battle for Otherworld had changed old allegiances and the Alliance was about forging a new future. "I see no reason why we cannot be friends."

To her horror, Lorcan caught her up in a hug and kissed her cheek. Affection, even toward those closest to her, was something Vashti found profoundly uncomfortable. She broke free of the embrace as quickly as she could, mumbling an excuse about needing to get a drink. In reality, the last thing she wanted was any more of the heady brew that tasted of sour apples.

When she reached the long table that held the barrels of beer, she snatched up one of the lanterns placed on its wooden surface and wandered a few hundred yards along the path to a point overlooking the bay. No one would miss her and a bit of solitude was exactly what she needed.

Yet when she reached the curve in the path, a tall figure was leaning against one of the trees, looking out over the still waters. Stifling an exclamation of annoyance as she recognized Jethro, Vashti prepared to stealthily make her way back. It was too late. He turned at the sound of approaching footsteps and, when he saw Vashti, his neutral expression changed to one of distaste.

"Coming back to the Isle of Spae must remind you of the last time you were here. The night you helped your father escape from justice."

He could not have said anything that would more effectively enrage her, and he knew it. There was no way Vashti could defend herself against the false allegation Jethro repeatedly insisted on making. How could she possibly prove Moncoya had tricked her into letting him go that night? Her anger kicked up a notch. And why should she have to defend herself to Jethro of all people?

"When do we set off in search of the challenger?" Two could play at this make-your-blood-boil game.

By the light of her lantern Vashti saw something shift in the midnight darkness of his eyes. Something dangerous. "Why did it have to be you?"

All around them the night was haunting in its perfection yet they remained inside their own little bubble of tension. Vashti had no idea what he meant. "Pardon?"

"Why do you have to be the one who comes with me? The Council could have sent anyone."

"My people have the most to lose if you find the challenger. I want to be absolutely sure you get it right."

"Ah, yes. I was forgetting. You will cease to be a princess if his claim to the throne is proved. That must sting."

His barb struck home. Vashti felt her own rage light up the night skies almost as effectively as the fireflies dancing around them. "You sanctimonious bastard."

Why must he persist in ascribing such hateful motives to her actions? It was the legacy of being Moncoya's daughter. Everyone assumed she was as evil as her father, yet somehow it hit harder when it came from Jethro. Or maybe he was prepared to be more honest than most and say exactly what he thought of her.

Jethro grinned, his anger dissipating as quickly as hers ignited. "Tomorrow." Vashti blinked at him, not comprehending this sudden shift in the conversation. "I am setting off in search of the challenger first thing in the morning."

"Okay." She turned away, but his next words brought her back to face him again.

"And, Princess, just so you know? Despite what you

think, you won't be able to keep up with me on this quest…and I have no intention of waiting around for you."

"Is that a challenge?" She flashed the words right back at him.

"You can count on it."

As the night wore on Vashti noticed the party had dwindled to a few hardy souls. A group, including herself and the bride and groom, sat in a circle, earnestly discussing the matter of the challenger for the faerie crown.

"Surely there are other topics of conversation you'd rather engage in on your wedding night?" Cal asked Lorcan.

"I can think of one or two." His friend grinned. "But Tanzi has a theory she wants to share."

Tanzi looked beautiful and happy as she sat between Lorcan's raised knees and leaned back against his chest. Vashti thought she had never seen her sister so relaxed.

"It may be nothing," Tanzi explained, "but when Ailie tried to gain an impression of the missing heir, she said he doesn't look like a faerie."

Known for their powers of healing and intuition, the Spae had been persecuted as witches in the mortal realm and driven to make their home here in Otherworld. They lived in isolation on this island, refusing to engage in the politics and fighting that drove the other dynasties.

Ailie, a woman with an open, pleasant face and a kindly manner, nodded her agreement with Tanzi's comment. "When Lorcan asked me if the true heir was still alive, I tried to discover what I could of him. Although I couldn't see him clearly, what came through was that he doesn't look like a faerie."

"It seems a strange thing to focus on." Jethro was

the only one of the group standing, his broad shoulders propped against the wall of one of the cottages.

Trust him to feel the need to look down on the rest of us. Vashti's earlier anger toward him might have dulled, but it was no less dangerous for having lost its edge.

"I've thought about it a lot since then," Ailie said. "The fact I gained that impression of him, above all others, makes me think he must look *nothing* like a faerie."

"Yet he is a pure-born faerie, so his looks must make him stand out among other faeries. And the Goddesses of Fate told me Lorcan already knows him." Tanzi spoke up again.

"Even though I actually have no clue who he is," Lorcan reminded everyone in a long-suffering voice. "What's this theory of yours, *Searc*?"

"Has anyone here ever met a pure-blood faerie who *doesn't* look like a faerie?" Tanzi's glance took in each of them in turn. The question stunned them all into silence.

Stella was the first to speak up. "You're right. Even I look a lot like a faerie and I'm not a pure-blood. My father was mortal. I'm a hybrid. The challenger is faerie royalty. He should definitely look like a faerie."

"He doesn't know who he is. He may not mix with faeries. Bloody hell—" Cal ran a hand through his hair, his expression increasingly incredulous. "He probably doesn't even know he *is* a faerie."

"Since I'm the one with the task of finding this mystery man, can we rewind a bit while someone gives me a refresher on the difference between faeries and sidhes?" Jethro's calm tone cut across the conversation.

Cal answered him. "All sidhes are faeries, but not all faeries are sidhes. The faeries are a dynasty, one of the largest in Otherworld, with many nationalities within it. The sidhes make up the majority of the faerie population.

Although Moncoya was elevated to the faerie gentry when he took the throne, he is a sidhe and his background is not royal…a fact that infuriates him. The challenger we seek does come from the original royal family.

"All faeries are endowed with incredible physical beauty, all have the power to enchant—known as faerie glamor—and all are able to coexist with humans. Like Tanzi and Vashti, sidhes have the ability to shape-shift, other faeries don't. Sidhes have a pronounced ring of fire around the iris of their eyes. Faeries have it, too, but their eyes are green, like Stella's, so the color makes the ring of fire appear fainter, possibly even nonexistent."

Vashti felt her lip curl. They were going to send a man who didn't understand something so fundamental about her people in search of this challenger? Her father was unlikely to have anything to fear. Which wasn't exactly a good thing for her people.

"But Lorcan and I do know someone who fits that description. Someone who doesn't look like a faerie." Tanzi turned her head to look up at her husband. "Aydan."

"Who is Aydan?" Jethro asked.

Lorcan turned his head to look up at him. "A prominent member of the resistance in Barcelona. We've worked together many times, fighting against Moncoya and his henchmen. Tanzi's right, he doesn't look like a faerie. He barely has a ring of fire around his irises. Aydan could pass for a mortal any day."

"You mentioned Aydan to me when I said I was losing my right-hand man now that you were coming to live here on Spae. You said Aydan would be the perfect replacement," Cal said.

"And he would. Brave, sensitive and totally reliable. I'd trust him with my life." Lorcan's voice resonated sincerity. "Hell, I have trusted him with my life. Many times."

"What's his background?" Cal asked.

Lorcan shrugged. "Sure, haven't we always been too busy kicking the shit out of Moncoya's henchmen to find time for a bonding session? I assumed he was one of the Iberian sidhes. Most of the resistance are."

"But his eyes are green," Tanzi insisted. "I noticed it the first time I saw him, which is why I think he is a faerie."

Cal looked thoughtful. "I'm a great believer in gut instinct. Is it worth you checking him out before you go to Avalon?" he asked Jethro.

"Sure. I can check out everyone Lorcan knows who doesn't look like a faerie, if you like." Jethro pushed away from the wall, standing straight and tall, looming over the rest of the group as they sat on the grass. Vashti was reminded once more of his sheer size and latent power. "But I thought we were up against the clock?"

"We are. We need to try to find the challenger before the elections for the Council leadership take place in a month," Cal said.

"I have to go home before I set off for Avalon, so it won't cost too much time for me to do a detour to Barcelona to see Aydan. I can sound him out about his background without coming right out and asking him any direct questions."

"Home?" Without thinking, Vashti had spoken directly to Jethro.

"Home." He repeated, his eyes flickering over her with their customary lack of interest.

"Where is home?"

"Maine." When she returned an uncomprehending look, he continued, as if speaking to someone of limited understanding. "In the United States." When she continued to stare at him, he spoke more slowly again. "Of America."

"This is a place in the mortal realm?"

"Of course." His voice was openly contemptuous now. "I'm mortal. Where else would I live?"

Before she could utter a scathing reply, Cal interrupted. "We're in agreement, then. Jethro will speak to Aydan before he sets off for Avalon. If there's the slightest chance he's our man, bring him to the palace so I can see him for myself. Use the excuse Lorcan has already given us. I'm seeking a new right-hand man and Aydan comes highly recommended." He rose, reaching down a hand to Stella. "Come on, let's get you to your bed."

Vashti watched as the group split up, wandering away to their separate cottages. She stayed where she was, shifting position slightly so she could sit with her back against the cottage wall. Hugging her knees to her chest, she rested her chin on them and remained that way for some time, wrapped in her thoughts.

"Why didn't you tell him of your fears?" Ailie's voice interrupted her musings as the older woman came to sit next to her.

"I don't know what you mean." Vashti retreated behind her usual combination of arrogance and belligerence. It was generally effective at driving people away. Why did she get the feeling it wouldn't work with this woman?

By the combined light of the moon and the lantern Ailie placed on the ground, Vashti could see the sympathy in the Spae leader's eyes. "Of course you do. It is natural to fear the unknown. There is no shame in it. Why not tell Jethro you are dreading this journey to the mortal realm?"

Vashti snorted. "You've met him. He's not exactly Mr. Approachable."

"There is a coldness in his manner, I agree. But I think you can trust him. Although he may not always use them wisely—" Ailie broke off as though chasing an elusive thought. Shaking her head slightly, she continued. "He has goodness, a strong sense of what is right and the ability to draw others to him that is unlike anything I have known before."

"He hates me." Where had the sudden wobble in her voice come from? "He thinks I am working for my father to undermine the Alliance."

"In that case, is it wise for you to go with him on this quest?"

Vashti sighed. "I have to go. Because it means more to me than anyone else. Except perhaps Tanzi, but she has other commitments now." She turned slightly so she was facing Ailie. "Jethro thought it meant so much to me because I will lose my royal status if the challenger is found."

"That hurt you." It was a statement not a question.

"I know what people think of me. I'm Moncoya's daughter, a spoiled-brat princess with no thought beyond her own comfort. But that?" Vashti shook her head. "He couldn't have shown his contempt for me any more clearly. I have to see this through for the sake of my people. If this man is found, he has the potential to tear the faerie dynasty apart in a way even my father couldn't achieve with his ambition and cruelty."

"And you see it as your duty to try to hold the faerie dynasty together?"

"If I can."

"Yet the thought of going into the mortal realm terrifies you." Ailie's soft voice became even more gentle. "Why is that?"

Vashti hunched one shoulder. "When we were children,

our father instilled a fear of mortals into us. They were the enemy, to be feared and avoided. I've been into the mortal realm before, but in the past I have always been escorted there and back, and protected the entire time. My interactions with the earth-born only occurred when I was required to kill or kidnap them."

"Yet violence toward the earth-born is not the true faerie way. In the past faeries and mortals have lived in harmony."

Vashti's lips twisted into a wry smile. "My father does not subscribe to the old ways."

Ailie nodded. "I have heard as much. What I don't understand is how Tanzi had the same upbringing yet, when she fled from your father, she voluntarily went to the mortal realm to escape him."

"Tanzi was desperate. And she was with Lorcan, a man who had sworn to protect her."

"While *your* journey will be undertaken alongside a man who is antagonistic toward you."

Vashti laughed. "That's his approach to me when he's having a good day."

"And your pride will not allow you to try to break down these barriers between the two of you?"

"Not in this millennium. Probably not in the next."

Ailie shook her head sadly as she stood. "Then I wish you luck."

"I have a feeling I'll need it."

Chapter 3

The next morning Vashti cautiously approached a very angry Jethro, who seemed to be taking his frustration out on Cal as they stood on the village green. "Is this some kind of joke?" Jethro's expression resembled a thundercloud. "You're telling me there is a portal direct from where we are now to the mortal realm, but it will take me to a remote Scottish island?"

Cal sighed. "The Spae originated as mortals on the Isle of Orkney. Centuries ago, when they were persecuted by witch finders and forced to flee their home, your convenience and ease of international travel were probably not uppermost in their minds. They were more concerned with their own safety."

"What is the problem?" Depositing her bag on the grass, Vashti surmised they were not likely to be departing immediately.

"The problem is I will waste time getting from Orkney

to mainland Scotland, then from there to a major US airport, where I'll need to get another flight to Maine. Allowing for connections and delays, it will take the best part of two, possibly even three, days."

Since Vashti had no concept of mortal time, Jethro's frustration was meaningless to her and she turned to Cal for an explanation. "It would take as long if Jethro returned to the palace with Stella and me to use the portal at La Casa Oscura. From there, he would enter the mortal realm in Barcelona and travel from Spain to the US. Either way, the journey is a long one. Which leaves me with one question." He turned back to Jethro. "Since we are, as you said, up against the clock, do you have to go home first?"

Something shifted in Jethro's expression. The irritation was replaced by a guarded look, as though shutters had been abruptly pulled down. "Yes."

"When it comes to being stubborn, you remind me of someone I once knew." Cal's voice held a trace of frustration.

"Who was that?"

"His name was Arthur." Cal's annoyance shifted and became a reminiscent smile. "He didn't turn out so bad."

Hoisting a large backpack onto one shoulder, Jethro held out a hand to Cal. "Sometimes stubbornness works. Have my money ready. The next time we meet, I'll be bringing you your challenger."

Gripping the outstretched hand, Cal nodded. "Blind, arrogant confidence. King Arthur had that, too. It's what we need right now. I guarantee Moncoya has it in abundance. Before you go, I need to have a few words with Vashti." Jethro started to turn away but Cal stopped him. "You need to hear this." Beckoning Vashti closer, he held up a small leather bag. "This contains a few items you will need." Opening the bag, he began to produce the contents one by one. "Cash. US dollars. Do you know how to use this?"

Conscious of Jethro's disbelieving eyes on her face, Vashti tried to sound nonchalant. "Is it money? I've heard of it, but I have never used it."

"Be careful with it. Keep it safe. If you wave it around, someone will try to take it from you. And, while I'm fairly sure you'll be able to stop them in their tracks, you don't want to draw attention to yourself by killing a mugger."

Cal reached into the bag again. "This is a credit card. When the money runs out, you use this to get more. Jethro will show you how." His eyes flicked over to Jethro. "Won't you?" The response was a curt nod. "These are the papers you will need so you have a mortal identity. And, finally, this is a cell phone. Use this if you need to keep in touch with Jethro."

Vashti took the little gadget from him. "Can I use it to contact you?"

Cal did his best to hide a smile. He didn't quite succeed. "The signal here in Otherworld tends not to be great."

"A word. In private." Jethro drew Cal to one side.

Vashti couldn't catch everything that was said but she was fairly sure it was about her from the turbulent set of Jethro's features and the occasional phrase such as "got to be kidding me" and "a babysitter for your observer." Whatever Cal said in reply appeared to have a calming effect. Nevertheless, Jethro's muttered comment reached her as the two men made their way back to her. "It was your decision to send her with me. If something happens to her, she's your responsibility, not mine." Vashti suspected she was meant to overhear it.

Cal scanned her face. "Sure about this?"

"Absolutely." She gave him her brightest smile. "At least I already know what the worst part of the journey will be."

"What's that?" He lifted her bag and handed it to her.

She cast a look at Jethro, whose expression refused to lighten. "The company."

Jethro watched Vashti surreptitiously as she leaned against the rail of the boat, allowing the brisk breeze to catch her face. It was hard not to watch her. She had a sort of mesmerizing quality that drew his gaze even when he tried to fight it. He'd met plenty of faeries in his time, but she seemed to have more enchantment about her than all the others put together. As if this job wasn't complicated enough already.

He felt his initial annoyance at not being able to get a flight from Orkney to Glasgow dissipating with each mile the ferry covered. It was one of the most infuriating things about what he did. It should be simple. He wanted to get from one place to the next in the most direct way possible. Other people got paid to take him there. Yet there always seemed to be a problem. Patience wasn't high on Jethro's list of virtues. Over the years he'd developed his own ways of getting around inflexible travel schedules, but today money and intimidation hadn't been options.

They had passed through the portal from Spae to Orkney just in time to find out they'd missed the only flight leaving the island that day.

Swallowing his annoyance, Jethro had resorted to finding an alternative. "It's an island," he'd said to the airport ticket agent. "There must be other ways of getting off it."

"The ferry to the mainland leaves in an hour," she'd told him, a trace of disappointment in her eyes as she'd looked him up and down. "I hope you'll visit Orkney again soon."

Now that he'd managed to phone ahead and get arrangements in place for the next stage of the journey, Jethro allowed himself to relax. Well, as close as he ever came to that sensation. What he did for a living never allowed him to completely unwind.

"I'm going to get something to eat." He raised his voice slightly above the noise of the engines, the wind and the cries of the gulls. "Since you're following me, I thought you might want to join me?"

Vashti turned her head and he was caught in the headlamp stare of those incredible eyes. Lighter and bluer than the sky above her head, they had a feline tilt below slightly slanting brows. The give-away sidhe ring of fire around her irises blazed bright, making the blue even clearer. Damn. He had a feeling those eyes were going to give him all kinds of problems.

"I'm not a child in the schoolyard, tagging along behind you because I want to." Her voice was haughty. "I'm observing you because it's my duty."

He grinned. "Perhaps you'd like to observe me while I eat a burger?"

Her expression was thoughtful. Then she nodded. "I'm hungry, too."

They made their way down to the boat's restaurant. "Is it true what they say about faeries?" Jethro paused as he studied the self-service menu. "If we eat together, will I belong to you forever?"

For the first time since he'd met her, Vashti smiled. It was an expression filled with genuine amusement and a hint of mischief. And it lit up the beige plastic and dull chrome environment like a flare launched into the midnight sky beyond the portholes. "Only if I want you."

Jethro returned the smile. He had no choice. It was irresistible. "I guess I'm safe?"

"Totally."

And in that instant, in that bland environment smelling of fries and cheap coffee with dispirited travelers milling around them, Jethro felt something shift ever so slightly. It was a tiny glimmer of something other than animosity. He wasn't quite sure what it was. Interest? He knew what Lorcan would say. He could hear his friend's long-suffering voice chiding, "Sure, can't you be around a good-looking woman for more than five minutes without trying to figure out how to get her into bed?"

But it wasn't that sort of interest. Call it curiosity. Vashti had taken him by surprise. He hadn't expected her to have a sense of humor. That was all. She usually hid it so well with that whole pain-in-the-ass royal thing she had going on.

"So are we going to get some food?"

Aware that Vashti was regarding him with a bemused expression, Jethro gave himself a mental shake. *So much for the ever-alert mercenary.* Just as well neither Iago nor Tibor had been around while he was gazing into Vashti's eyes, intrigued by this unsuspected facet to her personality. *I'd have been sprawled facedown with a knife between my shoulder blades or my throat ripped out before the girl behind the counter had time to ask if I wanted my coffee regular or large.*

"Yeah, let's do that."

The food was as sterile and uninteresting as their surroundings and they sat at a table offering them a view of black nothingness. Jethro was glad Vashti seemed content not to speak. Company on his travels was a new experience. Unwanted, unwelcome company in the form of Moncoya's daughter had to be the worst kind of intrusion. At least he didn't have to talk to her. No sooner had those thoughts passed through his mind than Jethro found himself wanting to question her. To discover what was going on behind those flawless features. To find out more about this exquisite enigma who, with her twin, had been Moncoya's trained assassin.

He couldn't talk about the night Moncoya got away. That would incite her to instant, boiling fury. In fact, it was probably best to steer clear of anything to do with her father.

"What was it like training with the Valkyries?"

Vashti withdrew her gaze from the darkness beyond the porthole and Jethro was conscious of that blue gaze assessing him. He was fairly sure he fell short of the required standard. "Demanding." She turned away again.

"And growing up in the faerie palace?"

There was that stare again. Bland, blue and impossible to read. "Luxurious."

This was becoming a challenge. *Get her to say more than one word.* "It must have been hard when your father was defeated."

"Are you making conversation?"

He grinned. "I'm trying to."

"Please don't."

With a feeling of amused irritation—*the princess has spoken, I've been dismissed*—Jethro lapsed into silence.

So far Vashti had survived her first forty-eight hours in the mortal realm without anything too alarming taking place. The noise and the sheer number of people moving around were the hardest things to deal with. How they could possibly know what they were doing, where they were going and how to avoid bumping into each other, was beyond her comprehension, yet somehow it seemed to work.

Although she would never admit it, Vashti was glad of Jethro. Keeping up with his long strides as he'd marched first through the ferry terminal, then the airport, had given her a sense of purpose that meant she hadn't stood in the midst of the chaos simply gazing around her like a lost soul. He'd even taken the trouble to explain that extreme reactions like drop-kicking the woman who'd jostled her at the airport check-in desk or throat-punching the man who'd regarded her appreciatively before stepping uncomfortably close as they'd boarded the plane would be considered inappropriate in the mortal realm. They would even, he explained with unexpected patience, attract undue attention and land her in trouble.

"They should keep their distance," she had grumbled as they'd taken their seats on the plane.

"They don't know you're a princess. To them you're an ordinary person."

Frustrated when her seat belt didn't do what she wanted it to, Vashti tried to wrench it out of place. With something that sounded suspiciously like a long-suffering sigh, Jethro had showed her how to fasten it.

"Oh." She had leaned back in her seat, digesting the information. *Ordinary.* She had been described as many things during her life. Never that.

Jethro had slept during much of the long plane journey. He'd slumbered like a cat, falling asleep instantly and deeply, but waking alert and watchful. While he'd dozed, Vashti had watched movies and observed her fellow passengers.

The man who had eyed her up earlier was seated across the aisle and one row in front. He was tall and slender with long, fair hair. He was traveling with a woman and the two of them seemed to exist in their own separate bubbles. Together yet apart. Vashti speculated on their relationship. As if aware of her gaze, the man looked in Vashti's direction. Recognizing her, he grinned admiringly. The scowl she gave him in return seemed to have the desired effect and he turned away once more.

Each time Jethro did stretch his long body and open those melting dark eyes, it seemed to Vashti a flight attendant appeared as if by magic. "Do women always look at you like that?"

"Like what?" He paused in the act of devouring a sandwich.

She wrinkled her nose in an effort to find the right words. "Like they want something from you."

His lips twitched and she got the distinct impression he was trying not to laugh. "Sometimes."

She sighed. "I will never understand mortals."

"We're a fairly uncomplicated lot if you give us a chance." He jerked a thumb toward the plane window. "The United States. Home."

Vashti leaned across him to get a better view. "I have heard of it even in Otherworld. It doesn't look uncomplicated to me." It looked like an uneven jumble of architecture and water and greenery. *What if I get lost down there?* She turned her head to voice the question but the words died on her lips.

Her face was inches from Jethro's, her shoulder pressed against his. Physical contact that was uncomfortably pleasant. It was a first. Something strange started happening inside her chest. As if her heart was insistently trying to pound its way out of her body. His nearness was delivering sensory overload. Every part of her was achingly aware of his scent, as though she had imbibed it through her pores. Not the smell of his cologne. Beneath that. The scent of *him*. Dark, spicy and seductive. It made her shudder ever so slightly. At least, she hoped the quivering movement was slight. She would hate to think Jethro could feel it.

Her eyes were drawn insistently to his mouth. Why had she never noticed the perfection of that luscious slope to his lower lip? Or the stubble outlining his upper lip that had darkened as their journey progressed. It was so tempting to reach out her finger to find out if the bristles were as coarse as they looked. She actually had to fight the impulse at the same time she was resisting the urge to trace the small cleft in his chin with her fingertips. And his eyes...

"Dark and bright at the same time." *Tell me I didn't say that out loud.*

"Pardon?"

Aware that she was still nestled close against him, Vashti sat up straight. "Is this our destination?" In an effort to distract him, she pointed at the city unfolding below them.

Jethro shook his head. "No, that's one more stopping-off point."

"Tell me we don't have to stand in another line."

He grinned. "Sorry."

Vashti groaned and slumped back in her seat. The action drew the attention of her admirer across the aisle and he turned his head again. "That guy over there keeps looking at me," Vashti complained in an undertone to Jethro.

"Vampires," he said it dismissively. "They've been with us since we stepped through the portal on Orkney."

She took a moment to digest this information. "They are *following* us?"

"Well, if we're going to be precise about it, they're following me. Blatantly. They do it all the time."

"Why?" She gave the vampire another glare and he mimed placing a hand over his heart in mock hurt.

"Because your friend the vampire prince has sworn to have me killed. Every vampire from here to the far end of Otherworld will earn their master's undying—no pun intended—gratitude if they can present Tibor with my head."

"So why doesn't this one kill you now and get it over with?"

Jethro grinned. "I'm a necromancer. I'm not that easy to kill. Tibor sends his bloodsuckers along to remind me of his pledge. It's a little game he likes to play."

It might be a game, but the smug vampire was seriously annoying Vashti. "I'll fix them."

She unbuckled her seat belt and made a move to rise from her seat. Jethro grabbed her around the waist, pulling her back down and holding her still when she tried to squirm away from him.

"You are playing by mortal rules now. Murdering two people in full view of the other passengers on an international flight tends to be frowned upon."

"Even vampires?"

He started to laugh, the sound vibrating through his chest where it came into contact with her shoulders as he held her against him. It was an effective way of distracting her from thoughts of vampire killing.

"Even vampires. The other people on this plane don't know those two are vampires. Tibor and his followers have evolved to the point where they can spend time in the mortal realm and blend in here. It's daylight. That guy doesn't need a coffin filled with the soil of his homeland. I could produce a crucifix right now and he'd only look a bit queasy. If you drew a silver dagger on him, he'd put up a hell of a fight. If you won—and I'm sure you would—he'd die like a mortal." He cast a glance across the aisle at the back of the vampire's head. "But, unless you staked and decapitated him, he'd rise again. They haven't evolved that far."

"Tibor isn't my friend." Vashti didn't know why, but it mattered to her that Jethro should understand that. "Why does he want you dead?"

Jethro let her go and she tried to quell the tiny feeling of disappointment. "Do you remember his human servant, the one called Dimitar?" Vashti nodded as she buckled up again. "Dimitar suddenly decided he wanted to be my servant not Tibor's. I have no idea why. I didn't want a servant...but we became friends." His mouth thinned into a hard line. "Tibor had us hunted down. Dimitar lost his immunity to a vampire's bite once he left the prince's service. Tibor's followers captured us and chained us up in a dungeon in Tangiers. They couldn't exert any mind control over me, so they beat me and made me watch while they came every night and bit Dimitar."

"How did he manage to chain you? I've seen you fight. You can overpower half a dozen men. You can certainly take out a few vampires."

Was it her imagination or did Jethro look slightly sheepish? "I was tricked. There was this girl and, well... it's a long story. Let's just say I wasn't concentrating."

Vashti took a moment to assimilate what he was saying. "Oh. How did you escape?"

"Lorcan freed me, but it was too late for Dimitar. His transformation was complete by the time Lorcan arrived."

"So he is one of them now?"

Jethro's eyes seemed darker than ever. "No. I couldn't let that happen to him. As a vampire, he'd have been Tibor's plaything for all eternity. That blood-sucking bastard would have made him pay daily for switching his allegiance."

"What did you do?"

"I staked and decapitated him. Then Lorcan and I buried Dimitar in Tangiers before we left."

It occurred to Vashti that she should say something comforting. That was what Stella would do. It seemed to be the mortal way. So she searched around for a form of words that sounded right. "That's what friends are for."

Jethro's helpless laughter continued almost until they landed. When they left the plane they were in another airport, similar to the one they had departed from but larger and busier. Vashti moved surreptitiously closer to Jethro. "Does Tibor have you followed everywhere?"

"Pretty much. Although I'm honored this time. He doesn't usually send two."

Sure enough, they had to wait in another line. It must be a mortal thing. "How do you stand it?"

Jethro shrugged. "At least, being a necromancer, I can spot a vampire easily. They are the undead. They can't sneak up on me. My other stalker poses more of a problem."

"Iago?" The powerful sorcerer who was in league with Moncoya had sworn to kill Jethro, Lorcan, Cal and Stella in revenge for the death of Niniane, the Lady of the Lake, during the great battle for control of Otherworld.

"Yes. He's a sneaky little trickster. The guy thinks it's funny to take on different guises to keep his opponents guessing, and he's good at it. He could be anyone in this line. Or he could be the dog that snaps at my heels in the park, the seagull that shits on my head, the cop that gives me a ticket, the man-eating lion around the next corner... You get the picture." He glanced around, lowering his voice so no one else could hear. "My necromancing powers don't work against him. I have to rely on brute strength, which is fine if he's in his own form, not so great if he decides to be a grizzly bear. And here in the mortal realm, I'm on my own. At least in Otherworld, we were four against one. Those are the kinds of odds we need against Iago."

"You aren't on your own." Jethro raised his brows in response to her words. "I'm here."

"Does this mean I have a Valkyrie-trained faerie princess on my side?"

"No, it means I won't stand by and watch while you get killed." They reached the desk and the conversation halted while Vashti produced the documents Cal had provided her with.

"Isn't that the same thing?" Jethro asked as they finally exited the vast building.

"If I observe while Iago kills you, you won't find the challenger. That's not the same as me being on your side. You haven't found yourself a new friend."

"Funnily enough, I wasn't considering you as a replacement for Dimitar. While I might be glad of your help against Iago, I don't think you'd make great sidekick material."

It was a good thing Jethro knew where he was going. The noise and bustle had increased to a whole new level. Vashti paused, looking around with a mixture of trepidation and wonder. "I'm not. You'll have to be the sidekick."

Chapter 4

Vashti looked from Jethro to the small aircraft and back again with an expression of disbelief. "*You* are going to fly this thing?"

After they had made their way out of the large airport building, Jethro had made his way through the crowds of people to a bus. This had taken them across the vast airport complex and deposited them on the other side. Trying not to show her confusion, Vashti had followed Jethro as he showed identification to a guard on a gate and then made his way onto an airfield.

He grinned. "Are you asking to see my pilot certification?"

"No, I'm walking away."

Jethro shrugged, throwing his bag into the plane. "Seems a strange way to observe me—particularly since you don't know where I'm going—but, as I said, I'm not waiting around for you."

Vashti bit her lip. The message was clear. *Go with him or be stranded.* "You really know how to do this?"

"I have over a thousand hours flying time and a commercial pilot's license."

He swung into the cockpit. Swallowing her nervousness, Vashti walked around to the other side of the aircraft and clambered into the passenger seat. It was a cramped space. Behind the seats there was a small space, barely large enough to stow their bags. She watched Jethro's hands as they busied themselves checking the various instruments. They were strong, capable hands and she was about to place her life in them. "What does that mean?"

"It means if I wanted to, I could make my living as a pilot."

"Wouldn't you need your own plane to do that?"

"This is my plane." His glance flickered her way briefly. "One of them."

Vashti studied his profile. The concentration on his face was absolute. She started to relax. "Maybe you should think about doing this instead of being a mercenary."

"It doesn't pay as well." One corner of his mouth lifted in a wry smile. "Although it would be a hell of a lot safer." He held out a pair of headphones. "Put these on. Once the engines start, you'll need them. It gets noisy and the only way we can talk to each other will be through the microphones."

After a few final checks, Jethro started the engines and the little craft juddered into life. Completely at home with the confusing array of controls, he steered it out onto the open runway, listening to the instructions in his earpiece.

"What are we waiting for?" Vashti frowned as they stopped.

"Our turn. We're in a queue."

"Can't we go to the front anyway?"

"No, because we have a thing here called manners."

She groaned and rolled her eyes. "I wish I was mortal so I could wait around in more lines."

Jethro took his eyes off the runway long enough to cast a sidelong glance in her direction. "Just what I don't need when I'm trying to concentrate…a sarcastic faerie in my earpiece."

They were moving forward again now, gaining pace rapidly, and Vashti forgot her impatience as the plane rose off the ground, wobbling from side to side as it seemed to struggle to find its balance. The airfield below them grew smaller and then the world tilted as Jethro banked the plane around to the right. Vashti fought the impulse to grab his arm and force him to bring it back so it was level again. The contrast between the jet they had traveled on earlier when there had been no sensation of movement and this plane that swayed and bobbed as it climbed higher into the blue sky could not have been more marked.

"How long will it take?" She was suddenly aware of feeling intensely tired. Perhaps it was as a result of not having slept for two nights. Or maybe it was the nerves caused by wondering if this fragile little craft was going to hurtle to the ground at any minute.

"It will depend on the wind, but it's not too bad today. Less than an hour."

An hour of living on a knife edge of pressure. *I can cope with that.* And there were compensations. Being this close to Jethro wasn't the hardship she had always imagined it would be. *How have I gone from loathing physical contact to craving it in such a small space of time?* She studied her own slender, jeans-clad thigh as it bumped against the muscular length of Jethro's leg with the movement of the plane. But it wasn't just anyone she wanted in her personal space. It was *him*. The thought annoyed her as much as it thrilled her. *I don't even like this man, yet here I am hoping he'll tilt the plane again so I get thrown up against him! How pathetic is that?*

Nevertheless, she took the opportunity to lean across him to ask questions about various landmarks, reveling in his warm breath on her cheek and his upper arm resting casually against her breast. *Having never been a schoolgirl, I didn't get the chance to have a schoolgirl crush. I'm making up for lost time with a vengeance.* Her body seemed to be suddenly awakening to a world of new possibilities. All of them directed toward the wrong man.

Vashti was starting to enjoy the soaring, swooping sensation of the flight when she felt a light touch on her shoulder. Swinging around with a sense of shock, she found herself face-to-face with the smug vampire who had followed them from Orkney. She recoiled in horror. There was no way he had been in the plane with them when they'd taken off.

"How the hell did you get in here?"

Her voice in the headphones alerted Jethro and he glanced quickly behind him. It took only a few seconds for them to reach the same conclusion. They spoke into their microphones at the same time. "Iago."

Right first time. Although they couldn't hear him above the sound of the engine, Iago mouthed the words. Silent laughter racked his body. The sorcerer was clearly enjoying himself at their expense.

Jethro's voice was a furious growl. "Tibor *didn't* send two vampires to follow me. The woman was my tail. This trickster bastard obviously tagged along then used his invisibility to sneak into the plane." In time with Jethro's words, the vampire's features changed, shifting and becoming Iago's sharp-featured, black-bearded face. She would know that face anywhere. It was imprinted in her memory from the first time she'd met him when Moncoya had brought him to Spae before her father escaped imprisonment. Iago's green eyes gleamed with enjoyment.

"Leave this to me." Vashti unbuckled her seat belt.

"Don't be so fucking—"

She didn't stick around to hear the rest of what Jethro had to say. Discarding her headphones, Vashti scrambled over the back of her seat. It was a tight squeeze and she landed in an undignified heap in Iago's lap. It wasn't the best way to intimidate someone, but it did have the element of surprise, particularly as Iago, without the benefit of headphones, hadn't been expecting her.

In one fluid movement she curled into a ball, gripping the sides of the rear seat on either side of Iago's thighs and bringing her knees up hard under his chin. The sorcerer's head jerked back and Vashti was willing to bet he saw stars. With grim satisfaction, she watched the smile disappear from his face.

The little aircraft rocked wildly from side to side as Jethro craned his neck to try to get a glimpse of what was going on behind him. Willing him to trust her and keep his attention on the plane, Vashti focused on her task. Iago had so many tricks at his disposal she had to neutralize him as quickly as she could. Not an easy feat in such a tight space. Since Moncoya had ensured his daughters were trained in every aspect of combat, Vashti was as comfortable wielding a samurai sword as she was in a boxing ring. Her instructor's words about being trapped in a confined space with a larger opponent came back to her now. *If you can't outrun him, go for the eyes first then the groin.*

Launching herself at Iago with her thumbs extended, Vashti prepared to put her training into practice.

* * *

Jethro had flown planes in some tricky situations. There had been that one time he had been caught in a violent sandstorm over the Sahara. Or the other when he'd been forced to make an emergency landing on a deserted highway when the canopy flew off just after take-off. And who could forget the death-defying spiral he'd had to fight his way out of when his rudder pedal had jammed on his first solo flight? But trying to control a plane while a faerie princess and a sorcerer slugged it out behind him? It was new situation. Not one he had foreseen and certainly not one he relished.

The worst aspect was Jethro could neither see nor hear what was going on. All he got was an impression of bursts of activity and the occasional elbow or foot in the back of his neck. Scanning the ground below him for somewhere to land, he saw nothing suitable. Iago had timed his appearance to perfection. They were flying over a built-up area.

Jethro risked a glance over his shoulder and winced as Iago caught hold of Vashti from behind, with a hand around her throat. She responded by bringing her elbow up and jamming it into his windpipe. Iago quickly released her.

Trying desperately to keep his concentration on not killing them all by nose-diving into the ground, Jethro was jostled into almost losing his grip when Vashti tumbled onto the passenger seat next to him. Iago followed close behind, hurling himself on top of her.

Iago wasn't a big man and his skill came from his ability as a sorcerer rather than any physical strength. He was also a coward, known to flee from a situation when things got physical. Nevertheless, he outweighed Vashti and he wasn't allowing chivalry to stop him. Using his fists, he was systematically pounding any part of her he could reach.

Out of the corner of his eye Jethro saw Vashti trade blow for blow, giving as good as she got. He felt an oddly proprietorial sense of pride in her. That was until she opened the passenger door. At that point any pleasure he might have taken in her accomplishments turned into instant fury.

"What the hell are you doing?" She couldn't hear him, of course. A series of expletives aimed in Vashti's general direction burst from Jethro's lips anyway. Somehow it made him feel better.

A torrent of icy air rushed into the cabin. At the same time Vashti caught hold of Jethro's arm, turning his attention to her. *Hold me.* She mouthed the words at him.

"Are you out of your fucking mind?" Amorous encounters in midair might be an exciting proposition in some situations. Not this one.

Even though she still couldn't hear him, Vashti seemed to get the gist of that question. Shaking her head impatiently, she tugged at his arm again. Iago, doing what he did best, had given up on traditional methods and had begun to shift from human to animal form. Within seconds, in addition to the turbulent, swirling wind inside the cockpit, they had a snarling leopard. This would make a great story to recount to other pilots over a few beers. If he survived to tell it.

His teeth already chattering wildly with the cold, Jethro grabbed Vashti's upper body, hauling her close and pinning her to his side with one arm as he did his best to steer the plane with the other.

Catching Iago unawares before the sorcerer had fully shifted, Vashti clung to Jethro's arm as tightly as she could, using both feet to kick the snarling leopard toward the open passenger door. Predictably, the cat didn't go without a fight. Gripping Vashti's right calf with its claws, it was about to close its teeth on her ankle when she launched into another kick with her left foot. Pushing back against Jethro with all her strength, relying on him to keep hold of her, she caught the leopard full in the face. Releasing her with a guttural cry, there was nowhere for the cat to go except out the open door.

Another kick from Vashti sealed its fate. As he began to free fall from the plane, Iago shifted briefly back into his own form. Swiftly, he changed again, stretching out his arms to become a soaring eagle. For a moment or two he flew ahead of the plane, then, wheeling nonchalantly away, he took a different course and disappeared from view.

Moving out of Jethro's hold, Vashti slowly altered position until she was slumped in the passenger seat. Her movements were weary and uncoordinated.

Jethro wasn't sure if the change in her manner was caused by cold, shock or the injury the leopard had inflicted on her leg. The priority had to be to try to get that door shut so he could find out. It was not going to be an easy task. His hands were numb on the controls, his facial muscles stiff with the effects of the glacial temperature. The frigid air was turning his labored breath to vapor in front of him. He couldn't hear anything in his headphones and he doubted his own ability to speak coherently to air traffic control even if he was able to make contact. His brain was stubbornly refusing to process the information on the tracking system in front of him. There was no way he was capable of landing this bloody thing with neither his hands nor his brain working properly.

How long did they have in these conditions? Jethro had no idea. He was flying as low as he safely could. There was still nowhere to land. His pilot's training had covered a number of emergencies, but nothing like this. Stories of doors flying off or being deliberately damaged merged together in his befuddled mind. But his door was intact and still there. Flapping wildly, but firmly attached. He just had to find a way to get to it without letting go of the controls. If he could hook something around the door handle, maybe he could pull it closed. His whole life was a series of long shots. As shots went, this had to be one of the longest.

Tapping Vashti on the shoulder to get her attention, he mimed what he wanted her to do. She stared back at him with wide, uncomprehending eyes. He tried again. Something flickered into life behind the blue blankness of her eyes. The sidhe ring of fire began to blaze brighter. Her gaze dropped to his waist. Then, to his relief, she nodded.

At first it seemed Vashti's fingers wouldn't work as she tried to undo Jethro's belt. With painstaking slowness, she managed to get the buckle open. Jethro lifted his hips up from his seat so that she could slide the belt out through the loops of his jeans. More agonizing minutes ticked away while Vashti struggled to make a loop in the end of the belt. Once she was done, she nodded at Jethro.

Catching hold of her by the waistband of her pants with one hand while he once again flew the plane one-handed, he watched out the corner of his eye as she leaned as far out of the open plane doorway as she could get. The strain of holding on to her was almost too much for the numb muscles of Jethro's right arm and, as Vashti angled out and tried to loop the belt around the door handle, he once or twice almost lost his grip on her. Finally, on the sixth attempt, she got the belt around the door handle and, battling against the wind, pulled it closed. Instantly the tornado that had been tearing through the cockpit died away.

Slumping into her seat, Vashti picked up her headphones. "So—" her teeth were still chattering like castanets as her voice sounded in Jethro's ear "—if flying is the safe option, tell me about a day in the life of a necromancer."

The gouges in the flesh of Vashti's right calf were deep and bloody. Her black jeans hung in ragged strips below the knee on that leg and she winced as Jethro swabbed the wounds with a sterile wipe.

"Serves you right." Now that they were safe on the ground, he seemed determined to fire a series of grim questions and allegations at her. "What the hell possessed you to open that door?"

"I thought it would be fun." From the scorching look of fury on his face as he glanced up from his task, Vashti gathered he was not in the mood for humor. She sighed. "I knew Iago was about to shift into something deadly. I was all that was stopping him getting to you. Opening the door and pushing him out seemed to be the only way to get rid of him."

Was it her imagination or did his expression soften ever so slightly? It was still stony, just perhaps not as granite-edged as it had been. "You were lucky he chose a leopard. You'd have lost this leg if he'd decided to become a tiger instead."

"I think his choice was dictated by the space available. He didn't have room to shift into anything bigger."

They were still inside the plane. Jethro had insisted they weren't going anywhere until he'd taken a look at her leg. Having cleaned up the scratches, he was now searching through the first-aid kit he kept on board the plane.

"I need to put a temporary dressing on your leg. When

we get to my house, I can take another look and decide if you need to see a doctor."

"I'm fine." It felt strange to have those big, capable—surprisingly gentle—hands on her flesh.

"You won't be if these cuts get infected."

"How far are we from your house? Tell me we don't need to do any more flying."

He grinned and she thought how much smiling suited him. It took that hard edge off his looks. She wanted to tell him to do it more often, then she remembered they didn't have that sort of relationship. It was strange how sharing a plane journey with him and a leopard had made her forget that Jethro was almost a stranger. And an antagonistic one at that.

He returned to his task, his fingers deft as they placed sterile dressing pads over her wounds and bandaged them in place. "No, just a motorbike ride followed by a short boat journey."

"Now I know why you were so angry about the distance from the portal to your home." Vashti remembered Cal's question—"Do you have to go home first?" And Jethro's brusque response—"Yes."

She wanted to ask him more. Like, "Why, when time is so important, are we starting our journey here in Maine?" She suspected, since Cal, who was his friend, had gotten the almost-silent treatment, she wouldn't fare any better. No doubt about it. The man was an enigma. "I didn't realize it meant you had to travel from one end of the mortal realm to the other."

Jethro had finished tending to her leg and was surveying her ruined jeans with a grim look about his mouth. "Nothing I can do about them. You may get some strange looks, but I'm sure you can give them one of your haughty royal stares in response. Can you walk?"

"There's only one way to find out."

His eyes lingered on her face. "You are a very unusual girl, did you know that?"

"I've had an unusual upbringing."

Something changed then in the dark depths of those eyes. It was as if he withdrew from her without moving. "So you have. I almost forgot." The words seemed to rouse him into action. "Wait there."

After Jethro had landed the plane he'd taxied straight from the runway into a private hangar. His booted footsteps echoed now on the concrete floor as, having jumped down from his side, he walked around the front of the aircraft and opened the passenger door. "Give me your hands."

Vashti hesitated a moment. Her fierce independence went to war with the fear of looking foolish. What if she found she couldn't walk and fell flat on her face? Pride won. Placing both her hands in Jethro's, she allowed him to assist her out of the plane and onto the ground. To her intense relief, her legs, although shaky, held her weight. She leaned against the side of the plane while Jethro retrieved their bags from the space behind the seats, the scene of her recent fight with Iago. Her muscles were stiffening and she was going to have some serious bruises tomorrow to remind her of that encounter.

"Will Iago come after us again?" She would need all her strength if he did.

"Sooner or later, yes. All I know for sure is he'll do it when we least expect it." Jethro moved to another part of the hangar. Pulling back a tarp to reveal a mean-looking motorbike, he quickly checked the machine over. Apparently satisfied, he beckoned Vashti over and handed her a helmet. "Put this on."

She glanced around the hangar. There were numerous

other large, vehicle-size, canvas-covered shapes within the building. "Is everything in here yours?"

Jethro was stowing their bags in a cargo box on the bike, but he glanced up at that. "Yes. Why?"

"Necromancing must be a lucrative business."

There was that grin again. The one she had thought, until so recently, she hated. Now, all of a sudden, it managed to turn her insides to liquid. Vashti wasn't sure she liked the change. She didn't have time to examine her reasons, but it felt a lot like control had somehow been handed over to Jethro.

"It pays the rent."

Once they were out on the open road, Vashti found some of the tension that had gripped her oozing away. The greenery and freshness reminded her of home. Perhaps the mortal realm wasn't so different or threatening, after all. If you took Iago out of the equation. She had been here before, of course. Moncoya had used his daughters to intimidate and threaten—sometimes to kidnap or assassinate—his enemies. On those occasions, Vashti and Tanzi had been closely guarded. Their focus had been on their assignment not their surroundings.

Vashti remembered a conversation with her father about those missions.

"Why do you send us and not your sidhe warriors?"

Moncoya's eyes had narrowed. Those eyes were as blue as her own and with the same sidhe ring of fire, yet subtly different. Probably because Moncoya wore eyeliner and Vashti didn't. "Do you question my judgment?"

"No. I'm not stupid enough to do that." It was true. Vashti might be more defiant than Tanzi, but she never deliberately incurred his wrath.

He had laughed. "You are my statement to the world. My beautiful twin daughters. My perfectly matched pearls. No one expects you to also be my killing machines. Each time I send you into the mortal realm, it gives two messages. One is about your loyalty to me. The second goes deeper. It tells the world the faerie race is not what legend would like mortals to believe. We do not sit at the bottom of the garden benignly waiting to bestow our favors upon the earth-born race. We have stepped out from between the pages of a child's tale. Yes, we still look good—" he'd waved a hand to encompass them both "—but we can kill a mortal with one hand."

Even though, at that time—before she had known the full scale of his villainy, including the fact he had murdered their mother—her loyalty to Moncoya was absolute, the words had caused Vashti to shiver. Yet she knew there had been a time when faeries and mortals had coexisted amicably. Their childhood nurse used to tell Vashti and Tanzi tales of the old days. Days before Moncoya's rule. It was dangerous talk, but she had risked it. Vashti knew Cal hoped the challenger—if he could be found—would restore some of that lost harmony between mortal and fae. *It isn't lost. It has been systematically destroyed by my father.* It had never occurred to Vashti to question the origin of her father's hatred for mortals.

Cal and Moncoya were half brothers, sharing the same faerie father. While Moncoya's mother was a sidhe, Cal's mother was a mortal woman, a nun who had hidden her talented sorcerer son away from his scheming father during childhood so he could not be given to Satan as part of an evil pact. Cal had grown up to become Merlin, the great sorcerer and now the leader of the Otherworld Alliance. Moncoya, through his ruthless drive and ambition, had usurped the faerie throne in a bloody coup. They might share a father, but no two brothers had ever been less alike. Perhaps the fact the brother he hated was half mortal explained Moncoya's all-encompassing loathing for the earth-born.

Under Jethro's skillful handling, the powerful bike purred along the country roads like a dream, eating up the miles until they reached a rugged stretch of coast. They followed the scenic route, hugging a dramatic shoreline of soaring, jagged rocks and gunmetal waters on one side and patchwork trees in every shade of green, gold and orange on the other. Finally, Jethro pulled into a narrow lane and halted the bike alongside a wooden boathouse. On the pebbly shore where they stood, the little building was level with the ground, but, as Vashti walked around to stretch her aching limbs, she saw it extended out into the water on raised stilts. A small motorboat, big enough for two people, was pulled up onto decking at the rear of the boathouse.

"Don't tell me. This is your place and that's your boat." She was beginning to wonder if Jethro had transport tucked away all over the mortal realm. But surely she'd heard it was meant to be a big place and that would be beyond his means?

Jethro nodded as he wheeled the bike into the boathouse. He indicated the boat. "Twenty minutes and we'll be there."

Where is "there"? Vashti supposed she would find out soon enough. When Jethro had finished stowing their bags in the boat and locking the bike away in the boathouse, she joined him in the little vessel. "It feels like we've been traveling forever."

"Welcome to my world." He started the engine and the boat was soon skimming over the dark waters. Behind them the coastline with its tall pines and dramatic rocks began to fade. Ahead, an island, roughly horseshoe in shape, covered in the same spiky pines, came into view. "Home."

There was something in Jethro's voice as he said that single word. A note Vashti had not heard before. Emotion was something she still could not fully understand, but she had a feeling she was witnessing it now in its rawest form.

As they drew closer, she could see a jetty poking out from the island into the water. Above that, there was a single wooden house. Tall and majestic, set like a jewel among the encircling pine trees, with the sun's dying rays glinting on high, arched windows. It was hauntingly beautiful.

"Who else lives there?"

"Just me." Jethro steered the boat toward the end of the jetty. "Welcome to de Loix Island."

Vashti shook her head. "You own this?"

He laughed at her expression. "I'm a loner. I don't like sharing. Besides, it belonged to my parents before me." He brought the boat to a halt alongside the jetty. Springing lightly onto the wooden boards, he reached down a hand to help Vashti.

"A fleet of planes. Motorbikes and boats strategically placed where you need them. Your own island. I may not know much about the mortal realm, but I know enough to know none of those things are normal." Her hand was still in his as she gazed up at him. "Who are you, Jethro de Loix?"

"Just an ordinary boy—" his irresistible grin appeared; the one that made her want to grab him and kiss him until he begged for mercy "—who happens to have outrageously wealthy parents and kick-ass necromancer powers."

Chapter 5

Jethro leaned his forearms on the deck rail and looked out over the darkened water. The half-empty glass of Scotch whiskey in his hand was doing its job, as was the feeling of being home. Cal had asked him if he had to come back here. The answer was simple. Yes, he did. He had to remind himself every now and then that life wasn't all about fighting monsters. That peace and beauty still existed. That his own little corner of tranquility was here any time he wanted it. And he had to check everything was right in his world. This time, of course, he had another reason to return. One he hadn't divulged to Cal.

Who are you, Jethro de Loix? He'd given Vashti his standard, flippant response. It was the answer he'd honed over the years. Because the truth was too difficult to contemplate explaining to another person. *I don't know who I am. How crazy does that make me sound?*

Most of the time it didn't bother him. He didn't think

about it. Then there were times—like now—when Jethro was reminded of the kindly, elderly couple who had brought him up and the unanswered questions would buzz around inside his head like an annoying, trapped fly. He knew he had not come into their lives by any conventional means. The thought made him smile. His parents—Bertha and Gillespie de Loix—had been older than the grandparents of other boys his age…and they'd both looked younger than their actual years. There had been no baby pictures, no anecdotes about first steps or first words, and no family tree to help him establish his place in the world. Jethro had grown up knowing that, despite their wealth, he meant more to them than gold.

Bertha and Gillespie had done their best to give him a conventional upbringing, yet they had been overawed as they'd watched him grow up to be stronger, faster and smarter than his peers. Gradually their pride had become tinged with fear when it became obvious he had other talents.

How many other children who, having just learned to speak, spent hours sitting alone in the graveyard holding lengthy conversations with unseen companions? When Bertha's aging tabby cat had been trampled by a horse, it should have been dead. It *was* dead, she'd insisted later to Gillespie. But after Jethro had whispered a few soothing words and laid his hands on the poor, broken creature, old Mitzi was like a kitten again.

And they never mentioned—because it would really be too foolish to dwell on it—the woman Gillespie had seen in the woods here on their holiday home island. A woman with white hair and pale skin, dressed all in white. She'd reached out her hands to Jethro, beckoning him to her and, enthralled, Gillespie had begun to walk toward her, leading his son with him. It was only when they'd gotten close that her expression had become a mask of malevolent triumph. Too late, Gillespie had realized he was walking into a trap with no way of escaping. At the last minute Jethro had stepped between his father and the apparition and spoken in a language Gillespie hadn't recognized. The woman froze. When Jethro spoke again—in a voice of command—she had simply vanished.

"What did you say to her, son?" Gillespie had asked later, when he had recovered from the shock.

"I told her to go away. Didn't you hear me?" Jethro had regarded his father with mild surprise.

Now Bertha and Gillespie were gone from this world, and the only identity Jethro had was his power as a sorcerer. The status conferred on him by his ability to control the dead defined him, and he loved and loathed it in equal measure. Unlike other necromancers, it had never been enough for him. He had always been searching for something more, but what that something might be he had yet to discover.

For a long time he thought what he craved was danger. Money wasn't important to Jethro, but his skills were highly prized in Otherworld. The more perilous the mission, the bigger the purse. He gained a name for himself as the mercenary who would take any necromancing job… for the right price. He knew other necromancers—purists like Cal and Lorcan—looked down on his lifestyle simply because they never understood why he was prepared to sell his skills for money. If they knew he was already a wealthy man, they would understand it even less. And Jethro, the most intensely private of a solitary group, wasn't about to confide in them. That had been before the great battle for control of Otherworld, of course. Before he had put himself on their side in the attempt to topple Moncoya from his throne. That attempt had not been wholly successful. Moncoya had escaped from the battlefield. He was still the King of the Faeries. Just because he was in hiding didn't mean he was any less of a threat. *Still, I suppose we should thank the evil little shit for bringing us all together. Bonds deeper than friendship were forged that day.*

Lately, Jethro wasn't so sure it *was* adventure he sought. The adrenaline rush of a new mission was still a high. Confronting and defeating a hostile undead being gave him a sense of a job well done. Even a day like today, one that brought an unexpected brush with death, was a white-knuckle ride he would miss if he gave it up. But that niggling sense of missing something fundamental was increasing...

A sound behind him made him swing around. Vashti had finally emerged from the hot bath where she had been attempting to soak away the effects of the beating she had taken earlier. Her face was showing signs of bruising and she walked stiffly. Wrapped in one of Jethro's robes, which looked ridiculously large on her, she appeared unbelievably fragile. Jethro felt his features soften into a sympathetic smile.

"Better?"

"I feel like I've been trampled by an elephant."

He grimaced. "Ouch. Come and sit down." He pointed back inside the house. "I need to take another look at that leg."

Obediently—she must be tired, he decided, since submissiveness was not the first word he associated with her—she followed him into the family room and settled into one of the cozy corner sofas. Angling a nearby lamp so he could see, Jethro pulled up a footstool. Lifting her foot and placing it on his knee, he turned her leg so he could view the gouges in her pale flesh. Somehow they looked worse in the soft, golden lamplight. His mouth hardened. That bastard Iago was going to pay for a lot of things, but this came high on the list.

"You said I might need to see a doctor, but I can't. Any mortal doctor would know in an instant I'm not earth-born."

Jethro glanced up at her. "There are mortal doctors who will treat other races...for a price. But I don't think you're going to need medical treatment. Not tonight, anyway. I'll put a fresh dressing on these cuts then you can get a good night's sleep."

Vashti sighed, her whole body appearing to relax back against the cushions. "That sounds like heaven." She watched as he busied himself with his task. "What do you do while you're here?"

"On the island? This was my parents' vacation home. We'd relax. Do some fishing, swimming, walking, sailing, read a ton of books, go across to the mainland and visit friends. Just unwind."

"Oh." She wrinkled her nose.

"You look like you have no idea what I'm talking about."

Because she did it so rarely, when Vashti smiled it was like the sun had broken through storm clouds. "I suppose people might think unwinding would come naturally to a princess. Perhaps for most princesses that might be true. But Tanzi and I are Moncoya's daughters. We've spent our whole lives on a tight schedule."

Something in the matter-of-fact words tugged at a chord of sympathy deep within him. Who'd have thought? Empathy toward the faerie princess. He'd have to watch himself. Vashti was still Moncoya's daughter. Like her father, she was beautiful, destructive and untrustworthy. He had seen that firsthand on the night when Moncoya escaped from captivity on the Isle of Spae. Vashti had claimed her father held her at knifepoint, but would any father do that to his daughter? Surely even Moncoya wouldn't stoop so low. No, she must have helped him and lied about it later. Now was a good time to remind himself of that…while he was gazing up into those incredible blue eyes with his hand encircling her ankle. It probably wouldn't hurt to give himself regular warnings while he was in such close proximity to her.

"Speaking of tight schedules, I expect you're wondering why I've made this detour when Cal wants the challenger found urgently." Why was he explaining himself to her? She had chosen to tag along. It wasn't like he'd invited her.

"It crossed my mind."

"There is someone here I need to see. Someone who may be able to help with this mission." Vashti was clearly waiting for him to say more, but that was enough for now. It felt like too much. It felt like intimacy. Something Jethro didn't do. "I'll show you to your room."

Her tiny, indrawn breath as he released her and rose indicated Vashti had also felt something more than their usual antagonism. Damn. Coming home was supposed to make life less complicated. Coming home and bringing an achingly beautiful faerie princess for company was starting to look like it might have the opposite effect.

Vashti awoke from a sleep so deep it felt like she was being pulled down into quicksand. Fighting her way to the surface, she became conscious of two things. The smell of fresh-baked bread and the sound of tuneless humming. Both seemed to be coming from the kitchen, which was directly below her room. She lay still for a few minutes, gradually allowing the memories of the last few days to infiltrate her lethargy. With the recollection of Iago came a resurgence of her aches and pains and she groaned, levering herself out of bed. There was a mirror over the dresser and a glance at her reflection confirmed the worst. Her face was an interesting array of bruises.

As she dragged on her clothes, every muscle screamed in protest. *Remind me again why I was so keen to be the one to accompany Jethro on this mission?* She peered inquiringly into the mirror once more, directing the question to her battered reflection. *Oh, I remember now. It's my duty. I need to see this through for the sake of my people. Once this challenger is found, the faerie dynasty will be plunged into a bloody civil war. I know my father well enough to be certain of that. He will not go without a fight. And I wanted to make Jethro de Loix suffer. He accused me of helping Moncoya escape from justice. I owe him a little pain, and how better to cause that than by inflicting my presence upon him?* She winced as she moved toward the door. *So why the hell am I the one hurting?*

Navigating the spiral staircase felt like she was descending one of the great mountains around Valhalla. Used to her well-trained limbs doing exactly what she wanted them to, Vashti was impatient of injury. After the battle for control of Otherworld, she had been close to death. It was only through the skill of the faerie doctors and Tanzi's patient nursing that she had survived. It had not been through her cooperation or adherence to their instructions.

She found Jethro in the kitchen. This was the biggest room in the house, running the entire length of the rear of the property with spectacular views across the bay to the mainland. Vashti blinked in surprise at the sight of him removing a loaf of bread from the range oven.

"You should have stayed in bed." He looked up in surprise as she limped into the room.

"If I did, how would we find the challenger?"

"*We* are not going to find the challenger. *I'm* going to find the challenger and you are going to watch me." The familiar arrogance was back in his tone.

"While serving up a delicious meal?" She gestured to the bread.

The arrogance vanished and was replaced by a smile that was almost—she hesitated to use the word in relation to Jethro—*shy.* "My mother used to bake. It's therapeutic." He pointed to another loaf standing on a cooling rack. "Want to try some?"

Vashti's stomach gave an enormous rumble in response, and she tried to remember the last time she'd eaten. It was on the plane when the flight attendant had been so attentive to Jethro while casting an occasional dismissive glance in her direction. She nodded and, within minutes, she was seated at the vast, scrubbed table with a cup of steaming coffee and a plate of bread and butter in front of her.

"You do not strike me as the domesticated type."

Jethro lounged in a chair opposite hers, his long legs extended in front of him. He wore a white shirt and his biceps stretched the thin material of the rolled-up sleeves to its limits. The V shape of the buttons left open at his chest revealed dark hair. His broad chest tapered to a narrow waist and flat stomach. He had obviously recently showered since his still-wet hair hung loose and slightly wavy below his collar. The crisp scent of citrus reached Vashti's appreciative nostrils. Big, dark and dangerous, he invaded her senses. Domesticated was about the last word she would have applied to him.

"You can't see me in a flowered apron?"

She pretended to consider the matter, tilting her head to one side. "Not flowered, no."

He quirked an eyebrow. "But you do see me in an apron? Now that's an interesting fantasy, princess."

Vashti, who had taken a bite of bread and butter, choked as his meaning dawned on her. At least dealing with the coughing and the streaming eyes gave her time to consider how to respond. She decided the best plan was *not* to respond. To pretend she hadn't heard or she didn't understand what he meant. That sort of banter was probably like breathing to Jethro. All that thrumming masculinity needed an outlet and any woman, even one he disliked as intensely as Vashti, would do. At least the redness of her face could be ascribed to her mild choking fit and not extreme embarrassment at the image—vivid and suddenly very tempting—of Jethro in an apron and nothing else.

"What's the plan for today?" Vashti asked when she had gained control over her voice.

"Yours should be to rest." Jethro's gaze skimmed the bruises on her face.

"Can we skip the bit where we pretend that might happen?"

He paused in the act of gathering the empty coffee cups. "Have you ever listened to advice from another person?"

"Only one."

"Moncoya?"

Vashti shook her head. "I used to do as he asked if it was also what I wanted. But my father and I are equally stubborn." A slight smile lifted one corner of her mouth. "Our fights were legendary. No, when we were children, Tanzi and I had a nurse who cared for us. She was probably the only person I listened to."

Jethro's expression was inscrutable. "It sounds like you were fond of her."

She gazed out across the dark blue water. The memories—or rather the recollections of which they'd been deprived...the mother they'd never known—didn't get any easier. "We both were. Our mother wasn't around, you see. At the time we believed she'd left our father when we were babies. Now we know he murdered her when she tried to leave and take us with her. Rina was the closest thing we had to a mother."

"Rina?"

Vashti turned back to look at him. There was a slight frown in Jethro's eyes, as though he was searching for something just out of reach. "Our nurse. Her name was Rina." The frown persisted. "What is it?"

"That name. It seems familiar, but I can't place why."

"It is unusual, but not unique."

He nodded, the frown clearing. "If it's important, I suppose it'll come back to me. Now, back to your question about plans for today. If you insist on coming with me, we're going visiting."

When they reached the sleepy mainland town of Darwen, Jethro left the motorbike close to the town square, complete with its decorative bandstand, and led Vashti along the main street. He carried a small, flat box made of polished wood, but didn't reveal its contents. The street boasted a handful of shops and a few bars and restaurants. A sign outside one invited them to a cider tasting evening. Another boasted it served the best lobster in town.

Vashti was conscious of a few stares directed her way and tugged her knitted cap farther down over her ears. *It won't be far enough to cover what they're looking at,* she thought glumly. *I'd have to wear a mask to do that.*

As a fae, she would heal quickly, but not fast enough for her liking. Perhaps those watching them thought Jethro was guilty of inflicting her bruises? He seemed unaware of the interested looks. Oblivious, in fact, that there were other people around at all.

Once they were away from the main street, the road climbed steeply and colorful wooden houses lined wide tree-lined streets.

Vashti had to quicken her pace to keep up with Jethro's purposeful strides. "Who are we going to visit?"

He glanced down at her and she got the distinct impression he had momentarily forgotten she was there. "Some people I know."

Well, that was helpful. She resisted the temptation to say the words aloud, sensing something within him. Some inner turmoil. And that in itself was unusual. Sensing anything about the feelings of others was new to her. She wasn't sure she liked it. Intuition wasn't for her. It brought with it a responsibility toward the other person she didn't want or need. And when that person was Jethro, things could start to get complicated. On the whole, she'd have preferred to remain detached.

Exactly how did *you see this mission unfolding?* She supposed that, at the outset, she'd started out with a vague hope of catching Jethro if he tried to deceive the Alliance leaders in some way. Or at least of imposing her presence on him so he had no way of engaging in a hoax. *I never imagined a situation where I'd have to interact with him.* A second inner voice chastised her. *That's because you didn't think this through.* She had been so focused on her anger, so determined to punish him for his sneering, taunting approach toward her. What would happen once they set off and were alone together had never crossed her mind. The fact he might have redeeming features, some of which she might even like, had never crossed her mind. She had certainly not envisaged a situation where she might actually be intrigued by him or—heaven forbid— care about how he was feeling.

The houses were larger and farther apart now, the trees older and taller. Pine and spruce stood proud and green. The shorter beeches and maples were showing the first signs of changing to autumnal shades of red and orange. Branches stretched across the lane above their heads, meeting and, in some places, entwining to form a tunnel of green and gold. The sunlight barely penetrated and Vashti shivered slightly as a sudden chill touched her face. That was new, as well. A sense of foreboding. This strange, fluttering awareness that something about this place just wasn't right. An impression of being watched by unseen eyes. *I'm not sure the mortal realm agrees with me. Within the space of a few days, I've been beaten black-and-blue and developed an imagination, among other characteristics I never knew I had. The sooner we set out for Otherworld, and I can return to normality, the better.*

They had almost reached the top of the hill and Jethro stopped, looking back down upon the town. The views were incredible, affording a sight of fishing boats huddled into the tiny harbor and beyond to the wide expanse of bay dotted here and there with pine-coated islands. Vashti got the impression Jethro had not stopped to admire the vista. *Here we go again. Perception. Awareness. Just because you've discovered it, does that mean you have to use it?* Clearly she did. It was unshakable. She knew what Jethro was doing. He was mentally preparing himself for whatever was coming next.

He pointed up through the canopy of trees. Vashti followed the direction of his finger. Barely visible through the leaves and fronds, she could just make out a pointed roof topped by a rusted weather vane. "That's where we're going."

"What is it?"

"It's a house. The oldest and largest in this area. It was built in 1830 for one of the wealthiest landowners in Maine, and it stayed in the same family for generations. It fell into disrepair after an arson attack."

"How horrible." Vashti watched Jethro's face. There was something behind his expression she couldn't understand. She got the feeling there was more to this story than his curt words were telling her. "Why would anyone deliberately set fire to a family home?"

"There have always been rumors about this house. Locally, it has always been known as a haunted house and a place of bad luck."

"And is it?" If anyone should know the answer to that question, surely it would be a necromancer.

"Yes and no." Jethro dragged his gaze away from the pointed rooftop and smiled down at her, genuine amusement lighting his eyes. "Yes, it's haunted. No, it's not a place of bad luck." He held out a hand and, surprised at the unexpected invitation, Vashti entwined her fingers with his. "Don't be scared. Let me show you the place where I grew up."

Chapter 6

As they crested the hilltop, the house came fully into view. Even in its neglected state it was a magnificent sight. Built in a quirky, individual style, the main house was three floors high. Vashti's eyes scanned the building, taking in such unusual features as the fact that each window was of a different design and the colored roof tiles were laid out in a mosaic pattern. In addition to the central property, with its wraparound porch and the pointed tower they had glimpsed from the road, there was a separate long, low building jutting out at right angles. This looked like an overlarge summerhouse, and it appeared to have escaped the fire damage that had left sections of the main house blackened and charred.

"It looks like—"

"Something out of a fairy tale?" Jethro interrupted her. "And you should know, I suppose?"

She ignored the deliberate gibe. "I can see why mortals

might believe it to be a place of evil. I have heard they are a superstitious lot."

He gave a harsh laugh. "Yes, that's us mortals. Forever avoiding walking under ladders and staying indoors on Friday the thirteenth."

"Am I supposed to understand what you are talking about?"

He shook his head. "Never mind." They made their way along a drive fighting a losing battle with weeds and creepers. "It's always the same. Whenever I come here, it's like I've ceased to live in the here and now. I get transported back to different points in my life, depending on what my mind decides to dwell on each time. So many memories come back to me."

"What are you recollecting now?"

He pointed to a broken-down gatepost. "I was running along the drive here, chasing a butterfly." He raised a brow as Vashti made a suspicious choking sound. "Are you laughing at me?"

She did her best to keep her expression prim but it didn't quite work. "Maybe a little bit. It's a new image, one that will take some getting used to. How old were you?"

"I'm not sure. I was very young. Anyway, I tripped and went headfirst into that post. I still have the scar." He turned his head.

Vashti stood on the tips of her toes so she could see the white mark above his right cheekbone. Some primeval instinct deep within her, a powerful urge she had never experienced before, prompted Vashti to reach out one fingertip and lightly trace the crescent-shaped scar. Jethro jerked beneath her touch, his eyelids fluttering closed. Raw heat arced from her finger to him and back again. It sparked through their bodies in a series of low-level electric currents. Although Vashti wanted to break the contact and stop the storm of sensation coursing through her, the force compelling her was too strong. Helpless to do anything else, she placed her other hand on Jethro's shoulder, clinging to him as her body shuddered in time with his.

Jethro's eyes flew open, their expression unreadable. He caught hold of her wrists, moving her away from him. One final surge crashed through them and then the contact was broken. Jethro released her. "What are you doing?"

"I don't know." Vashti felt the blush rise from her neck, heating her cheeks.

"It's a bit late to try to cure my hurt, if that's what you were attempting." His eyes continued to probe her face as though seeking an answer there. "Is it true the touch of a faerie has healing qualities?"

"It may have been once, way back in the mists of time. You've met my father, the great modernizer. He has no use for the old ways. I can fight half a dozen men, but I have few of the traditional fae powers. I couldn't heal you any more than I could enchant you with my touch." And yet, hadn't that strange, lightning-bolt instinct been telling her to do both those things? She tilted her head back, looking away from him and up at the cloud-scudded sky. "It wasn't about your scar."

"What was it about?"

She shook her head, frustration making her tongue-tied. "I wish I knew." How could she put into words something she didn't understand herself?

"Which powers do you have? Cal said you could shapeshift."

Vashti cast a glance toward the house. It loomed over them, watchful and waiting. Patient. It had all the time in the world. Was Jethro interested in her abilities or was he finding a way to postpone the moment when they would walk up those lopsided steps? "I can shift, but not in the way true shape-shifters do. My body doesn't change. Because I am fae, I can create the illusion of shifting instead. So I fool those around me into thinking I have changed rather than actually changing. It is something Tanzi and I taught ourselves to do when we were children, a talent we kept hidden from our father. Oh, and I can levitate. I always wanted to be able to fly like the faeries in the tales, but I can only manage to rise a few feet off the ground." She gave him the benefit of her mischievous grin. "It comes in handy if I have to fight someone taller than me."

Jethro's features relaxed as he returned the smile. "If we ever get into a fight with each other, I'll remember to chain you to the ground first." Sighing, he looked back at the house. "Let's get on with this."

"If the house is derelict, who are we going to visit?" Vashti walked beside him along the last few feet of uneven path.

"My parents."

It had always been a matter of pride to Vashti to be the best at everything. As children, she and Tanzi had been fiercely competitive, and it was a trait Moncoya had encouraged. He had wanted to ensure that, beneath their delicate, ethereal beauty, they were hardened killing machines, devoid of feeling. That was why it had come as such a shock when Tanzi had tumbled headfirst in love with Lorcan Malone. That was why now, as she stepped onto the porch of the de Loix mansion, Vashti was stunned at the violence and range of emotion ricocheting through her.

I'm not meant to be like this. I'm meant to be the best

at being a hard-hearted, brutal warrior. It's what I do.
If I don't have that, who am I?

This property refused to be ignored. It oozed character, yet it didn't have the sort of atmosphere Vashti had expected when Jethro spoke of a haunted house. This unconventional mansion seemed to leak a thousand family memories into the ozone. Some of them happy, some of them sad. All of them powerful. None of them frightening. As she looked up at the uneven chimney pots and the once bright, now faded paint on the eaves, she envied the childhood Jethro must have had and the contrast to her own rigid upbringing. She was conscious of him watching her face, measuring her reaction. As if it mattered to him.

"It's—" she searched for the right word, sensing the importance of what she said next "—extraordinary."

His expression held a world of memories. "Ordinary is certainly not a word I'd use to describe it. Shall we go inside?"

The front door gave a classic horror-movie creak as he opened it and stepped aside to let Vashti go first. She was inside a narrow hall, gloomy because of a thick film of dirt on the huge, arched window above the turn on the stairs. Motes of dust danced in the air and mingled in her nostrils with the scents of dried apples, wax candles and mildew. Old newspapers were stacked in piles on the uncarpeted stairs and leaves, blown in from outside, lay scattered over the worn floorboards. The paint on the walls was cracked and peeling, its original color an indeterminate shade somewhere between gray and green. If Jethro was serious about his parents living here, they needed to hire themselves a decent housekeeper.

"Through here." He indicated a set of double doors to the left of the staircase. Vashti heard the breath he took, as if steeling himself for an ordeal, before he opened the doors and stepped inside.

The room they entered was a shabby museum piece, a perfectly preserved century-old parlor, cluttered with dark wood furniture, pictures, framed photographs and knick-knacks. Worn velvet drapes hung at the windows and rugs were scattered in threadbare pools of faded color across the floor. A huge, black-leaded fireplace dominated one wall, although no blaze warmed the room. A large piano stood in one corner, its once glossy surface dull and dusty.

A woman was seated at a small table near the window. She was clad in a full-length, high-necked black gown, and there was an air of quiet elegance about her. Apparently unaware of their entrance, she continued dealing out cards from a pack at her elbow and studying each intently. She hummed a tune under her breath. As they drew closer, Vashti saw that the cards she drew were from a tarot pack.

"Bertha." Jethro spoke her name with infinite gentleness.

She paused, tilting her head slightly as though listening for a distant sound. Without replying or acknowledging them, and without interrupting her humming, she returned to the cards.

"More and more often these days she retreats into her own world."

The man who entered the room was tall, handsome and very old. Despite his age, he had a proud, upright bearing that made Vashti think he must have been a military commander in his younger years. As he moved forward, Vashti took in the faded blue of his eyes, the pallor of his skin and the graceful way he moved. She turned wide eyes to Jethro as realization hit her.

"But where are your manners, my son? Who is this lovely lady you have brought to visit us?"

Either his eyesight was fading or his old-fashioned courtesy prompted him to stretch a point. "Lovely" was the last word Vashti would have chosen to describe her bruised and battered appearance.

"This is Vashti." She knew why he didn't use her title. Even here in the mortal realm, association with Moncoya could be dangerous. "My parents… Bertha and Gillespie de Loix."

"You are welcome, my dear." Gillespie bowed with old-fashioned courtesy. His eyes narrowed. Even without her title, her name was too well-known to escape attention. "I have heard of your father, of course."

Although he was currently in exile, Moncoya was well-known throughout Otherworld. His fierce ambition had driven him to clash with most of the other leaders at some time or another. He wanted to be the undisputed ruler of all Otherworld. He made no secret of it. How could he, when he repeatedly invaded the lands inhabited by other dynasties? It was how the faerie territory had grown to be the largest and most powerful in Otherworld. It was why Moncoya was the most feared and hated of all the leaders.

Moncoya's political machinations were also legendary. His two main allies were the vampires and the wolves. Unsurprisingly, these were—apart from Moncoya himself—the most bloodthirsty and ambitious races in Otherworld. Moncoya switched allegiance as often as he changed his clothes. He thought nothing of signing a peace agreement one day and invading the territory of the dynasty with whom he had made the pact the next. But there was one dynasty he could not predict or manipulate. One ruler he could not outmaneuver. The ghost lord was one of the few leaders who was not an aggressor. For that reason Moncoya had misjudged him and thought he could be bullied. He was wrong. The ghostly realm had stayed quietly neutral throughout all the bloody conflicts that had marked the centuries of Moncoya's domination of Otherworld history.

So, it was no wonder that Gillespie de Loix had heard of her father. Because Gillespie de Loix was a ghost.

Jethro watched his mother out of the corner of his eye while his father talked to Vashti. It was a surreal situation. For obvious reasons he'd never pictured himself introducing anyone to his parents. He was shocked when he realized the way Gillespie's mind was working. Was it appropriate for Jethro to intervene and state this was not a bringing-a-girl-home-to-meet-the-folks thing? He decided to leave it alone. Vashti could look after herself. She might look like a delicate flower, but she had the hide of a rhino. And if Gillespie thought there were going to be bridesmaids and wedding bells in the near future...well, he'd have to think again. Jethro almost laughed aloud at the whole image, anyway. If he ever did get married— and that "if" wasn't just big, it was a yawning chasm of immensity—the groom's side of the church was going to take some explaining.

"Have you met the ghost lord?" Gillespie had gestured to Vashti to take a seat on the studded velvet sofa near the window. He had taken a winged chair at right angles to her. Jethro remained standing.

"I have not met the new leader of the ghosts, although I did meet his predecessor a few times. Before he went into exile, my father often entertained the leaders of the other dynasties." Vashti smiled. "He believed in keeping his friends close and his enemies closer."

Gillespie laughed. "I was under the impression Moncoya did not have many friends."

"He liked to keep up the pretense."

"So, our new leader—" Gillespie seemed reluctant to let the topic go. He tented his fingers under his chin, his eyes probing Vashti's face. "What have you heard about him?"

"Very little. The change has been recent and unexpected. All I have heard is the former leader grew tired of the machinations of those such as my father and Prince Tibor and decided it was time to retire. His replacement is well respected among the phantom race." Jethro sensed she was choosing her words carefully and was surprised. Diplomacy was not a skill he associated with Vashti. "I always think those leaders who have followers in both Otherworld and the mortal realm have the hardest task. The vampire prince and the wolf pack leader are ruthless in their authority and, whenever there is a hint of trouble in the mortal realm, they are quick to stamp it out. It is more difficult for the ghost lord."

"Why is that?" Gillespie's piercing eyes focused on her face.

"Because ghosts do not dwell in the mortal realm for the same reasons vampires and werewolves do. They do not come here to feed or for sexual gratification. Ghosts choose to be here for many reasons, as individual and personal as the lives they left behind. It is said the new ghost lord follows the example of the previous leader in doing a good job of respecting that. As long as his people do not transgress on the lives of the earthbound, he is content to allow them to live here in peace."

"And yet there *are* cases of ghosts crossing the boundary and causing problems. Poltergeists, for example." Jethro knew how much his father loved this sort of debate.

"In that case, we must rely on this recently appointed ghost lord to deal with those cases swiftly and effectively. Now and then, they will inevitably come to the attention of mortals before he can intervene." Vashti's face was earnest. "Merlin Caledonius was speaking about this the other day in a Council meeting. Just as the occasional vampire, werewolf, even faerie, on the loose in the mortal realm is inevitable, so, too, is the random haunting. On the whole, these things are contained."

"There are those who advocate employing someone such as Jethro here to rid the mortal realm of ghosts, vampires and lycanthropes. I have heard it said the Dominion, the Angels of the Fourth Choir, would support such a move."

Vashti looked surprised. "I am the faerie representative on the Alliance and I have not heard this proposal. Besides, a necromancer would only be effective against those who are undead." She glanced in Jethro's direction. "He could not remove faeries, witches, elves, or so many other races from the mortal realm."

Gillespie turned that direct gaze in Jethro's direction. "Did you hear that, my boy? There may no longer be any use for your services."

"Don't try and drag me into this debate. There will always be a use for my services, but I hope I've never been guilty of trying to banish a harmless ghost to Otherworld against his or her will."

"That was almost diplomatic. And most unlike you." Gillespie shot a searching glance at Jethro. "Why have you brought that?" The change of subject brought about an abrupt transformation in mood as Gillespie pointed to the wooden box Jethro had placed on top of the piano.

"I may need it."

"That is not an answer."

"I need to ask Bertha a question." The words hung in the air alongside the motes of dust for a long, silent moment. "You know I would not do this if it wasn't important."

Finally, Gillespie sighed. It was the same sound as the brittle leaves on the path outside. "Tell me."

Even though he knew Bertha was locked in her own world and couldn't hear him, Jethro lowered his voice. "When I was a child, before her mind started to fade, she used to tell me the most fantastic stories."

Gillespie's smile was laden with sad reminiscence. "She was a wonderful storyteller."

"The best ones were always about the court of Good King Ivo." Jethro noticed Vashti sit a bit straighter. "Bertha weaved a world around the Seelie Court and King Ivo's Code, the rule by which the good faeries lived." He laughed. "I can still quote the values I learned from those stories now... 'Death before dishonor, love conquers all, beauty is life and repay all debts.' As I grew older, I knew what Bertha was doing, of course. Through her stories, she was instilling my own moral code into me."

The angular lines of Gillespie's face softened. "She did a good job."

Involuntarily, Jethro's eyes flickered to Vashti's face. Would she agree with that summary of his character? She still saw him as the notorious necromancer who sold his skills to the highest bidder. Unlike Gillespie, she had no idea what he did with that money. Those glorious eyes were fixed on his face as she listened intently.

"I was fascinated by tales of King Ivo's battles with his enemies. They were the evil faeries of the Unseelie Court. Their code was the opposite of his. They believed chaos was mighty, kindness to mortals was a sin, honor was a lie and passion came before duty." Again he glanced at Vashti. Was it his imagination or did a faint blush touch her pale cheeks? Was she thinking of Moncoya and recognizing him in the Unseelie code? *Don't get your hopes up. You are not on a campaign here. Converting Moncoya's daughter is not the purpose of this visit.* "In the stories Bertha told me there were constant plots by the followers of the Unseelie code to overthrow King Ivo."

"And, of course, the stories she told you all had a basis in truth."

Jethro looked again at the solitary figure by the window. Bertha turned another card and hummed her melancholy lullaby. "Which is why I need to speak to her. Do you remember my favorite bedtime story when I was young?"

Gillespie frowned in an effort of recollection. "Something about a lost prince?"

"It was the tale about the great massacre. The night on which Moncoya led his followers into King Ivo's palace and slaughtered the king, his family and all his followers. It brought about the end of the Seelie Court and the beginning of centuries of domination over the faerie race by the Unseelie Court." Vashti's long eyelashes fluttered down, hiding the expression in her eyes from his view. "But a baby—one of King Ivo's great nephews—was smuggled out of the palace by his nurse and taken to a place of safety. I always thought my mother made that story up, but now I know it really happened."

"And why does it matter so much?"

"I have been given the task of finding that last remaining member of King Ivo's family. Don't you see what it means? It's not just about challenging Moncoya. This is a chance to restore the Seelie Court to its former glory."

Gillespie frowned. "What makes you think your mother can tell you any more now than she did then?"

Jethro drew a deep breath. "Because, from some of the things she said, I think Bertha knew where the child was taken."

"She is too fragile." Gillespie's face was anguished.

"I swear I won't hurt her." If she hadn't heard it for herself, Vashti never would have believed Jethro's voice could be capable of such gentleness.

"I thought you didn't use the dark arts of the ancient necromancers." Gillespie pointed to the box. "If that is so, why do you need that?"

"I need to try to restore her memory for a brief period of time. We both know she won't respond if I simply speak to her as I'm talking to you now. That is because her mind was already damaged when she died, the decline had begun before she crossed over." Jethro shot Gillespie a look from under lowered brows. "And, if you'll let me, I can get her to release her grip on this house and send her to Otherworld where much of her consciousness will be restored."

"I promised her I would never make her leave here."

"Some promises are made to be broken." The softer note was back.

"I will permit you to question her, as long as you stop immediately if she becomes distressed."

Jethro nodded.

Vashti noticed Gillespie made no further reference to Jethro's offer to remove Bertha from this house and Jethro didn't try to force the issue. It seemed to be a well-worn subject between the two men.

"That goes without saying." Jethro undid the brass clips on the case and opened it. The interior was divided into compartments lined with worn, red velvet. Unable to contain her curiosity, Vashti rose from her seat and came to stand closer. Some of the compartments contained bones, others small jars with symbols etched on yellowing labels. One contained a large book, another a folded cloth and in the center there was a large, black candle. Aware of her scrutiny, Jethro turned his head. "Many people believe necromancy is simply another form of witchcraft." He lifted the cloth from his case as he spoke and spread it over the piano top. It was a delicate, shimmering silk, embroidered all over with celestial symbols. "It is easy to dismiss that which we don't understand as evil, and necromancers have been viewed throughout the centuries as masters of the dark arts. But we are not witches. Our gifts are sacred and noble. They confer upon us the power to channel the spirit world according to our wishes. The responsibility that brings is huge."

"But you don't use these methods—" Vashti indicated the candle he was now placing in the middle of the cloth "—all the time?"

"No. Necromancing is rare. There are very few of us around and the best of us—me, Lorcan, Cal and Stella—don't use the older forms of the art often. Nevertheless, there are times when nothing else will do." He lit the candle and an acrid smell, like stale, dried herbs, made Vashti wrinkle her nose. Jethro looked at Gillespie. "I need some of Bertha's hair. From when she was alive."

With the unusual movement that was somewhere between gliding and walking—the one that had first alerted Vashti to his undead status—Gillespie left the room. When he returned, he brought with him a silver-handled hairbrush. Strands of long, black hair clung to its bristles and he hesitated before handing it to Jethro. He cast a dubious look at the items on the piano before taking up a protective stance close to Bertha.

"You know I would never harm her. She means too

much to me." Jethro extracted several hairs from the brush and placed them in a small copper dish. Opening several jars in turn, he added a few grains from each to the dish. Extracting a taper from the case, he held it to the candle's flame, a frown of concentration on his face. Pausing, with the lit taper an inch or two above the dish, Jethro chanted a few words in a guttural language Vashti had never heard before. When he finished, he set light to the contents of the dish. Blue flames and white sparks shot into the air and a loud hissing noise ensued. A strong scent of sulfur filled the air.

"Mother." As soon as he said the word, Bertha paused in the act of dealing her next card and looked up. A smile as sweet as the happiest dream dawned on her face.

"How long will the sorcery last?" A single tear tracked its way down Gillespie's cheek as he watched his wife.

"Not long." Jethro took the chair opposite his mother at the table. "It will be as if she has been hypnotized. She will be unable to lie to me while she is under the influence of this spell."

Bertha appeared not to hear him. "My boy—" although she was unable to touch him, her hands hovered an inch above Jethro's on the tabletop "—I've missed you."

The shadow that crossed Jethro's face caused something hard and tight to form inside Vashti's chest. "Whenever you need me, I will be here. Can I ask you a few questions?"

Bertha laughed, a high, musical sound that dispelled some of the grief in the atmosphere. "Why so formal? Surely you know you can ask me anything."

Vashti flinched. *She doesn't know. Oh, dear Lord, she has no idea what's going on here.*

"It's about the story you used to tell me of King Ivo's lost heir."

A cautious look came over Bertha's face and her hands fluttered nervously. "I'm not sure…"

"Do you know what happened to him after he was smuggled out of the palace on the night of the massacre?"

A soft sigh of resignation escaped her lips. "Yes, I do."

Vashti leaned forward. She wanted to jump in with a dozen questions of her own. How could Bertha possibly know what had happened that night? The massacre had taken place in another world. In the end, there was only one question that mattered and Jethro asked it next. "Where did his nurse take him?"

Bertha's eyes darted around the room. "I can't say."

Jethro frowned, his eyes moving from Bertha's face to Gillespie's. "She should not be able to evade my questions. Not unless there is some powerful force at work preventing her from answering."

Vashti ventured a suggestion. "Perhaps if you ask her specific questions, so she has to answer yes or no?"

Jethro nodded. "Was he taken to Avalon?" Bertha continued to gaze around the room, anywhere other than meeting his eyes. "To another location in Otherworld?" Bertha began to rock back and forth. "To the mortal realm?" Bertha started to sob quietly.

"Enough." Gillespie placed his arm around Bertha's shoulder. "Even if she knows the answers, it is clearly causing her pain to think of it."

Although Jethro ran a hand through his hair in a gesture of frustration, he inclined his head in acceptance and rose. "She will be lucid for a few more minutes. We'll leave you alone." He drew Vashti away so Gillespie could talk privately to his wife. "I feel like I just wasted over a week of our precious time."

"You know her better than I do, but it seems to me she was afraid to tell you what she knew."

"Whatever her secret is, it must be huge if she has never confided in Gillespie about it." He looked across to where Bertha was gazing up at her husband with shining eyes. "Shit. We're right back to square one."

Are we? Vashti wanted to point out his use of the word "we" felt like a step in the right direction to her. *Are we becoming a team?* The thought made her want to laugh out loud. She didn't, because her attention was drawn to Bertha, who'd returned to her seat and, after glancing around with an expression of bewilderment, resumed her humming and card sorting.

"I'm sorry." Jethro packed away his necromancing artifacts and shook his father's hand in farewell.

"I know you would not have done it if it wasn't important." A slight smile touched his lips. "And those few minutes were very precious." Gillespie turned to Vashti. "The circumstances were unusual, but it was a pleasure to meet you, my dear."

They were almost out of the room when Vashti spoke again. "Wait a moment." She left Jethro waiting by the door.

She returned to where Gillespie stood watching his wife as she dealt her cards and hummed her endless tune. He looked up as Vashti approached. Although she couldn't touch him, she went as close as she could so he could feel her presence. There was a question in his eyes.

"For what it's worth, I believe the ghost lord chose the right successor. I think you will do a good job."

The smile lines around his eyes deepened. "How did you know?"

"Intuition." She shocked herself with her use of the word. *I don't do intuition.* Her eyes dropped to take in Bertha. "You should think about Jethro's offer. Otherworld isn't perfect, but she would have more of a life—"

Gillespie raised his brows and she smiled "—okay, a *death*, there than she has here."

"I will consider it." His expression told her he was serious. "Will I see you again, Vashti?"

"If you ever join the other leaders around the Alliance table, most certainly."

He lifted his eyes to where Jethro—a silent, brooding figure—stood watching them. "That is not what I meant."

Vashti felt the tell-tale blush creep into her cheeks. Oh, good heavens, how was she going to explain to this dear, sweet ghost that he shouldn't regard her as daughter-in-law material? She was surprised he couldn't pick up on the fact Jethro had no romantic inclinations toward her. Ghosts must be immune to those sorts of undercurrents. Or had he sensed she was attracted to his son? Was it a diplomatic way of probing her feelings?

"This is work." Her voice was firm. "For both of us."

Dusk was falling as Jethro cooked dinner while Vashti watched him. She got the feeling this was what he did to calm down after a bad day. He must have had days that were more violent and energetic, but he could not have had many as intense as the one he had just spent watching his mother climb out of her decline before spiraling back into it. A dozen questions rose to Vashti's lips but Jethro's expression was closed and distant. She knew that look. She had used it herself often enough.

Eventually he opened a bottle of red wine, poured two glasses and handed one to her. "Go ahead."

Vashti didn't pretend to misunderstand him. "When did your parents die?"

He grinned at her, tilting his glass in a mock salute before gulping down half its contents. "Good question, and not the one I thought you'd go for first. What really you mean is 'what's a nice mortal boy like me doing with a couple of ghosts for a mom and dad?'"

Vashti didn't answer. She was surprised to experience a pang of sympathy for him. He was trying to pick a fight with her, that much was obvious. Maybe she should let him take his anger out on her. She could be his verbal punch bag, if that was what he needed. Except she didn't think using her as a distraction from his emotions *was* what he needed. And there it was again. Since when had she become the expert on what was best for Jethro de Loix? When had he gone from being someone she hated to some who intrigued her, to someone whose feelings she cared about? And how the hell had the transition happened so fast?

The pause while she went through those thoughts seemed to work. Running a hand through his hair in the gesture he used to signal frustration, Jethro turned to gaze out the window at the darkened landscape. "Would you believe me if I told you their deaths happened almost a century ago?"

Treading carefully around the feelings of another person didn't come naturally to Vashti, but she understood what she said next mattered. More than mattered. It might make the difference between whether this intensely private man opened up to her—perhaps the only time he had ever opened up to anyone in his life—or clammed up forever. "I have no reason not to believe you, but I'm not sure I understand."

He kept his face averted. "I'm not sure how long I've been alive."

Vashti dug deep into her memory, dredging up everything she knew about necromancers. "Isn't it true that necromancers, although born mortal, will, along with their powers, have immortality conferred upon them?"

"Yes."

"Forever is a long time. I don't know many immortals who count the passage of time in mortal years." Jethro didn't respond. "Perhaps you are right. Asking how long ago your parents died was the wrong question. Tell me about your childhood."

His laugh was bitter. "Oh, you're good. Whatever Moncoya did to try to destroy your fae-ness—is that what you call it?—it didn't work."

He was trying to drive her away with his harshness, but she wasn't going anywhere. Among the many traits she had inherited from Moncoya, tenacity was the one she could put to good use in this situation. "Believe it or not, it did. I'm usually crap at intuition, but it must have been lying dormant inside me all along. Today, for some reason, it seems to have surfaced with a vengeance. You get to be on the receiving end."

"What the fuck does that say about me? I'm such a sad specimen even the most unfeeling faerie around gets pity vibes from me?" Jethro's hand shook slightly as he took another gulp of wine. "Sorry, that was uncalled for. Okay, my childhood." He shrugged. "It was unremarkable."

Vashti tried a different approach. "You said the house was built for a wealthy landowner. What was his name?"

His eyes narrowed. This was it. He was either going to answer her or storm out into the night. After a moment, during which he appeared to be fighting an internal battle, Jethro gave a bleak laugh. "Let me serve this food and then we can eat while you interrogate me. How does that sound?"

Vashti hadn't realized she was hungry, but, at those words, her stomach gave a rumble so loud she was surprised Jethro didn't comment on it. "It sounds wonderful.

On one condition." He raised his brows. "I interrogate. You answer. Truthfully."

"You are one bossy faerie. Has anyone ever told you that?"

Vashti grinned at him over the top of her wineglass. "All the time…but you're the first person to mention it today."

Was he going to tell her? All of it? And why her? After a lifetime—and, let's face it, a bloody long one—of determinedly *not* sharing, why was he contemplating opening his heart to Moncoya's daughter, of all people? *Ridicule. Humiliation. Public scorn. Have those things been missing from your life? Because, once she knows, they will become a permanent feature. Everything you've worked so hard to avoid will be a reality.*

At the same time as Jethro's rational self was trying to warn him against confiding in Vashti, something deep inside him, something basic and primeval, was refusing to listen. He didn't just *want* to tell her. He needed to. Had to. Had no choice. The force dragging him to her was like the pull of the earth's magnetic field. He could fight it, but it was a battle he was never going to win. He'd heard about faerie glamour, but having never seen it used or been on the receiving end of it, he'd always been skeptical about its potency. Was Vashti using it on him now? If she was, he suspected she didn't know. Which somehow made it more frightening.

When she didn't question him further as they ate, he actually found himself becoming impatient. *What the hell is wrong with me?* Having made the decision that he was going to do as she'd asked and tell her everything, he suddenly wanted to get on with it.

"This is delicious." Vashti gestured to the plate of pasta in front of her. "You are full of surprises."

"You're not exactly predictable yourself." His eyes lingered on her face, enraptured by the purity of her complexion. An impulse to reach out his hand and run the back of it down her unbruised cheek—just to feel if her skin was as soft as it looked—surged through him and, with an almost superhuman effort, he fought it. Because he knew he wouldn't be able to stop there. He'd have to move on to check if those tempting lips tasted as sweet as they appeared. And if those high, pert breasts fitted into his hands as neatly as they did in his imagination…

"Do you?"

Jethro realized Vashti had asked him a question and he had no idea what it was. What the hell was going on here? He didn't do fantasizing about women. If he liked someone, and the feeling was mutual, they did something about it, then moved on. It was as uncomplicated as that. If the feeling wasn't mutual… He frowned. Had that ever happened? Not that he could recall. He wasn't vain. At least he didn't think he was. It was the way his life had always been until this damn faerie had come along. She wasn't even his type. Petite. Ethereal. Uptight. Know-it-all. Hell, she was the complete opposite of his type.

"Well?"

Oh, shit. She was still waiting for an answer to the question he hadn't heard.

Vashti frowned. "Are you listening to me?"

No point lying about it. He grinned. "No." Gazing into her eyes, Jethro cursed himself for feeling the way he did right now. Something about *this* woman brought a range of new and disturbing emotions storming through him. His need for her was primal, raw and exposed. God knew, he was no stranger to sex, but he had never felt like this before. An insane, intense urge was driving him to carry her up those stairs, throw her down on his bed and bury himself inside her. To shut out the world and lose himself in her.

Vashti slumped back in her seat, regarding him in astonishment. "Why not?"

"Because I couldn't stop thinking about how much I wanted to do this."

Her eyes widened as he leaned forward and, lifting his hand, ran his knuckles down her cheek. Her skin was as smooth and inviting as he'd imagined. When she didn't move away, he brought both hands up to cup her face, his touch gentle because of her bruises, drawing her to him so he could crush her lips beneath his. A tiny exclamation of surprise escaped Vashti before she twined her arms around his neck, pressing closer to him. His mouth caressed and demanded and he was delighted at the willingness with which her lips parted for him.

Hesitantly at first, Vashti's tongue met his, becoming bolder as they twisted and swirled in an ever more frenzied dance.

Jethro felt desire spiral harder and faster than anything he'd known before. Everything changed in that instant. Not just his relationship with this woman. Everything Jethro knew about himself, his world and his feelings shifted and was centered on this moment. On Vashti. There was nothing else. And, if he'd been frightened before, he was fucking terrified now.

He broke the kiss and moved away from her.

"What just happened?" Vashti's voice was husky, her eyes slightly unfocused.

"It was a kiss. That's all." All? Who was he kidding? That had been *the* kiss. The one poets clutched their brows over and singers poured their hearts into lyrics about.

That once-in-a-lifetime, perfect kiss. Why the hell did it have to happen to him with a woman he didn't even like?

"I know that. I meant…is it always like that?" A blush tinged her cheeks with pink, making her appear suddenly vulnerable.

"Haven't you ever kissed anyone before?"

Vashti shook her head shyly. "No. You have, I know."

This was it. His way out. The coward's way. He grabbed it. "Yeah, hundreds of times. It's pretty much always the same. No big deal."

Surely he was about to be struck down for a lie of such enormity? Nothing. No thunderbolt, no pit of hell opening beneath his feet. Of course, he was in deep shit when she kissed someone else and discovered the truth, but Jethro comforted himself with the thought that he was unlikely to be around at the time.

"Oh." Her long lashes swept down, hiding her eyes momentarily. "So you mortals do that sort of thing all the time?"

"Yes." He decided to drive the message home further. "It doesn't mean anything."

The lashes lifted. Those eyes were like headlamps pinning him in their glare. "In that case, can we do it again?"

Jethro tried to maintain his blasé attitude. It was a task made more difficult when her words prompted an instant erection so enormous it seemed to be making its own superhuman efforts to break free from the restraining confines of his jeans. It made even talking a monumentally difficult task. Because there was nothing in the world he wanted to do more than to kiss Vashti again. Except keep kissing her, then maybe take her by the hand and lead her up the spiral staircase to his bedroom…

"I'm going for a run." Anything to take his mind off the throbbing ache in his groin.

"Okay." Should his ego be dented by the fact she didn't appear the least bit concerned? One minute she wanted to kiss him again, the next she was scraping her chair back from the table as if nothing had happened. *I thought I was more memorable than that.* It seemed an encounter with a faerie princess was an effective way of deflating his ego...but not his cock. That remained stubbornly hopeful. "I'll come with you."

"No!" He needed to put some distance between them. "I prefer to run alone."

Vashti shot him a sidelong glance. "I'll clean up here." He'd almost made it to the staircase when her voice halted him. "And, Jethro? I don't know if the kiss was meant to be a distraction. If it was, it was a pretty successful one, but I haven't forgotten. You still owe me some answers."

Chapter 7

You still owe me some answers. Vashti pressed her fingertips to her lips long after Jethro had departed the house. *Leaving aside your strange family life, Jethro, let's start with how you can kiss someone like that and walk away completely unaffected.* How could he be unaware he had turned her life upside down with that first touch of his lips?

Mortals do that all the time? It doesn't mean anything? She gave a soft, disbelieving laugh. If that was the case, why was her whole body on fire with a restless, burning longing, the source of which she didn't understand, but at which she could hazard a pretty good guess? *I'm not mortal, so perhaps that's why I felt it so powerfully? Who cares? You made me want you, Jethro de Loix. Not only that, you made me determined to have you.* Her chin tilted stubbornly. *You don't know me very well...but, when I want something, I get pretty tenacious about it.*

How long could one man run for on an island this size? And what was he running from? It was fully dark now and Vashti gazed out the full-length window. The bay was an inky nothingness, lit only by the moon. Jethro must know the path around the island's perimeter like the back of his hand to be able to do this. She was glad now he had gone without her. Glad of this time away from him to gather her thoughts. It hadn't made her change her mind about her feelings toward him, it had just calmed the raging need to hurl herself at him and beg him to kiss her again. She was glad she had found the strength to restrain herself when he'd refused. It had been difficult, but she had managed it. Moncoya had taught his daughters to behave with dignity at all times. She doubted her father had been thinking of quite such an occasion as this when he'd insisted on etiquette lessons. Nevertheless, she silently thanked him.

To her surprise, about an hour after he had set off, Jethro came down the spiral staircase. Clearly having just emerged from the shower, he was clad only in sweatpants and had a towel slung around his shoulders. The hair on his hard-muscled chest curled damply and the ridges of his abdomen rippled as he moved. It took every ounce of restraint Vashti possessed not to throw herself at him and crawl all over him like an out-of-control kitten. She attempted to view the situation dispassionately. Vashti had always ruthlessly suppressed her own femininity. As she'd grown up, she had been as disappointed as Moncoya that she was not the son he craved. Most of her life had been spent trying to prove she could do anything a man could do. And more. Now, all of a sudden, she found herself rejoicing in the fact she was a woman. Because she wanted this man with a fierceness that was sweet agony.

I might just not mention it to him yet. Her newfound intuition was working overtime.

"I thought there was only one door."

Barefoot, Jethro crossed the kitchen to the coffee machine. "No, you can get into my bedroom through the deck on the upper floor."

He held up the coffeepot in invitation and Vashti nodded. It was incredible the way his presence filled a room. As if every speck of light and matter was suddenly concentrated on him and everything else faded into nothingness. *Is it just me he has that effect on?* She decided not. She had witnessed firsthand his effect on other women. *I am one of many.* The thought didn't enhance her self-esteem. Then Jethro smiled at her as he handed her a mug of coffee and nothing else mattered.

They took their drinks over to the sofa in the family room. "You wanted answers."

"And you wanted to avoid giving them." *Is it weird we're sitting this close and not mentioning the kiss? Is he even thinking of the kiss? How can he* not *be thinking of the kiss?* She was lurching from one emotional high to another without pausing for breath. It was the most exhilarating yet alarming thing she had ever experienced. Like being on an out-of-control roller-coaster ride.

"I'm not great at a lot of things. I don't do opening up to other people. I don't do love." He turned side-on so he could watch her face. When she didn't respond to that blatant warning, he continued. "And I'm not great at sharing."

"I can relate to that." She shot him a glance that was pure mischief. "As a child my motto was always 'Why have half a cake, when you can grab the whole thing and outrun your twin sister.'"

Jethro's laughter was infectious. "Let me ask you something."

Vashti frowned. "When did that become part of the deal?"

He grinned. "Do we have a deal? It seems I'm not the only one who doesn't like questions."

She made an attempt at appearing casual. "Ask away."

The grin deepened. *Damn the man.* He clearly wasn't fooled by her fake nonchalance. "Why does it matter?"

The confusion she felt must have appeared on her face, because Jethro clarified, "Why do you want to know about my life?"

Ah. It was a good question. One she should spend a little time considering carefully. "Because Bertha and Gillespie fascinate me."

It was true. It just wasn't the whole truth. Although she was being unfair to herself by dismissing her interest as being just about Jethro. Bertha had clearly had some involvement, however minor, in the life of the true heir to the faerie crown. It was frustrating Jethro had been unable to discover the extent of his mother's knowledge. But did that mean they'd reached a dead end with this line of inquiry? Only by finding out more about his fascinating family could she learn the answer to that question.

"Okay. Ask away."

Vashti studied his face briefly, an occupation that did strange things to her heart rate. His expression was unguarded, yet it gave her no clue about his feelings. What had brought about this sudden change in approach? From extreme reluctance to easy openness. Was it the kiss or the run that had changed things? Or something else of which she was unaware? She returned to the question she had asked before dinner. "What was the name of the wealthy landowner who built the house we visited today?"

Jethro's eyes were fathomless pools of darkness. "I think you've already figured that out."

Vashti went with what her instincts were telling her. "Very well. If I'm right, his name was Gillespie de Loix. Did you father build the house in 1830?"

It was as if her words released a world of tension inside him. Although they were more than a foot apart, she felt his whole body relax. "Yes."

The next question followed seamlessly. "How long after that did you run into the gatepost?"

"You are scarily good at getting to the point." There was a pause then Jethro released the long, shuddering breath he'd been holding. "It was the day we moved in."

"So you were a young child in 1830, but you don't know exactly how old you were?"

Jethro had decided he needed whiskey instead of coffee and he came through from the kitchen carrying a bottle, an ice bucket and two glasses. Resuming his seat on the sofa, he set the glasses down on the table and commenced pouring them both a hefty measure of the amber-colored liquor.

"No. I've never known that." Jethro tilted his head back on the cushions so he was looking at the ceiling. "I don't believe Bertha and Gillespie were my real parents."

"Ah." That explained a lot, while deepening the mystery. "Did you ever ask them outright if you were adopted?"

"I tried to raise the subject once or twice, but it wasn't easy. They loved me very much, you see." A reminiscent smile twisted his lips and he sat straighter so he could take a drink. "And they gave me everything a child could have wanted. It always felt like a betrayal to cross-examine them about my birth. As though I was saying they weren't enough for me. Does that make sense?"

"Yet they must have anticipated you would want to know."

"I'm not so sure. For a number of reasons. First, there would have been nothing formal about my adoption. Think about it. As you've so astutely figured out, I was born before 1830. How long before is anyone's guess. There were no adoption laws back then."

Vashti wrinkled her brow in confusion. "I have to confess I struggle with the concept of mortal time. We are talking many mortal years between then and now, I take it?"

"Several mortal lifetimes. So, however it was that I came to live with Bertha and Gillespie, it is highly unlikely there was any legal contract involved. Although I don't know exactly how old I was when we moved into the old house, I have always believed I was born in about 1825."

Because his face was in shadow, Vashti couldn't read his expression. "What makes you think that?"

"I'm a necromancer. Our immortality works in a specific way. We progress into adulthood at a normal rate and then simply stop aging. That day in 1830 is my earliest memory, so I guess I was born not long before that."

"You must have inherited your necromancing powers from your birth parents." It was a fascinating story, one that went some way toward explaining the enigma that was Jethro de Loix.

"From one or both of them. I'm one of the strongest necromancers around, part of an elite group that includes Stella, Cal and Lorcan—and Iago—so it's possible they both had the power."

"You said there were other reasons that led you to

believe Bertha and Gillespie might not have expected you to ask questions about your birth parents," Vashti reminded him.

"Yes. And those are to do with my necromancing powers. I think I was under some sort of spell during my childhood. A spell that was intended to suppress my abilities. It's precisely because I *am* so powerful that my abilities were able to override the spell." He sighed, leaning back again. "I've been over and over it. I think it's possible Bertha was so desperate for a child—and Gillespie would do anything to make her happy—that she tried to erase all trace of my background so I wouldn't ask questions."

"But you did question it?" Vashti had never drunk whiskey before. It was having a curious effect, spreading mellow warmth through her veins.

"It was hard not to. They were so old, you see. It was obvious Bertha adored children. She'd devoted her whole life to them, yet she had none of her own. It didn't take much imagination to work out she couldn't have a child of her own. There was no way I was the late arrival in their lives they claimed. I wish I had been. If anyone deserved happiness, it was them." He took a long slug of his drink. "Then Bertha's mind started to go and it wasn't possible to ask her anything. You saw what she was like."

"When did they die?"

"They were killed in 1918. I was away, fighting on the Western Front in Europe." At Vashti's look of confusion, he explained further. "The mortal realm was involved in a great war and I fought as an enlisted soldier. When I returned home, it was to find Bertha and Gillespie had been brutally murdered."

"My God! Who did it?"

"I never found out, but I will never stop trying." Jethro turned his head on the cushions so he was looking directly at her. His face was a mask of sorrow. "This is harder than I imagined it would be. I've never spoken about it before."

Her eyes widened. There it was again. That huge weight of responsibility. The importance of getting it right. "Is that why they stayed? Because they have unfinished business here?"

"They didn't remain in the mortal realm out of any desire for revenge. Even in death, she refused to leave the house she loved. And she couldn't let go of the charity work to which she'd devoted her life." His laughter was affectionate, the sadness gone now. "She insisted on being around to make sure her good work continued. Over the years, Gillespie became more involved in what was happening in the Ghost realm in Otherworld, but Bertha has steadfastly refused to leave here. Her mind had started to deteriorate when she was alive, and strangely, the decline continued after her death. Even when the dementia took a hold so firm she was scarcely recognizable as the strong woman we once knew, she made us promise we would never make her leave her home. Which is why Gillespie is still adamant she must be allowed to stay."

"And the fire you spoke of? That really was an arson attack?"

"I think so. It happened a few years ago on Halloween—" he groaned at her confused expression "—talking to you is like a minefield. I feel like I have to start every conversation with Mortal Culture 101…"

"You do know I have no idea what you are talking about, right?"

"Introductory college classes are traditionally numbered 101. It was my feeble attempt at a joke."

"And Halloween?"

"Much more interesting. Essentially, it is the Celtic

pagan festival of Samhain, which celebrates the end of harvest season. It is the time when the walls between our world and the next become porous, allowing spirits to pass through. They return to life on the day of Samhain to bring mischief to the mortal realm. The name Halloween comes from the words All Hallows Eve. It has become a commercialized festival in recent years."

"Sounds like a lot of fun. Particularly if the burning of houses is involved."

"As I told you, the house has always attracted a lot of superstitious attention locally. That intensifies around Halloween, which, coincidentally, is tomorrow night. I believe it was a random act of vandalism. Am I sure?" He shrugged. "As far as I can be. So there you have it. My life story…what I know of it."

Vashti scanned his shadowed features. Why did she get the feeling he was still keeping something from her?

"Any questions?"

"Just one." Jethro quirked a brow at her. "Why did you change your mind and decide to tell me this, after all?"

Instead of answering he leaned closer, reaching for her hand. "Because I think there is an affinity between us."

Vashti's breath caught in her throat and she swallowed hard. "You said it was just a kiss. The kind of thing mortals think nothing of."

His smile gleamed, full of darkness and promise. "That's not what I meant. When I stepped out of the shower, I took a look in the mirror." He lifted her hand to his face and Vashti's eyes widened in amazement as her fingertips connected with the smooth flesh of his right cheekbone. "My scar is gone."

There were too many questions raging around in Vashti's mind for her to contemplate how to start unrav-

eling them. One minute, they had been caught up in con-
troversy, the focal point of which was Jethro's past life,
then, without warning, it had shifted and become about
Vashti herself. She was still struggling to understand how
the change in focus had happened.

Jethro had asked only one simple question. "Do you
know how you did it?" In response, she had given a help-
lessly noncommittal shrug. He seemed to understand she
was incapable of further discussion about the matter.

Now, alone in the pleasantly cozy guest room, she lay
back on her bed and tried to make sense of a day that had
contained very few rational moments. Her mind insisted
on replaying only those events involving Jethro. *I have
managed to progress through my life so far without ex-
hibiting any of the traditional traits of the fae. Now, in the
few short days I have been in close proximity to Jethro de
Loix, I have discovered a hitherto unsuspected side to my
personality.* Intuition, the power of healing, the glamour…
all the legendary characteristics of the members of the
Seelie Court seemed to be emerging from within her,
prompting a question that could not be ignored. Was Jethro the catalyst for this change?

If she had never met him, would she ever have become
aware she possessed these qualities that had once been
so revered by her race? Somehow she doubted it. Setting
aside the kiss—even though her mind showed an alarming tendency to return to it every few minutes—he had
the ability to light her up from within with just a look or
a touch. *He does something to me no one else can. And
whatever it is appears to have awakened a fundamental talent within me. Something that must always have
been there, lying dormant. Something that was always
meant to be.*

Although her restless thoughts found no answers, they

did come up with another question, one that would not be
banished, no matter how hard she tried to drive it from
her mind. *Why does he have this effect on me?* Was the
answer all too obvious? *Let this not be about how much
I want him. Because surely that will go away once I get
this mad longing out of my system.* Whereas the fact that
her proximity to Jethro appeared to be effecting these
deeper changes to her psyche, suggested something more,
something she didn't want to probe any further. *He said
he doesn't do love. Good, because nor will I.*

Impatient and agitated by a problem she couldn't solve,
Vashti rose from the bed and, opening the sliding door,
wandered onto the balcony that encircled the upper floor
of the house. She was wearing only a thin cotton nightshirt and the cool fall air made her shiver slightly. Leaning
on the rail, she gazed out into the darkness. The uninterrupted silence wrapped itself around her, eerie, yet
strangely comforting. The lake was a glassy reflection,
bouncing back a perfect image of the moon and stars
above her head.

"What are you doing out here?"

Because she hadn't heard Jethro approach, he was right
behind her before she felt his presence. When he spoke,
his voice was a soft growl in her ear. His hands came
down firmly on the rail on either side of her, imprisoning her in the circle of his arms. Vashti attempted to turn
so she was facing him, but he pressed himself hard up
against her, imprisoning her against the balcony rail with
his body. His erection pressed into her spine, signaling
his intentions. A storm of desire shuddered through her
whole body as his teeth nipped at the back of her neck.

She wanted to speak, to protest at his high-handed as-
sumption that this was what she wanted. But wasn't this
exactly what she wanted? What she had been hoping for?

As one muscular arm slid around her waist and the other hand moved to under the hem of her nightshirt to caress her thighs, the only sound she could manage was a helpless whimper.

"Let go of her, you trickster bastard." It was Jethro's voice. Icy with pent-up fury. A few feet away from where Vashti was standing. Yet weren't those his fingertips sliding just inside the elastic of her underwear? What the hell was going on here?

"Must I? We were having so much fun." The voice in her ear was mocking and all too familiar. It took a moment or two, but then the reality of what had happened sank in. With a furious exclamation, Vashti brought her elbow back hard into Iago's stomach. Too late. He was already gone. Only the sound of his derisive laughter lingered briefly in the still night air.

Red-hot heat flooded her face as she turned to face the real Jethro. "I thought it was you…"

Oh, dear God! That didn't make it any better. She might as well admit she would be happy to let him bend her over the balcony rail and take her any time he wanted. Despite his anger, the brighter flare in the dark depths of his eyes was a brief acknowledgment Jethro knew exactly what she was saying.

Drawing in a deep breath to cover her embarrassment, she tried for a more composed tone. "How do you suppose he found us?"

"Your guess is as good as mine." Some of the tension in his frame relaxed slightly. "He could have been with us the whole time. We don't know if he's gone away now."

Vashti brought her hands up to her upper arms, hugging herself against the breeze that suddenly seemed to chill her flesh through the thin fabric of her nightshirt. "That's a horrible thought."

"Would you put it past him? From what I saw just now, I reckon he'd be quite capable of joining you in your bed or in the shower."

Vashti cast a glance over her shoulder. He was right, of course. Iago would try any trick to unnerve them, no matter how devious or dirty. "That settles it. We're swapping rooms."

Jethro shook his head. "It doesn't matter what room you're in, if he wants to find you, he will. And I've had a thought more horrible than yours. He can impersonate me, but he can imitate you just as easily. I don't like the idea of waking up with Iago's tongue in my mouth…or elsewhere. This might seem like a massive U-turn considering my opposition to the idea of you accompanying me on this mission—" he reached out a hand and, much to Vashti's surprise, caught hold of her wrist "—but I'm not letting you out of my sight from now on."

Chapter 8

"I still don't see how locking the door will work if he's already in here with us." Vashti flopped wearily into a chair beside the bed as Jethro prowled around his bedroom, checking the windows.

"If the slimy little bastard is in here, he'll have to show himself sooner or later. That way I can get my hands around his scrawny throat before he has another chance to escape." He flicked a glance in her direction; she looked tired but unbearably desirable. Although he couldn't quite figure out why that should be the case, since she was wearing a perfectly respectable nightshirt that kept her covered from neck to knee.

"Why don't we make this easier? I promise faithfully *not* to try to seduce you during the night. Now, if anyone does slide into bed with you, you'll know it's Iago." Vashti smothered a yawn behind her hand. "Mind you, if he's listening to this conversation, he'll know he's lost the element of surprise. I expect he'll be plotting some-thing else instead." She gave a mischievous chuckle. "Al-ways supposing cozying up to you was his intention. I hate to be the one to break this to you, but you might not be his type."

Her laughter was infectious and Jethro couldn't help smiling in response. "That's the problem. Now he knows where we are, we have to expect the unexpected. All the time." He quickly became serious again. "We also have to assume Iago is not the only one who knows our whereabouts."

Vashti's eyes went to the window, as though she ex-pected to see someone standing in the darkness outside looking in. Even before she spoke, Jethro knew who she was picturing. "My father?" It was as if those two words had drained all the life from her. The laughing sprite of seconds earlier was replaced by a colorless shadow. If the mere thought of Moncoya could do that to his own daughter, was it any wonder Cal didn't want him ruling the faerie dynasty?

"He and Iago are allies. As soon as Moncoya gets an inkling of this mission to find the challenger, he'll do ev-erything he can to put a stop to it." He drew the drapes, shutting out the darkness and, hopefully, Moncoya's image with it. "I think it's time to move on, don't you?"

"Do we have to go right now?" Vashti cast a longing look in the direction of the bed.

"Tomorrow will do. There is something I have to do first, and I want to see Gillespie again before we go."

"Why?"

Why indeed? Jethro wasn't sure he could answer that question. He just felt there was unfinished business back at the old house. What it was, he couldn't say, or even guess at. "To make sure Bertha isn't suffering any ill effects." It was the truth, but not all of it. "And I suppose I need one final attempt to get him to let me send Bertha to Otherworld."

Vashti glanced around the room again. "Iago isn't in here."

"What makes you say that?" He came to sit near her on the bed, so close their knees were almost touching. Her eyes were huge in the pale oval of her face, the sidhe ring of fire blazing brighter than ever.

"I just feel it." She shook her head. "The fae has never been strong in me, but, since I've been in the mortal realm, its force has been growing more powerful all the time. A minute ago, when I said he wasn't here, I was fairly sure I was right. Since you sat down there, I've become absolutely certain of it." Her eyes scanned his face. "Could your nearness affect my ability?"

Jethro shrugged. "I'm not dismissing the idea, but I don't know. It's not something I've experienced or even heard of."

Vashti stretched her arms above her head. "Maybe I'm being fanciful and I just need to get some sleep. Since you've locked me in here, do you mind explaining the sleeping arrangements?"

The bed was huge, but Jethro very much doubted she'd be willing to share it. On one level, he felt a sense of regret. He had a feeling sharing a bed with Vashti could turn out to be a life-changing experience. But was life-changing what he wanted—or needed—right now? On a purely physical level, there was only one answer to that question. It started with *hell* and ended with *yeah*. Of course he did. His rational mind attempted to restore a sense of balance. Life was complicated enough. Distance was what was needed here.

"You take the bed." He pointed at the sofa Bertha had

lovingly restored many years ago. He knew from experience it was the most uncomfortable item of furniture in the house. "I'll sleep there. And just so we're clear—" Vashti glanced up at him, a question in her eyes "—that promise you made works both ways. I won't be sneaking in beside you, either."

She blushed. "I'm so tired I wouldn't notice."

Just as he'd decided to be sensible and keep his distance, some roguish impulse prompted him to see if he could deepen that blush further. "Oh, you'd notice."

Sure enough, the soft tinge of color in her cheeks darkened to a deep rose and she drew in a ragged breath. Jethro decided it was the most enticing sound he had ever heard. Unfortunately, the success of his tactics meant he was now going to endure a night tormented by erotic fantasies instead of getting the decent sleep he desperately needed. It was worth it, to see that look of delicious confusion spread across her face.

"Sweet dreams, Princess." Grabbing a pillow and blanket from the top shelf of the closet, he settled into his makeshift bed.

Jethro gulped coffee and groaned, stretching his limbs. Every muscle seemed to cry out in protest after possibly the worst night's sleep he'd ever had. And that was saying something when he considered some of the places he'd been forced to get his head down in the past.

Vashti, who looked bright-eyed, regarded him over the top of her coffee cup. "I slept really well."

"Yes, my bed *is* comfortable, isn't it? At least your slumber was uninterrupted by Iago."

"Completely uninterrupted." She placed her coffee cup on the counter, casting him a sidelong glance as she did. "By anyone."

"Hey—" Jethro held up a hand in a mock defensive gesture "—I told you I wouldn't be sneaking in beside you." He watched her face, sensing the change in mood as she fought some sort of internal battle.

Vashti took a deep breath, turning to face him. "Maybe I hoped you would."

Damn. It took Jethro two steps to close the space between them. This wasn't what he needed…so how come he had never needed anything so much in his whole life? He didn't so much meet Vashti halfway as collide with her as she cast herself into his arms. Why had he wasted hours on that rock-hard sofa last night torturing himself with fantasies, when this was what she wanted, too? That was the last coherent thought he had for some time.

Vashti rose on the tips of her toes, pressing her lips to his. It started tender. Just a simple kiss. No pressure. But the tingle her touch sent through him stripped the last remnants of Jethro's willpower away. His mouth possessed her. With a murmur of approval, Vashti slipped her arms around his neck. The kiss peaked and became dizzying. Her lips parted to the insistent demands of his and, when his tongue swept inside, she responded instantly. Each time his tongue glided across hers, Jethro felt a tremor run through her in response. He broke away, panting harder than after his run the previous night.

"Sure about this?"

"Do I look like someone who's having second thoughts?" Since her fingers moved to the button on his jeans as she spoke, he assumed the question was rhetorical.

Jethro didn't need any further encouragement. Tugging Vashti's nightshirt up, he grasped her around the waist, lifting her onto the counter. His fingers scrabbled frantically at his zipper, freeing his erection. Thanking past experience for the foresight that meant he always had a condom in his pocket, he fumbled with the foil wrapper. Standing between Vashti's thighs, he gripped his latex-sheathed cock in one hand, positioning himself at her entrance. Vashti clutched his shoulders, meeting his gaze and giving him the permission his eyes sought. Clenching the powerful muscles of his buttocks, Jethro thrust into her. Her cry—a sound midway between pleasure and surprise—rang out as her head fell back and her whole body tensed.

"Did I hurt you?" It took every ounce of restraint he possessed to hold still.

"It's not that—" she caught her lip between her teeth "—it's just so much *more* than I expected."

"We haven't started yet."

Jethro's every muscle ached with the effort of keeping his raging desire in check. He desperately needed to finish this the way his body was demanding, to pound into her, to take her hard and fast and furious. Mindful of her inexperience, he knew he had to take it slow. Sliding his hands beneath her buttocks, he lifted her closer. Her flesh was silk beneath his hands, her unique fragrance seeped into his pores, her blue eyes claimed him.

He groaned as Vashti tightened her muscles around him. "What the hell are you doing?"

"Using my initiative." Her voice was unbearably husky. "Is that allowed?"

"Only if you're prepared to take the consequences." He pinned her with his gaze.

"I'll risk it." She gripped him harder.

Slipping partway out of her, Jethro thrust forward again, gritting his teeth as the need to lose control almost overwhelmed him. Her heat engulfed him, stiffening his cock, electrifying the nerve endings in his spine and drenching him in sweat. His erection jerked inside her and he dragged in a shuddering breath.

"Please..." Vashti begged, "I need you to keep doing that."

Needing no further encouragement, he held her in position so she was impaled on his cock and pistoned his hips hard and fast. Vashti's muscles clenched around his throbbing shaft as he stretched and then released her. She wrapped her legs around his hips, bucking in time with his rhythm, taking as much of his cock as she could. He drove into her as if he couldn't get deep enough, couldn't take her fast enough, couldn't get enough of her. As he ground his pelvis against hers, sparks of sensation shimmered from the point of contact between them to his nerve endings. Jethro's thrusts grew ever more frenzied, his cock thickening and his sac tight and aching. Vashti tangled her fingers in his hair and held on as her body shattered into orgasm, her body gripping him rhythmically and forcing him to join her. Panting, convulsed with pleasure, he buried his face in the curve of her neck, groaning as he emptied himself into her.

When he finally eased out of her and lifted her from the counter, Jethro held Vashti against him. The whirlwind of emotion coursing through him was like nothing he had ever experienced. What the hell was going on? This sense of completion went way beyond the fulfillment great sex—okay, amazing, earth-shattering sex—brought with it. This was a maelstrom of feeling that gripped him and flung him to the edge of euphoria. Whatever it was, Vashti was clearly feeling it, too. She clung to him as if she was buffeted by a storm and he was her sanctuary. If this woman was trying to drive him insane, she was doing a pretty good job. Already, the memory of the enchantment of being inside her was washing over him again.

She was invading his senses. The smell of her hair. The feel of that silken skin. The honeyed taste of her lips. His body was beginning to crave her again, mere seconds after withdrawing from her.

"Are you going to tell me mortals do *that* all the time?" Her voice was slightly stunned. "That it meant nothing?"

He gave a shaky laugh. "If I did, I'd be lying."

How could he explain his feelings to her when he didn't understand them himself? Cursing the set of circumstances that had brought them to this point in time, Jethro wished he could turn back the clock. To that Alliance meeting when he had negotiated this mad deal. Not because he wished the last half hour of his life undone. On the contrary, he wanted to repeat it. Every day. Forever. But that wasn't going to happen. This was Moncoya's daughter, for fuck's sake! She was probably going to one day marry some powerful Otherworld leader and preside over her own dynasty. Hell, she could end up reigning over the vampire territory as Tibor's bride. They could demand Jethro's head on a plate as a wedding gift and every undead being in Otherworld would be falling over themselves to provide it. *I'd have walked away from this challenge if I'd known she could make me feel like this.* Jethro had believed he was immune to the sort of lightning bolt that had struck Cal and Lorcan. He gave himself a mental shake. *I am* immune. *Just because we had great sex doesn't make us bonded together for life.*

Now he had to convince himself of that, before explaining it to Vashti. Just as he was pursuing that line of thought, Vashti lifted her head. The usually clear, pale blue of her eyes was darker and stormier, the ring of fire muted.

"We should get ready to leave."

Jethro nodded, releasing her from the circle of his arms

and watching as she walked away from him toward the spiral staircase. He had been about to say the same thing. So where had this overpowering sense of disappointment come from?

Vashti gave Jethro an incredulous look as he locked up the house. His jaw was tight, his expression closed and completely unreadable. *So, clearly we are going to continue as if nothing happened.* It was as if that tumultuous outpouring of passion between them had never taken place. Was he regretting it? It certainly looked that way. Vashti's pride kicked up a notch. *Who the hell does he think he is? Or is this what he does? Is he so used to having any woman he wants he doesn't acknowledge his partner has feelings?* True, she had been the one to withdraw from their embrace and walk away. But only because she had acted on the turmoil she sensed in him. Whatever inner battle he had been waging immediately after they made love, it appeared to have been resolved in favor of a return to taciturnity. Well, two could play at that game. No way was Vashti going to cling to him and try to cajole him into analyzing what had happened between them. No matter how much she wanted to.

Swinging her bag up onto her shoulder, she marched away from the house and out onto the jetty. By the time Jethro joined her, she had reached the foot-tapping stage of annoyance. Tanzi would have recognized the warning signs. Jethro barely glanced in her direction as he placed their bags in the boat. When he sprang lightly down into the little vessel and reached up a hand to help her down, Vashti ignored him.

He appeared not to notice, turning away to start the engine as she joined him in the boat. Once they set off, Vashti looked back at de Loix Island as it grew smaller

in the distance. From the water, it was easier to appreciate the beauty of the cedar-log house, sitting high on the
island, commanding views across the surrounding bay.
Despite Iago having found them there, it was the first
place in the mortal realm where she had felt safe. She had
also learned a thing or two about herself. She experienced
a faint tug of sadness knowing she would never return.
*Tanzi was right. We can care. We just have to be placed
in the right situations to discover it.* The thought no longer had the power to shock her. Instead it was strangely
comforting.

Risking a glimpse at Jethro, she found he was staring
at her. Even though his face remained impassive, there
was a searing intensity in the dark depths of his eyes. He
looked as though he was about to say something. Vashti's
breath hitched in anticipation…then the shutters came
down and he looked away.

When they reached the boathouse, Jethro finally spoke.
"Wait in the boat while I check the place out. Iago might
have been here ahead of us." When she opened her mouth
to protest, his expression softened slightly. "Please? I
know how the place should look. It will be quicker if I
do it alone."

Grudgingly, Vashti agreed. Jethro disappeared inside,
reemerging again after a few minutes to signal everything
was fine. Vashti tossed their bags up to him and this time
allowed him to take her hand so he could help her onto
the decking at the rear of the boathouse. Anything else
would have resulted in an undignified scramble. "Has
Iago been here?"

"If he has, I can't see any signs. I need to check the
bike over, but tampering with vehicles isn't Iago's style.
It's not theatrical enough."

They went inside and Jethro wheeled the bike out onto

the grass at the front of the boathouse. Vashti watched as he gave it a thorough examination before pronouncing it sound. She was struck again by his hands. She'd seen those hands do many things. They were strong and capable, nimble as they fiddled with the bike's valves and gears. Vashti recalled their gentleness with Bertha. Her mouth went suddenly dry as she thought of those long fingers on her own body…she looked away abruptly as a wave of pure lust hit her.

Oblivious to what she was feeling, Jethro stowed their belongings in the cargo box and handed Vashti a helmet. She remembered he'd said he had something he needed to do before they went to see Gillespie. "Where are we going?"

"It's something I have to do. A promise I made."

That was it? That was all he was prepared to tell her? He was still being strong and silent? Of all the emotions Vashti was feeling, frustration was the one that fizzed to the surface. "Do you have to do this whole enigmatic thing every time?"

He frowned. "What do you mean?"

"I mean why do I have to pry everything out of you? Just for once can't you volunteer something? A little snippet? Like where we're going? What you're doing? How you're feeling—?"

She broke off as he grabbed her by her upper arm, and hauled her to him. "You want to know how I'm feeling? Okay, I'll tell you. I'm feeling like my whole fucking world got turned upside down this morning. By you. Like I want you every minute, with every breath I take. I can't stand to be near you and not touch you." Just as Vashti relaxed against him, he let out a shuddering breath. "But I don't *want* to want you. I don't do needing. This is not who I am—"

His words were cut short as Vashti pressed her fingers to his lips. "I wanted information, not a grand declaration. This isn't the time for soul searching. Not with Iago snapping at our heels. Let's stick to where we're going, shall we?"

Some of the anguish went out of his expression and he gave a shaky laugh. "What the hell are you doing to me?" The words came out as though torn from him against his will. "Emotional speeches are not my style. Not usually, anyway." He released her, his expression still slightly disbelieving. "We're going to visit a place near the old village of Head Tide. It will take too long to explain, but it'll become clear when we get there. Now, can we get going before a deadly cobra emerges from the cargo box or Iago bursts out of the woods in his latest grizzly bear disguise?"

He didn't add, "Or Moncoya turns up with his henchmen in tow?" He didn't need to. They were both thinking it.

Once they were out on the open road, Jethro kicked the bike up a gear so the scenery flashed past. Vashti gave herself up to the sensation of speed and his nearness, splaying her fingers across the iron-hard ridges of his abdominal muscles. *So you want me, but you're fighting it? That's okay.* A smile touched her lips. *We both enjoy a challenge, and we're evenly matched. But just so we're clear, my big, hot necromancer, there will only be one winner in this contest. And she's sitting right behind you.*

Chapter 9

The mansion resembled a child's dollhouse with its square shape, symmetrical features and perfectly maintained white-clapboard exterior and extensive gardens. Beyond the house itself, Vashti glimpsed the sparkling curve of a river wending its way in the distance. It was an idyllic location and the sound of distant children's laughter filling the air added to the perfection of the scene.

Jethro left the bike in a small-car parking area and they followed a path around to the front of the house. A brass sign beside the door welcomed them to Toussaint House. A small plaque underneath bore the words "Established 1863."

"What is this place?" The atmosphere was so calm and tranquil Vashti almost felt she should whisper in case the sound of her voice shattered the peace.

"Toussaint House was originally the Toussaint Home for Young War Orphans. It was founded by Bertha during a civil war that tore this country apart." Jethro rang a bell at the side of the door. "Rather in the same way we anticipate your dynasty could be devastated if the return of the challenger is not handled correctly."

"Toussaint?"

"Bertha's maiden name. Her family were great philanthropists."

The sound of footsteps from within ended their conversation. The door was opened by a young woman whose face lit up when she saw Jethro. "Mr. de Loix, what a pleasant surprise!" Her hand went instinctively to her hair, smoothing it. "We weren't expecting you."

"This is a brief visit, Ella. I was in the area and I wanted to see if there was anything you needed."

They stepped into a wide, bright hallway. A broad arch spanned the center and the dark wood antique furnishings included a huge grandfather clock that sat on the first turn of the galleried staircase. A series of framed portraits lined the walls. The atmosphere was calm and organized; the air redolent of furniture polish and baking.

"Toussaint House is one of the few remaining privately run orphanages in the state," Jethro explained to Vashti. "Ella is responsible for the day-to-day running of the home on behalf of the board of trustees." Obviously feeling an introduction was required, he continued. "Miss—" he flashed a wicked grin in Vashti's direction "—Moncoya here is an independent observer. She's come along to assure herself I conduct all of my activities in an ethical manner."

Ella, who was clearly devoted to her employer, bristled slightly and regarded Vashti with a look that was decidedly less than friendly. "You are welcome to observe any aspect of what we do here. Perhaps you'd like to see the children?" Without waiting for an answer, she led them through the hall and into a vast dining room. Opening the French windows at the rear of this room, Ella gestured to Jethro and Vashti to step forward onto the terrace beyond.

The gardens, which sloped down to the river's edge, had been allowed to grow into a semblance of wilderness. Although there were pathways through the shrubs and trees, they were overhung with branches and resembled tunnels and mazes. Groups of children were engaged in various pursuits including climbing trees, wading at the water's edge and cutting back some of the thicker shrubs.

"We have up to thirty children here at any one time, varying in age from between five to twelve years," Ella explained as they observed the activity. "Our specialty is that we take children who are hard to place in foster care. Children who have, for whatever reason, been traumatized by their life experiences and may have developed behavior problems. Our goal is to place them with adoptive parents and we have a high success rate."

"You don't seem to use conventional teaching methods here," Vashti commented as a group of children pushing carts piled high with leaves walked past them. They were red-faced with exertion and their laughter and chatter was infectious.

"Our founder, Bertha de Loix, believed children who have experienced severe mental stress need to learn life skills and have fun before they can face academic learning. We use a combination of both types of education here."

As they watched, Jethro asked Ella questions about the administration of the orphanage. Vashti listened with half an ear. So this was the reason why he wanted that million-dollar bounty from the Alliance. He needed it to maintain this haven. And she had thought him grasping. The thought humbled her. Every day she was with him brought a fresh revelation about this man. Gradually the layers of privacy were being stripped away and she was seeing more of the real Jethro de Loix.

"We have to go." Jethro jerked his head and they walked back through to the hall.

Vashti paused in front of the portraits. The largest canvas was of a woman in a traditional pose. Although she had been much younger when the picture had been painted, Vashti recognized Bertha. It was the central portrait that drew her attention, however. Clad in a soldier's uniform and sporting a mustache, the man in the painting was unmistakable. The artist had perfectly captured the devil-may-care arrogance that was the essence of Jethro.

"The likeness is remarkable, isn't it?" Ella asked. "Everyone comments on it." She turned to Jethro. "This gentleman was…what? Your great-great-grandfather?" He managed a noncommittal smile as an answer. Turning to Vashti, Ella held out her hand in a formal gesture. "I hope your visit has been a productive one? Although I am surprised you have come so soon after your colleague."

"One of her colleagues has been here recently?" Jethro asked and Vashti's heart rate kicked up a notch as she sensed the matching tension in Jethro's frame.

"Yes, just yesterday. Such a pleasant man. He was so interested in everything we do." Ella turned her head to smile at Jethro. "I almost forgot. He asked me to pass on his regards to you. He was most insistent about it."

"Do you remember his name?"

Ella frowned in an effort to concentrate. "I don't. How odd. It's not like me to forget someone's name. I'm not sure he told me…but he signed the visitor's book." She led them to a grand oak desk at the side of the front door. Opening a book that lay on the polished surface, she tapped the page with one fingertip. "Here it is." A crease appeared between her brows as she read what was written. "I hadn't looked at it until now. What a strange thing to write."

Jethro leaned over so he, too, could see what had been written. Concerned at the sudden change in his expression, Vashti read the words aloud. "'They are all gone away, There is nothing more to say.'" She glanced from Jethro to Ella. "I don't understand. What does it mean?"

"It's a line from a poem by Edward Arlington Robinson who was born here in Head Tide in 1869," Ella explained.

"We have to get going. Right now." Grabbing Vashti by the hand, Jethro propelled her out the door. They barely paused to say goodbye to Ella, who stared after them in consternation.

Vashti was forced to break into a run to keep up with Jethro as they made their way back to the bike. "Is it Iago?"

"I'd put money on it."

"Where are we going?"

"Back to the old de Loix house." He paused next to the bike, catching his breath. "That bastard has gone after Bertha and Gillespie."

"How do you know?" The anxiety gripping his features was painful to see.

"Because the title of Robinson's poem is 'The House on the Hill.'"

The last time they had passed through Darwen, the town had seemed to be slumbering away a lazy, late morning. This time, when they arrived, the afternoon was well advanced and there was an energy about the place that was at odds with its former atmosphere. It wasn't a pleasant mood. There was a dark, sinister feeling that made Vashti want to keep glancing over her shoulder. Or maybe it was the knowledge of Iago's nearness that made her feel that way. Possibly it was the fact that the main street appeared to be filled with miniature ghosts, vampires and hobgoblins.

"Who are all these people?" Vashti moved closer to Jethro, eyeing the oddly dressed passersby with suspicion.

"Trick or treaters. It's a Halloween tradition. Don't worry, they're just kids dressed up. This is the early crowd. The serious ones come out after dark."

Vashti sidestepped a child in a bedsheet who carried a miniature bucket that was overflowing with candy. "I don't know. I've got a bad feeling about some of these."

"With good reason. There'll be some chronic stomachaches later." Although the words were light, that tension was still there. His whole body was like a coiled spring and Vashti knew that he was waiting for Iago to make his move. Or for what they would find when they reached the old house.

"Could Iago actually harm Bertha or Gillespie?" she asked as they commenced the steep climb out of town. The feeling of walking into peril took a grip on Vashti's imagination as the squeals and laughter of the main street faded. "They are already dead."

"As well as being a trickster, Iago is a necromancer. He's as powerful as I am. I haven't seen him at work, but Lorcan has. He told me Iago is capable of controlling a dozen zombies using the power of his thoughts."

Jethro's words conjured up an image too awful to contemplate. If Iago could wield that sort of power, what could he do to poor, confused Bertha and courteous Gillespie? "Why is Iago so evil? What made him this way?" All Vashti knew was that Iago's story was tied into the legend of King Arthur.

"He is one of the two sons of Mordred, the illegitimate son of King Arthur and the notorious sorceress known as Morgan le Fay."

That stirred something in the depths of Vashti's memory. "That can't be right. Morgan le Fay was King Arthur's half sister."

"They had a relationship before they knew they were related. Mordred was the result. Not surprisingly, it didn't make for a happy outcome."

Vashti grimaced. "And I thought my family was dysfunctional."

"Mordred was killed by Cal at the battle of Camlan, just after he struck the blow that felled Arthur. Bizarrely, when Cal took Arthur to Avalon, it was Morgan le Fay who nursed him. That's the point at which conflicting legends kick in. Some say she saved him and he still lives. Others say he died and was laid to rest on Avalon. Another story is he lies sleeping, waiting for a time when he is needed. When that day comes, Arthur will rise up and once again become the greatest king the world has known."

They had reached the point on the hill where the weather vane on top of the de Loix house peeked through the trees. The sense of malevolence was tangible. Vashti felt as if she could reach out a hand and touch the darkness created by Iago's hidden presence. The soaring trees hid their secrets well. Even the awakening creatures of the night fell silent in anticipation.

Just as he had done when they'd come to the house the first time, Jethro held out his hand and, with real gratitude, Vashti twined her fingers with his. Jethro raised his other hand and, in that way that was unique to necromancers, lit their path. When they followed the path to the house, despite the near darkness, the ramshackle old building looked much as it had the previous day. But it wasn't. They both knew it. The circle of menace was closing in on them.

"You said my presence strengthens your instincts." Jethro turned to face Vashti, taking both her hands in his. "What do you feel?"

The force of her response almost threw Vashti off her feet. "Iago. He is close and he is not alone."

"You asked why Iago is evil." Jethro's gaze locked on hers steadied Vashti's out-of-control emotions. "You were there, that day on Spae, when Iago told us he'd been raised on Avalon by Morgan le Fay and her half sister Niniane. Believe me, either one of those two could turn a saint into a sinner with a single look. Together they were concentrated malevolence. Give them a child to raise? If he wasn't determined to ruin the lives of people I care about, I could almost pity Iago."

As if on cue, and in mockery of Jethro's sympathetic words, an explosion tore the roof off the house, shattering the calm of the surrounding forest and sending a volcano of flames and sparks shooting into the darkening sky. It was a pyrotechnic spectacle of epic proportion. With one accord, Jethro and Vashti broke into a run toward the building.

When they reached the house, Jethro paused, holding Vashti back with an arm across her waist before she could bound up the steps. The sight that greeted them was pitiful. The blast had completely destroyed the roof, causing it to collapse in on itself. Bright cinders and billowing smoke were already pouring from the space. The air thrummed with the tang of wanton destruction.

Vashti placed a hand on Jethro's restraining arm, pointing toward the ruin. From within the clouds of smoke, Gillespie staggered down the steps and came toward them, carrying Bertha in his arms. She was struggling to get away from him.

"She wouldn't leave." The words were a harsh rasp, as if the smoke had penetrated his throat. "Even now, she refuses to be parted from her beloved home."

Jethro stepped forward, his face tight with a combination of pain and fury. Vashti sensed his frustration that he could not relieve Gillespie of his burden by taking Bertha from him. When a body had no substance, only another phantom could hold it. Her heart ached for Jethro, knowing he longed to comfort his parents with an embrace he could never give.

Instead, Jethro became brisk. "We don't have much time. The bastard who did this won't stop now. Let me send her to Otherworld. At least you know she'll be safe in the phantom realm."

"What about the two of you?" Gillespie glanced from Jethro to Vashti, concern on his face.

"We're looking forward to meeting up with him again," Vashti assured him, her voice grim. She hoped Iago could hear her.

"Very well." Gillespie nodded. "What do you want me to do?"

"Nothing. Ghosts are more fortunate than the rest of us. You don't need to find a portal to Otherworld. You can go there any time you choose. I'll persuade Bertha the time has come for her to leave the mortal realm for good. Then all you have to do is depart together."

"Will it hurt her?" Gillespie looked down at the figure in his arms. Bertha had begun to tire and her desperate writhing turned to quiet sobbing as she looked back at her ruined home.

"She won't like it, but she will not be harmed," Jethro promised him. Stepping closer, he held his hand above

Bertha's head. "*Afaran.* Depart this place." His voice was soft and compassionate.

Bertha shuddered into awareness. "No!" Her eyes were wide and pleading. She turned her head to look reproachfully up at her husband's face. "You promised I would not have to go. The fae one will seek me out..." Her voice drifted through confusion into nothingness.

"Take care, my son." Gillespie held up a hand in farewell as the two ghostly figures faded into the surrounding dusk.

As they faded away, Vashti spoke quietly. "How is it you don't do love when you have had such a perfect example of it before you all your life?"

"I've wondered about that. It's as if something deep inside me is broken." He looked down into her eyes. "Almost as if I've had a bad experience, but I've never been in love."

"Sorry. That question was way too deep for this situation." The two figures had gone completely now and Vashti reached out instinctively for Jethro's hand. "What now?"

His fingers closed around hers. "Now we wait."

While they waited for Iago to become visible and make his move, Jethro's emotions swung back and forth on a pendulum between relief he had Vashti, a seasoned and ruthless fighter, at his side, and concern for her welfare. How did that happen? At what point had he gone from feelings of irritation at having her presence forced on him to caring about what happened to her? And why the hell hadn't he noticed the change creeping up on him? Because now it was too late. He was backed into a corner with someone who mattered. A lot. And the evil trick-

ster who was toying with him would not only know it…
he would use it to his advantage.

"Shit!"

"What is it?" Vashti had been facing away from him
but at Jethro's exclamation, she swung around to face him.

He shook his head. How could he explain? The expletive had been wrung from him at the realization Iago
would sense Jethro's weakness and go after Vashti first.
Would the fact she was the daughter of Iago's ally, Moncoya, count in her favor? Jethro almost laughed aloud at
the thought. This was Moncoya. The King of the Faeries had killed his own wife when she tried to leave him.
He had tried to sell Vashti's twin sister to the devil. He
wouldn't think twice about sacrificing his daughter if it
meant winning a fight.

Could he tell Vashti to go? Get out of here? Leave him
to deal with this? Jethro almost laughed out loud. First, at
his chances of Vashti listening to him and, second, at the
possibility Iago would leave her alone so she could escape
to safety. No, they were in this together. He gripped her
hand harder and Vashti gave him a questioning glance.
Jethro returned the look with a reassuring smile. Despite
his misgivings, together was how he liked it.

"What did Bertha mean when she said the fae one
would be able to find her now?"

"Who knows? Her mind is so full of holes it's like a
fragile piece of old lace. Even when she does speak, she'll
say things that only make sense to her. I guess that was
one of those things."

He could see Vashti wasn't convinced, but a debate about the state of Bertha's mental health was not
to be forthcoming. There were voices—normal, mortal voices—coming toward them along the path that
lead from the road and he could see flashlights bobbing

through the trees. A dog barked and someone shushed it nervously. Obviously a group of townsfolk had decided to make their way up the hill to find out what was going on.

"Damn. I suppose it was too much to hope Iago's little fireworks display wouldn't attract attention down in the town." He sighed. "I do not want any innocent bystanders caught up in his games."

"I think it might be too late."

She was right. The shadows around them had started to undulate, flickering like candlelight in a breeze. Jethro could feel the darkness pounding in his blood. He knew that feeling. Vampires. Older than sin and twice as deadly. Within seconds there were dozens of beautiful vampires encircling him and Vashti, each one hell-bent on taking Jethro's severed head back to Prince Tibor. Even as he tried to count them and assess what he was up against, more appeared.

Jethro could control the undead, but this many at once? And while he was busy with the bloodsuckers, what would Iago be doing? The answer came sooner than he anticipated. It was not the one he wanted. The flashlights in the woods changed direction as the focus of the group from the town shifted abruptly away from the burning house and toward something else. An animal howled, a woman screamed and a flurry of activity ensued.

"Lord! Was that a wolf?" The man who spoke was clearly shaken. "Did anyone bring a gun?"

"Get me out of this circle so I can deal with Iago." Vashti kept her voice quiet and level.

"No way. Not on your own."

A scream from the depths of the trees followed his words. "He'll make us listen while he kills them one by one." The obscure figures around them drew closer, adding to the sense of urgency. "We have no choice."

She was right, of course. "Promise me you'll be careful." Who was he kidding? They both knew she wouldn't be careful.

"Just do it."

"Oflinnan." Jethro issued the halt command and the vampires closest to them instantly stilled. It was the most powerful word in the necromancer's armory. The ancient Anglo-Saxon language of his predecessors worked on the dead at a soul-deep level. Even in the case of vampires whose souls had long gone. Yet even this powerful trick was no match for the sheer number of creatures before him. As the front rank of vampires froze, the next line was moving closer. It was a carefully planned maneuver.

"Swactrian." Jethro gave the order to depart and the vampires under his control whirled obediently into their bat form, wings flapping as they flew away. This attack had Iago's signature scrawled all over it. Jethro would be tied up doing nothing but issuing instructions to vampires, his psychic energy slowly draining. Meanwhile, Iago was free to do as he pleased.

"Can I go now?" Pulling her hand free of his, Vashti was already poised to sprint through the vampires and head in the direction of the trees.

"Oflinnan. Wait. Let me think. *Swactrian."*

"Sorry. Thinking is a luxury we don't have time for." Without waiting for a response, she was gone.

Muttering a curse under his breath, Jethro returned to his alternating halt and retreat commands while trying to formulate a plan to break the cycle so he could follow her.

Chapter 10

Jethro took his responsibilities toward the dead seriously and always tried to keep his dealings with them ethical. It was his job to care for them in death as they wished to be cared for in life. That was the necromancer code. It included not raising the dead without good reason.

Yet faced with a never-ending swarm of barely visible vampires while Iago did God knew what to a group of innocent mortals, Jethro considered this situation a good reason. Having Vashti dealing with Iago alone counted as another—even better—reason.

He thought of the age-old question he and Lorcan debated now and then. Zombies versus vampires? Who would win that fight? The answer seemed straightforward. Vampires were possessed of immense strength, speed and intelligence, particularly now that darkness had fallen. Zombies, on the other hand, were slow, shuffling and operated on pure instinct. But they were hardwired to never give up. What would happen when an army of beautiful monsters faced a legion of unstoppable ghouls? It was time to find out. He wished Lorcan was here to see the end result. He wished Lorcan was here. Period.

Keeping up his alternating chant of ordering the vampires to freeze and then depart—while trying not to let his mind dwell on what might be happening to Vashti—Jethro introduced a new command, one intended for a different audience. He hated this part of the job. Zombies were easy to raise but they could be bastards to get back in their box.

"*Awacnian.* Awaken." Jethro raised his outstretched arms to shoulder height and bowed his head. "*Hidercyme.* Come here. Come to me."

They were on their way. Almost immediately he could feel their ghastly presence. The cemetery was close by. Even zombies, with their lumbering gait, would cover the distance in no time. He hoped no one was around to witness what was happening in Darwen's churchyard right now. It would be a Halloween to remember, that was for sure. The town would never forget the night every occupant of the graveyard rose and decided to go for a stroll...

The vampires quickly picked up on the change in mood. The circle moved closer to Jethro as those around him bared their fangs in an angry, collective hiss.

"*Fýrwylm.*" Jethro raised his hands, keeping his palms upward. Flames shot from his fingertips, engulfing the vampires, who shrank back with shrieks of rage. Fire wouldn't kill them, but it would hold them back until the zombies arrived. It sure as hell wasn't doing anything for their mood. The group of pissed-off, singed-around-the-edges vampires turned eagerly as wet, shuffling sounds signaled the arrival of Jethro's zombie army.

Zombies had no brains. Each individual zombie cell

was programmed to fight for the necromancer who controlled them. Their body could be hacked into pieces and each piece would continue to fight. As long as Jethro remained close by, he could leave his foul-smelling, brainless foot soldiers to carry out his bidding. He might not like them, but these zombies were the ultimate in blind, unthinking loyalty.

Jethro knew from experience it was best to keep zombie instructions simple. He couldn't tell them the truth. He couldn't say, "Gather round and listen up, guys. You can't kill these blood-sucking bastards. Not unless you stake them through the heart, then decapitate them." How did you explain a concept like that to a shuffling, snuffling mass who didn't share a single brain cell between them? The best he could hope for was that the zombies would keep the vampires occupied while he and Vashti got the mortals out of Iago's clutches and to safety. Dealing with the aftermath? He wasn't looking forward to that.

"Kill them." He pointed to the vampires. "All of them."

Raising their arms in front of them in the familiar zombie stance, his corpse fighters shambled forward to meet the whirling mass of vampires. Whatever the outcome, this was not going to be pretty. Wincing as the two groups met head-on, Jethro stayed for a few minutes to ensure the vampires really did have a fight on their hands before setting off in Vashti's direction.

When Vashti plunged into the forest she had no idea what she would find. She only knew she could not ignore that Iago was around here somewhere, torturing innocent mortals to get at her and Jethro.

"Pick on someone your own size, you evil trickster," she muttered, following the sounds of a struggle.

She could see lights weaving in and out of the tree

trunks up ahead and she made her way toward them. The shouts and exclamations continued, interspersed with the occasional scream. As she drew closer, Vashti could see about a dozen figures—men and women with one or two children—flailing wildly around. The beams of the flashlights added to the sense of chaos, as did the relentless barking of several dogs.

There was no doubt Iago had done this deliberately to separate her and Jethro. The sense she was walking into a trap laid by the most cunning opponent she had ever encountered weighed heavier with each step she took. *He might be sneaky, but he's also a coward*, she reminded herself. Iago didn't like face-to-face confrontation. Smoke and mirrors were his style, but, time after time, he'd chosen to run when the going got tough.

"What's going on?" She reached the group of mortals and raised a hand to shield her eyes as a flashlight was turned in her direction.

"Who are you?" The man's voice was high-pitched and jittery with nerves.

"I was passing and heard noises. I thought maybe I could help." She hoped he wouldn't notice she hadn't answered his question.

"There's an animal that keeps coming at us, snapping and snarling. Each time we think we've got a look at it, it vanishes into the darkness. It could be a big dog or even a wolf." This time it was a woman who spoke and, as Vashti's eyes adjusted to the gloom, she saw the speaker was carrying a young child on her hip.

Another man moved forward to stand alongside the woman. He had an air of authority that was explained by his next words. "I'm the rector. We've come from the church hall at the top of the road. The fun was just getting started when we heard the explosion up at the old de Loix place. Someone said maybe it was another arson attack, so we decided to come and see what was going on. We took a shortcut through the woods, then this happened. Is this someone's idea of a joke?"

Yes, but the sort of sick mind we are dealing with here makes a bit of trick or treating look tame in comparison. "Possibly. Why don't we get out of these trees? Whatever, or whoever, is causing the problem is using the cover of the woods. Out in the open it will be much harder to hide."

Making sure the group was with her, Vashti turned and led them back the way she had just come. Was it her imagination or did she hear a faint snickering sound behind her? Was Iago trying to get inside her head to convince her he was more powerful than he truly was? *I'm not falling for your hype.* She wanted to say it out loud, but decided talking to an invisible being was probably not the way to get these mortals to trust her.

When they reached the path, she had a decision to make. Head down the hill toward the town or take the upward curve to the de Loix house? It wasn't much of a choice. Not only was the route into town longer, it would leave them out in the open, exposed to any attack Iago might launch. Like it or not, her little group was going to have to take their chances with the haunted house, taking a detour around Jethro and the vampires, of course.

"Whoa." The rector drew alongside her. "Why are we going this way?"

Before Vashti could answer, one of the women pointed a finger. "What's going on over there? It sounds like the hounds of hell have broken loose."

A tall, familiar figure strode toward them. "Rival gangs." Jethro jerked a thumb over his shoulder in the direction of the mayhem. "They decided to join in the trick or treating and it got out of hand. I suggest we get the children out of the way. The summerhouse at the de Loix place hasn't been damaged by the explosion. You can hide out in there until the police have dealt with this." The rector looked skeptical, but there was no mistaking the sounds of bloodshed. The other mortals seemed only too eager to get away from a scene of carnage. Vashti slid her hand into Jethro's, gripping his fingers hard with relief. He glanced down at her with a slight smile before becoming serious again. "Shall we go?" She knew he was keeping his voice deliberately controlled, hiding any urgency from the mortals.

"What is it?" she murmured, walking alongside him toward the house.

"The sounds of undead flesh being ripped apart you heard back there? Vampires taking on zombies. Both sides will see this group of mortals as a moving feast. I can control the zombies, but if the vampires get their scent they'll forget to keep ripping apart the zombies and be up this hillside faster than you can blink."

"So what use will it be to get these mortals into the summerhouse?"

"Vampires can't cross a threshold unless the residents invite them."

"Clever."

"I do my best." He glanced over his shoulder at the group of mortals. They were approaching the old house now and the moonlight on their faces displayed a range of emotions. None of which could have been described as happy. "That just leaves Iago."

Vashti groaned. "Why does everything we do end with that sentence?"

The blaze had not fully taken hold of the main house and tendrils of smoke swirled sluggishly around them as they approached. The roof leaned at a dangerous angle and some fiery embers still burned bright against the night sky. By the combined lights of the moon and the flashlights, the summerhouse was a silent, empty outline, its many windows opaque with decades of dust. Jethro tried the door and it creaked open. He beckoned the others to follow him inside. The interior was stacked high with furniture and boxes covered by dusty tarps. It was obvious that, in life, Bertha and Gillespie hadn't believed in throwing anything away.

"This place became used for storage." Jethro stated the obvious as the flashlights illuminated the gloom.

"How come you know so much about this place? And why don't our cell phones work up here?" The rector came to join them.

Jethro drew him to one side and Vashti joined them. "I don't want to alarm your companions, but those gangs back there? They have some sort of weird Halloween thing going on. One group thinks they're vampires while the others are dressed as zombies. Just now, they seem totally focused on each other. I wouldn't like to speculate on what might happen if that gets out of hand."

The rector's expression took on a queasy hue. "You mean they could come after us? Enact some sort of sick ritual?"

"Let's hope not. Maybe we should be prepared, just in case? If they believe they are vampires, they could try anything. Let's play along. Do you and your companions wear crucifixes?"

The rector nodded, his pallor increasing with each passing second. "Good. Wear them on the outside of your clothing. Let your dogs go. They'll fend for themselves and find their own way home. I want you to sit in a circle in the middle of the room, facing outward. Put the children in the middle. Don't break that circle, no matter what you see or hear. Is that clear?" The other man nodded weakly. "And, Rector? Don't invite anyone in. No matter who they are or appear to be. Do you understand?"

Another nod. The rector swallowed audibly. "This is not a human gang, is it?"

"You might want to pretend it is."

It felt like the longest night of Jethro's life. Without Vashti at his side, it probably would have felt longer. They had walked around the exterior of the summerhouse in an endless circle. When the first vampire attack came, Jethro was almost glad. Anything to break the nerve-jangling tension and monotony.

The vampire who approached was newly transformed, inexperienced and overeager. Drawn by the prospect of mortal blood, he approached swiftly, ready to slash his way through any obstacle.

"Step aside, mortal." Fangs bared, the vampire drew himself up to his full impressive height, facing Jethro across a distance of several feet.

In reply, Jethro took a step forward, holding up his hands. The wooden stake and serviceable hammer he held were clearly visible in the moonlight. Vashti joined him, swinging the ax Jethro had unearthed from the barn at the rear of the old house. She studied the vampire with her head on one side before turning to Jethro.

"This isn't the sharpest ax, but one good blow should do it. Two at best."

Jethro gave an exaggerated sigh. "Remember what I said. Stake through the heart first. Then the decapitation. It has to be in the right order."

"Oh, yes. I forgot." Vashti looked the vampire up and down again. "What are we waiting for?"

With barely imperceptible movement, the vampire

whirled closer, his eyes boring into them. "You don't scare me with your mortal banter."

"If I was mortal I'd probably be shitting myself right about now. But they should have told you at bloodsucker school you can't use mind control tricks on a necromancer. Or a faerie."

"Let's get on with it. Do that thing that makes him into a statue, then we can put his head on a pole to warn his friends to stay away."

"Faeries." Jethro shook his head with mock sadness. "Good to look at, but no finesse. Now, where was I?" He stepped closer to the vampire, stake held high. After a brief hesitation, the vampire gave a furious hiss, then swirled away. He blended into the shadows before disappearing completely. "That was fun. We should do this double act thing more often."

"You let him get away." Vashti scanned the darkness, her eyes seeking any sign of movement. "We should have killed that one as a message to the others."

"For the sake of the mortals, I'd prefer to avoid a bloodbath."

She wrinkled her nose. "Are the earth-born really so squeamish?"

Jethro laughed. "They tend to shy away from acts like chopping the head off an undead monster."

Vashti considered the matter for a moment before shrugging. They commenced their pacing. Several more vampires approached in the night, relentlessly drawn to the summerhouse by the number of mortals in one place. Most were persuaded to leave. Two, overcome by their bloodlust, needed more drastic action. Jethro was able to freeze them before staking and decapitating them.

A faint glow was lighting the sky as he and Vashti washed the worst of the blood from their hands and arms under the old pump outside the de Loix house. "The vampires won't come now. What bothers me most is we've still heard nothing from Iago. Can you feel him?"

"He's still close by." Her expression was tense. "It's like he's toying with us."

"Sounds about right. I need to deal with the zombies." Jethro grimaced. "Wish me luck. This could go either way."

"Do you have to go and round them up?"

"Like some sort of freak show shepherd? Hopefully, I can exert enough control over them from here to send them back to their graves. The problem with zombies is that the longer they've been out of the ground, the harder it is to get them back in again. They don't so much develop free will—they have no will—it's more like they get some sort of blind, stupid obstinacy. They start resisting commands just for the hell of it. This lot has tasted freedom for longer than I'd like. Time to find out how they respond." He moved slightly away from Vashti, adopting the familiar stance, head bent, arms outstretched at shoulder height.

For several minutes he breathed in the darkness. It was fading now, but there was still more in the remaining gloom than most would ever know. Sunset wasn't a frightening or sullen time for the ones whose hearts beat to the rhythm of the night. With his finely tuned necromancer senses, Jethro could feel them going about their business. The children of the night. The vampires were retreating now. These were not Tibor's well-trained followers. They did not have the self-control to withstand the light of day. Coffins filled with their homeland soil sang to them.

Jethro turned his attention to the shambling mass of zombies. Damaged by the vampire onslaught, they shuffled close by—staggering and blundering into each other—awaiting his command. *You're not going to like this one, guys.*

"*Edhwierft.* Return."

The response threw him backward, almost jolting him off his feet. Zombies had no voice, no thoughts, no free choice, but their collective resistance was a silent scream echoing in his mind. It was his lone strength pitted against their sheer, bloody, brainless defiance. He had to win. If the zombies he had raised got into the town… No, that didn't bear thinking about.

"*Edhwierft.* Do it now." His voice was stronger, ringing out across the unseen distance between him and his undead followers. He had them this time. Breathing hard with the effort of keeping them under control, Jethro repeated the command once more. He couldn't afford to feel relief too soon. Nevertheless, his mind conjured up the wet flesh sounds and old-corpse scents of a zombie retreat. It was happening. They were going back to their graves. Dragging their feet—those who still had feet— but that was zombies for you.

Drained by the effort it had taken, Jethro sank abruptly to his knees, feeling the early morning dew soak through the cloth of his jeans. Vashti hurried to his side, pausing to glance around at the sound of applause ringing out in the murky half light. Although, its source unclear, the voice that accompanied it was all too familiar. Iago remained invisible. "Very impressive. But can you do this?"

There was a rustling sound in the trees, as if giant unseen birds were settling high above them. Eerie whispers filled the air, accompanied by rasping, sucking sounds. A smell—reminiscent of rancid meat—hung in the air, mingling with the smell of smoke from the house.

"My God. How low will he stoop?" Jethro's voice resonated with a combination of shock and disgust.

"What is it?" Vashti sounded like someone who knew she wasn't going to like the answer.

"He has called upon the Sluagh."

"What are the Sluagh?"

"They are the undead fae, so reviled even the Unseelie Court cast them out. These are souls so evil they aren't welcome anywhere after death and are forced into exile in the mortal realm. They can never be reincarnated into their earth-born forms or exist as ghosts. Yet their malevolence survives. They are envious of the souls that live in mortal bodies and want to drag those souls along with them on their endless journey.

"The Sluagh gather when the earth-born are dying. They arrive in the night on the westerly wind and enter mortal dwellings through open windows or doors that have been left ajar. Once inside, they will try to snatch the soul of the dying person before it has time to move on. The unwilling soul is forced to join the Sluagh and add to the numbers of the flock."

"What use can the Sluagh be to Iago if they only feast on the souls of the dying?"

"Generally, the Sluagh cannot pull the soul from anybody that is not dying. The will of the living is much too strong. It is when they arrive at dawn they are at their most dangerous." Jethro cast a look at the brightening sky, aware his words offered little in the way of reassurance. "Dawn is when they seek the souls of the living. And they need the support of a powerful being to assist them in their quest."

"Let me guess. That powerful being wouldn't happen to be a necromancer, would it?"

"Right the first time." He licked his finger and held

it up, testing the air. "Sure enough, the wind is blowing from the west. Every other necromancer I know has taken a vow that no matter how great the provocation, we will never call upon the Sluagh."

"I don't imagine necromancer ethics mean much to Iago. What can we do?"

"If we could somehow get word around the town, tell everyone to make sure their doors and windows are tightly closed…" He gave a laugh that ended on a groan. "They'll think we've gone mad."

Vashti gripped his arm and shook it as his rising panic communicated itself to her. "It's better than doing nothing. If the Sluagh are dead, you must be able to exert some sort of control over them. Can you hold them here while I take the mortals back to town?"

Jethro tilted his head back, staring up at the teal-colored sky. The sun's first rays touched his face with pale warmth as tendrils of early morning fog wrapped around his ankles. What would this new day bring? Could he hold a flock of Sluagh? Could anyone? He'd never heard of it being done. Vashti's upturned face was full of hope and trust. She believed in him.

"I'll try."

Chapter 11

Vashti gritted her teeth as the man known as Rector continued to question her plan. Dealing with humans was not as easy as it should be. She found this one particularly annoying.

"Can we talk as we make our way into the town?"

"I want to be absolutely sure it's safe before we leave here. There were some very strange sounds during the night. Screams and such like. Have those gangs really gone? And where is your friend?"

"Linus—" one of the women stepped forward and placed a hand on his arm "—these people have proved trustworthy so far. Let's go." The woman had obviously recognized Vashti was running out of patience.

He made a grudging harrumphing sound. Since Vashti had reached the point where she might need to start smashing things, his compliance came just in time. She

set off down the hill at a sprint and was forced to mod-
ify her pace when the mortals failed to keep up with her.

"Let me get this straight. You want us to knock on
every door and tell the occupants to make sure they stay
inside, with every window and door closed, until noon?"
The rector's voice was incredulous.

"Yes."

"And what reason will we give for this bizarre request?"

*How about I promise to keep my foot off your throat?
Is that a good enough reason?* Biting back the retort,
Vashti improvised. "Those gangs that were fighting up
on the hillside last night? They had gas canisters with
them. We overheard them threatening to release chemi-
cals into the atmosphere."

"Good heavens! There's not a moment to lose." He
quickened his pace, issuing instructions to his companions about which streets to take and what to say to the
residents.

Bemused, Vashti shook her head. She would never understand mortals. Ask them to trust and they dug their
heels in. Give them a fat, juicy lie and they were all eager
compliance. Why couldn't they obey blindly?

Her thoughts went to Jethro, facing the Sluagh all alone
on the hill. Her heart clenched with dread. *Dawn is the
time when they seek the souls of the living.* That was what
Jethro had said about the Sluagh. And she had left him
to face them alone. *Iago has succeeded. He has separated us.* The trickster had sworn to kill Jethro. *He never
wanted these mortals. He used them to get at Jethro...
and I let it happen.* Whirling around, she ran back up the
hill, her heart pounding in time with her footsteps. *Let
me not be too late.*

When she reached the de Loix house, Jethro was standing exactly where she had left him. His head was bent and his outstretched arms were held at shoulder height while a group of about twenty hideous creatures performed a freakish dance around him. The Sluagh were birdlike, haggard and thin, with skin barely clinging to bone in a pitiful version of what used to be the faerie form. They kept their leathery wings close, forming a weathered cloak around their bodies. What had once been hands and feet were now bony claws. Sparse strings of dark hair covered their exposed skulls and gnarled, pointed teeth protruded from their beak-like mouths.

Horrified at the sight before her, Vashti approached. Jethro lifted his head and she flinched at the agony in the dark depths of his eyes. "They are trying to tear my soul from my body." His voice was raw and filled with pain. "I don't know how much longer I can hold out against them."

Although the Sluagh croaked their annoyance at her intrusion into their circle, they did nothing to prevent her when Vashti approached Jethro. It was as if she didn't matter. *The outcome is decided. I cannot change it.* The thought chilled her.

"What can I do?"

"Get the hell out of here. Tell Cal I'm sorry."

"No." She slid her arms around his waist, pressing her cheek against his chest. "There must be something."

"He's right, you know." Iago's hated voice grated in her ear as he emerged from the shelter of the trees. "I do hate to interrupt this touching little scene, but the Sluagh are keen to finish this. As am I."

Vashti turned to face him, keeping her body in contact with Jethro's, hoping against hope that she could impart some of her own strength into him. "You bastard."

"I love it when you talk dirty." Iago's grin widened.

"And we'll have so many more opportunities with him out of the way."

"I was wrong. You're a *deluded* bastard."

"So fiery. Talking of fire, I really thought the house would burn to the ground this time," Iago said. "Yet it seems determined to resist my efforts—"

"Fŷrwylm." Jethro's voice was weakened, his hand only half raised. Nevertheless, the flames that shot out caught Iago unawares. The trickster went staggering back but he recovered quickly. Iago responded instantly. A fireball of his own, bigger and more powerful, came flying through the air. It would have hit Vashti full in the chest if Jethro hadn't caught hold of her upper arms and turned her side-on with his body protecting her from the flames. The impact of the fiery onslaught hit him in his upper left arm and he fell to the ground, writhing in pain. Vashti dropped to her knees beside him, sickened at the smell and sight of the burned flesh of his biceps.

"Finish it." Iago waved an imperious hand to the Sluagh. "He is all yours."

Triumphantly the creatures started to advance. Vashti leaped to her feet, standing guard over Jethro, who appeared unconscious. "Stay away from him!"

To her everlasting surprise, they stopped, cocking their heads as though listening to a silent voice. Quivering with anticipation, Vashti braced herself for a fight.

"You have got to be joking." Iago appeared to be talking to himself. "We swore revenge on all of Niniane's killers, remember? This one is ours for the taking. This had better be good." He tilted his head, much in the way the Sluagh had done. Then, clapping his hands, Iago drew the attention of the Sluagh back to him. "She has spoken. Not this one, my friends. Not this time."

Vashti watched in amazement as, with flapping wings,

screeching cries and a whirlwind of undulating shadows, the ill-begotten creatures rose, circled Jethro once and flew off. Iago strolled casually forward, glancing down to where Jethro lay.

"I don't know why, but he has been saved by one whose powers are greater than any of us can comprehend. You might be able to patch up his wounds, little faerie, but the damage inflicted by the Sluagh may go deeper than the physical. There is only one place to make sure he heals fully. You are commanded to bring him to Avalon. The time has come for the truth to be revealed."

His smile deepened and he reached out a hand to stroke her cheek. Vashti flinched away in a combination of shock and disgust. Iago's smile deepened. "You look at me like that now, but you will change. There is one on Avalon who awaits our mutual friend with great eagerness." He nodded at Jethro. "Trust me, you will not be able to compete with her. When he no longer looks your way—is no longer aware of your existence—you will be glad of my touch."

"Never." Vashti didn't try to hide the shudder his words provoked.

The smile became unpleasant. "How little you know. Yet you will learn. I will enjoy teaching you when we meet again on Avalon. She is waiting." With those words he was gone, fading into invisibility.

Stifling an uncharacteristic sob, Vashti turned back to where Jethro lay. His face was ashen in the pale sunlight. With his strong features, he resembled a fallen statue of a heroic knight from a bygone age. Kneeling beside him, Vashti pressed her ear to his chest. His heartbeat was faint, his breathing impossibly shallow.

Vashti acted on instinct. Through the unique bond they had, they could empower each other. She knew—without understanding *how*—that Jethro needed her touch to restore his strength. Lying next to him on the damp ground, she pressed her body against his and, holding her hands on either side of his face, kissed Jethro's ice-cold lips. For the longest time there was no reaction. He remained still and unresponsive, like the effigy she had imagined him to be. Then, very slowly, his lips parted and she was able to slide her tongue into his mouth. A shudder ran through him and his right hand reached up to clamp her waist. This was a kiss unlike others they had shared. This was no furious fusing of lips with a promise of further intimacy. In place of the immediacy of passion, this was slow, honeyed sweetness and a touch of magic. Blending her breath with his, Vashti used every ounce of her new-found faerie power to infuse the strength and life stolen by the Sluagh back into Jethro's body. As she did, she knew the most potent force of all was working its charm between them. *You have to live...because, unlike you, I do love. I love you.*

"What did you say?" Jethro pulled away from her, a frown in his eyes. His voice was weak, his face ghostly pale, but he was alive.

"I didn't speak." She felt bright tears sting her eyelids and blinked them away before they could spill over. "Now, can we get the hell out of here?"

At first Jethro was so weak he could barely stand. Leaning on Vashti and pausing for breath every few steps, he managed to falter his way down the hillside. When they reached the town square, all was thankfully quiet. Clearly the chemical warfare story had worked and the rector had done a good job of persuading his parishioners to stay indoors.

Vashti eyed the motorbike with misgiving. "Can you ride it?"

"Have to." The words were a faint croak.

"Maybe I could do it?"

A corner of his mouth lifted in a fleeting shadow of a smile. When he spoke again, his voice was stronger. "Mortals have laws, remember? The sort of day we're having, you'd get pulled over by highway patrol. Come on, let's do this."

As she climbed up behind him and slid her arms around his waist, Vashti felt Jethro's pain reverberate through her body. The Sluagh had damaged his soul. A ripple of panic ran through her. *Can I heal him?* Could her powers extend that far? There was no one she could ask. All she could do was trust her instincts. That fae sense that had lain dormant inside her for so long rose up now strong and true. It was telling her she could cure Jethro's injured psyche. More than that. It was urging her to do so. Deep inside her something was saying, *This was meant.* The implications of the message shook her to the core. *It feels like there was a plan. A plan that included me being here to save him.* How could that be the case, when the only reason she was here at all had to do with her own stubborn determination and antagonism toward Jethro?

They were fortunate that none of those highway cops Jethro had mentioned were around as they made their way along back roads to the nearest motel. It was a journey of epic proportions, though the distance was only a few miles. The bike weaved a slow, erratic path. Several times it came perilously close to the oncoming traffic. Once, they left the road completely and ended up in the undergrowth. Luckily, the vehicle wedged itself in shrubbery and remained upright. Vashti would not have liked their chances of lifting it had it fallen.

Just when Vashti was about to suggest abandoning the bike, they meandered into the parking lot of an unattractive motel. Jethro almost toppled headlong onto the asphalt. It was clear he had no energy left. Vashti left him slumped against a wall and went to deal with the very mortal matter of securing a room. She muddled through the whole credit card thing. The desk clerk's attitude was one of bored resignation.

Finally, she emerged with a key and was able to help Jethro inside the bland room. He collapsed onto the bed while she collected their belongings from the bike. When she turned her attention back to him, Jethro was asleep but shivering violently. When she touched him, his skin was icy though the room temperature was warm. She wanted to deal with the burn on his arm, but Vashti knew those chills were coming from deep inside him. If she didn't heat him up, and do it fast, he could die. Stripping off Jethro's clothes and then her own, she lay next to him, drawing the bedclothes over their naked bodies. Holding his juddering form in her arms, she willed her own warmth into him. Gradually, over a period of many hours, he grew still.

Later again, when they had both slept and the light through the thin curtain was beginning to fade, Vashti opened her eyes to find Jethro propped against the pillows, watching her. Relief flooded her veins. She moved into a half sitting position beside him. Before she could speak, he kissed her neck, dipping his tongue to the hollow of her throat. Her world spun and her heartbeat kicked up a notch. His stubble brushed her skin as he moved his mouth toward her lips.

"I want you…need you," he murmured before taking her mouth in a searing kiss. His laugh was a sigh against her lips. "But I'm as weak as a kitten."

Vashti kissed him back with everything she had, everything that had simmered inside her from the moment they'd met, everything she had refused for so long to acknowledge she felt. "I don't mind doing all the work."

Jethro's arms tightened around her as his chest rose and fell more quickly. With slow, deliberate movement, Vashti straddled him with her knees on either side of his hips. He made a low animal sound as he moved his mouth to her nipple. His tongue found the stiffened nub and circled it, lapping it with velvety smoothness as his hands held her hips, keeping her firmly in place against him.

"Are you strong enough?" Her voice was husky. Given the rock-hard erection pressing into the folds of her sex, it seemed to be a particularly unnecessary question.

"Being inside you is exactly what I need right now."

Needing no further encouragement, Vashti raised herself up and moved slowly down to feel his shaft against the heat of her core. Jethro lifted his hips and she took him inch by throbbing inch. She squeezed her muscles tight, drawing in his size and iron hardness, trying to control the pace as he pushed eagerly up. He moved one hand down to rub her clitoris with a fingertip and she lost control, crying out and driving up and down on him in time with his upward thrusts.

Jethro moved his finger to the point where his cock and her sheath were joined. "This is where the magic between us happens." He moved her hand up to his chest and held it over his heart before covering her left breast. "And here."

His words triggered an explosion that hit Vashti hard, radiating out from her core to touch every nerve. At the same time as she clutched him tightly inside her, Jethro's orgasm pumped and jerked out its rhythm, his cry of ecstasy mingling with hers.

"How does this work?" Jethro studied her face as—once the world had righted itself and she lifted her sated body off his—Vashti curled up next to him. "You are somehow able to restore my strength through amazing sex and mind-blowing orgasms?"

She grinned. "Are you complaining?"

"God, no! Just trying to understand."

"I don't know," she confessed, a slight frown wrinkling her brow. "It's almost as if there is a force at work within me, drawing me to you, urging me to make you stronger. And, right now, to heal you." Should she mention the other feeling? The one that told her this was *meant*? She decided against it. There was strange and there was downright odd. "I don't understand it."

"Nor do I." He pulled her into the crook of his arm and dropped a kiss onto the top of her head. "But I'm glad of it. I'm also hungry—" his smile, no longer a weak shadow of its former self, dawned "—and this time for food."

"Tell me again what Iago said," he asked after they had eaten a less-than-stimulating meal Vashti had procured from the motel's vending machines.

Jethro was still stunned by what had happened over the last twenty-four hours. He had no doubt Vashti had pulled him back from the brink of death—or something worse than death. The living hell of the Sluagh drawing his soul from his body inch by painful inch was a nightmare that would live with him forever. The agony inflicted by Iago's fireball searing his flesh was nothing in comparison.

Before Vashti had returned, he had tried several times to use fire against the Sluagh, but he had not had enough strength. Only with his body in contact with hers had he found the energy to send that fireball Iago's way and buy them a precious few minutes. Vashti had spoken about the way contact with Jethro made her powers stronger. It seemed to work both ways.

Vashti's healing techniques were unique. Sleep, food and sex. He doubted she'd ever get a license to practice. *And, face it, do I want my faerie therapist to work her magic on anyone else?* That thought triggered a series of don't-go-there others and he quickly turned it aside. The sleep and the food had been good. But the sex? That had been beyond incredible. And each time his body had grown stronger. So much so that now, just one day after that dawn encounter, he felt ready to face the world. His arm would be scarred forever by Iago's fireball, and perhaps his soul would bear similar wounds, but he was ready to continue his mission.

"He said you could only fully heal on Avalon." Vashti lay in his arms, but she tilted her head back so she could look at him. Her expression was filled with anxiety.

"It's as well that's where we planned to go anyway, isn't it?" Jethro felt his facial muscles tighten with anger.

"I didn't like the way he spoke of it. He talked of someone—a woman—who was waiting there for you." She raised worried eyes to his face. "Could it be Morgan le Fay?"

"Possibly. Although what would Morgan know of me? We've never met. I can't mean anything to her. Unless this is all about Iago's vendetta against me, Cal, Stella and Lorcan."

"You mean because they blame you for the death of Niniane?"

"Yes. Niniane—the sorceress known as the Lady of the Lake—was Morgan le Fay's half sister. And Morgan is Iago's grandmother. Niniane was obsessed with Cal. Centuries ago, when he was still known as Merlin, she imprisoned him in a cave at Darnantes because he refused to return her love. Cal was freed by the Dominion, the Angels of the Fourth Choir, on condition he kept his identity secret and worked for them to protect the boundary between Otherworld and the mortal realm. That's why he's been known as Cal ever since. When Niniane found out he had escaped, she swore revenge. During the battle for Otherworld, she tried to kill him and Stella. The three of us—me, Cal and Stella—joined forces and destroyed her. Although Iago includes Lorcan in his vendetta, Lorcan was actually on the other side of the battlefield at the time."

"If Iago has sworn to kill you, he could have done that easily yesterday. The Sluagh could have killed you at the de Loix house. You were unconscious, they were coming for you, then…" She floundered, as though seeking the words to explain what had happened. "They just stopped and flew away. Iago said you had been saved by someone powerful. He didn't say who saved you, or who the woman is that waits for you. He did say you would be unable to resist her and I would be forced to turn to him."

"Wishful thinking." The corners of Jethro's mouth turned down in distaste at the thought of Iago anywhere near Vashti. "Iago's got the hots for you. He knows you'll never feel the same way, so he's trying to come up with a scenario where he can get you in his power."

"Maybe." Vashti didn't seem convinced. She changed the subject. "You told Cal we would go to Barcelona and meet with Aydan before we set sail for Avalon. Is that still the plan?"

Jethro rose from the bed, flexing his injured left arm. It ached, but not too much. "That's the plan. Tanzi could be right. Aydan might be the challenger. It's a long shot, but it's worth checking out."

"In which case, we wouldn't need to go to Avalon at all." Her voice was hopeful.

"Challenger or no challenger. Money or no money. Iago has made this personal. This is between me and him now. He admitted he was the person who tried to burn down the old house. I'll be going to Avalon no matter what. And if Morgan le Fay wants to meet me, she can bring it on, as well." Jethro shot her a sidelong glance. "You've fulfilled your obligation to the Council to observe me. You must know you can trust me to see this through. I'm sure they won't hold this against you if you decide not to accompany me to Avalon."

"Are you kidding me?" Vashti bounced up from the bed. Standing beside him, she slid her arms around his waist. "To hell with observing you. We're in this together. I'm coming with you…whether you like it or not."

Jethro turned so he could pull her fully into his arms. "That's what I hoped you'd say."

Chapter 12

This time Vashti shared Jethro's seething impatience at the dawdling pace of international travel.

"How do mortals put up with this?" she asked as the plane they had boarded in New York finally landed in Barcelona as planned.

"They don't know any different," he pointed out.

As they left the airport and made their way into the city, Vashti regarded the people milling around them. While she might still dislike the bustle of the mortal realm, her fear of this place had dissipated. It didn't mean she wouldn't be glad to return to Otherworld, of course.

Lorcan had given them detailed instructions on how to find the resistance safe house, explaining the location was guarded by a series of complex spells designed by Cal himself. Following the directions he had given them, they found themselves in front of a tall, dilapidated house. The front door of this uninviting building might once have been red. Leading up to it was a series of worn sandstone stairs. A tub of listless geraniums sat on the top step, their roots anchored in a combination of cigarette butts and dust.

"You'd have to be pretty desperate to run to this place," Jethro commented as he raised his hand and knocked loudly on the door.

"From what Tanzi told me, most of the people who seek safety here have reached the point of despair." Vashti glanced up at the windows, all of which were shuttered. "Mostly because of the behavior of my father."

After a minute or two the door opened an inch. "You must be Pedro." Jethro addressed the aging sidhe scrutinizing them through the gap. "Lorcan Malone told me to say *hola*."

There was no response. "We have a letter from Lorcan." Vashti nudged Jethro and he reached into his jacket pocket, producing Lorcan's scrawled missive. He held it out and the sidhe extended a hand through the narrow opening. Once he had taken the letter, he closed the door again, leaving Jethro staring incredulously at the scarred panels.

"He should ask the charm school for a refund," Jethro commented with a grimace. "It's as well Lorcan already warned me his old friend Pedro takes incivility to a whole new level."

"Look on the bright side. At least this means we're probably in the right place."

Jethro tilted his head back to study the unprepossessing exterior of the building. "Would you call this a bright side?"

Before Vashti could respond the door opened again and Pedro jerked his head at them. *"Entrar."*

"Thank God for Lorcan," Jethro muttered as they

stepped inside. "Whatever his note said it seems to have done the trick."

The interior of the house, while not exactly luxurious, was more comfortable than the outside promised. Pedro led them down a long, narrow hall and into a large kitchen at the rear of the property. This was occupied by a portly woman, who was as wide as she was tall, and a number of cats. The woman paused in the act of chopping onions to wipe her eyes on her apron and study the new arrivals. She looked Vashti up and down several times, a confused look in her eyes.

"Searc?" It was the nickname Lorcan had bestowed on Tanzi when she was in hiding and her identity was a secret.

"No, I am her sister. We are twins." This must be Maria, Pedro's wife. Vashti knew her sister had struck up a bizarre friendship with this funny little woman.

"Twins? *Sí. Bienvenida.* Welcome."

Vashti momentarily feared Maria might start forward and embrace her. Before any such undesirable physical contact could take place, the door at the rear of the property opened and a young man walked in. He paused on the doorstep, staring at Vashti.

"Ah, pardon." Vashti was relieved when he switched to English. "I thought for a minute you were Tanzi, but I can see now I was wrong."

Vashti exchanged a quick look with Jethro. "If you know my sister's real name, I'm guessing you must be Aydan?"

He came into the room and Vashti got a good look at him. She liked what she saw. Aydan had an open face with regular features and an engaging smile. His features were pleasant without being precisely handsome. He had the sort of face you'd trust. Did he look like a long-lost king? That was the all-important, unanswerable question.

"Yes, I'm Aydan." Pulling out a chair at the large, well-worn table in the center of the room, Aydan invited Vashti and Jethro to join him. Once they were seated, he turned to Maria. "Is there any coffee in that pot, *querida*?"

With a glare that could curdle the freshest milk, Maria halted her chopping and brought the coffeepot and three cups over to the table. "*Sí, el jefe.*" Her voice dripped sarcasm as she poured the dark liquid.

"What did she call you?" Vashti inquired when Maria, with a dark look over her shoulder in Aydan's direction, stomped out of the room.

"*El jefe.* The boss or the chief. Maria misses Lorcan. She can't get used to me being in charge. I guess I don't have the same air of authority he had." His expression was rueful.

Jethro, who had been watching Aydan carefully, shot a meaningful glance in Vashti's direction at those words. She gave a tiny shake of her head in return. It was hardly conclusive. If Aydan didn't know he was the challenger, how could he be expected to know he should have an air of authority?

"How is Lorcan?" Aydan appeared not to notice the exchange. "Last time I saw him, Iago had infiltrated this house and with it, of course, the resistance movement. He pulled a mad stunt where he set a dozen zombies on us while pretending to fall down in a faint. Then he disappeared. Not long after that, Lorcan and Tanzi vanished, too. I'm guessing the two things weren't unrelated?"

Jethro managed to give the edited highlights of what had happened after Lorcan and Tanzi left the safe house. "Not entirely. Iago was working for Moncoya. Once he left here, he went straight to Moncoya with information about where Tanzi was. Lorcan escorted her to safety. They are married now."

"And Iago?"

"Still around. Still causing trouble." Maria made a truly disgusting cup of coffee and Vashti watched in some amusement as Jethro forced himself to finish the foul-tasting brew. "He has issued a challenge to us. We are to follow him to Avalon."

Aydan whistled. "Avalon? You won't go, of course." He glanced from Jethro to Vashti, then back again. "Ah, I see. You *are* going to Avalon. Good luck with that." Suspicion dawned on his face. "Why have you come here?"

Before they could answer him, a young woman came into the kitchen. "Aydan, I wanted to ask…" The words died on her lips as she paused in the doorway.

It would be hard to say the color drained from her face, because she was already so pale. Her skin was lily-white and her hair white-blond. In contrast, her eyes were so dark they appeared black. Her features were sharp, her limbs slender and willowy. Her looks were unusual yet curiously compelling.

Although her eyes flickered briefly over Vashti, it was undoubtedly Jethro who caused the new arrival to become frozen into immobility. Her gaze fixed on his face and her eyes widened. Vashti was getting used to women doing a double-take when they looked at Jethro. Or the occasional surreptitious glances in his direction. Even the open flirtatiousness. This was something more. This woman, whoever she was, was riveted to the spot by him. It was almost embarrassing. When Jethro smiled at her, a faint blush bloomed in her pale cheeks.

"Hey, Lisbet." Aydan held out his hand to her. His voice broke the spell and, dragging her eyes away from Jethro's face with an obvious effort, Lisbet turned to look at Aydan. "These are Lorcan's friends. This is Jethro and, in case you hadn't made the connection, Vashti is Tanzi's sister." For Jethro and Vashti's benefit, he added, "This is my girlfriend, Lisbet."

Lisbet's lips parted as though she was about to say something, then, without warning, she whirled around and ran back the way she had come. Her footsteps echoed on the wooden floorboards of the hall before pounding up the stairs.

Aydan's hand dropped back to his side. "I'm sorry." He addressed the words to Vashti. "Lisbet believed Moncoya sent Tanzi to infiltrate the resistance. Even when we discovered Iago was our traitor, Lisbet remained prejudiced against Tanzi. I can only imagine your likeness to your sister brought back the memory of that time."

Vashti inclined her head, as though accepting his explanation. Did Aydan buy his own account of what had just happened? Could he be oblivious to Lisbet's reaction to Jethro? She had barely glanced Vashti's way. *I doubt she noticed me, let alone realized I look like Tanzi.* No, Lisbet's whole body had undergone some sort of wild reaction in response to Jethro. *Which I fully understand, having been on the receiving end of his unique brand of alchemy myself. I just wouldn't have expected it to be so potent on first sight...or to be so devastating across several feet.*

Vashti glanced at Jethro. He was leaning back in his chair, apparently unaware of the devastation he had wrought on an unknown woman.

Aydan's voice brought her back to reality. "This is quite a detour. Would you care to tell me why you have come here on your way to Avalon?"

"It's a long story. Can we tell you later, after we've rested?" Jethro stretched his long frame with a yawn.

* * *

Maria showed them to a room on the top floor of the house. It contained a large bed with a brass bedstead and very little else. In her broken English, Maria informed them dinner would be ready in two hours.

"If we were into swinging cats, we wouldn't be able to do it in here," Jethro commented when Maria had gone. He glanced out the window across the jumble of rooftops.

"You mortals have some strange habits." Vashti kicked off her boots and collapsed onto the bed with a sigh of relief. "I thought you were fond of felines?"

He laughed. "I'm too tired to go there. What do you think of Aydan? Is he our challenger?"

"I thought we'd know when we met him. That we'd recognize him instantly because he'd have an aura about him. If that's the case, then it's a no. Aydan doesn't have that. But what if I'm wrong and the challenger appears to be an ordinary guy? That would make Aydan a maybe."

"If you take that line of thinking, anyone could be a maybe."

Vashti groaned. "I'm exhausted. Can't we sleep now and think later?"

Jethro came and lay down next to her. Vashti turned on her side, fitting her body into his embrace. It was scary how natural the movement was. The kiss they exchanged was a mix of comfort and intoxication. Vashti gave a soft murmur of pleasure when Jethro's tongue slipped into her mouth. She responded with all she had, stroking her tongue against his in a caress that told him everything she wanted to say out loud. Jethro broke the kiss, lifting his head slowly to stare down at her. His eyes told her he understood. Wrapping his arms tighter around her waist, he pulled her closer.

He raised his head, his eyes warm on her face. "How sleepy are you?"

"Very sleepy." Vashti's voice was husky in response. It wasn't true. Never had tiredness deserted her so swiftly.

"That's a shame." He ran his tongue lightly along her lower lip, then tugged it gently between his teeth.

"Why? Did you have something in mind?"

Jethro nodded, a slight smile tugging at the corner of his mouth. "Shall I show you what I was planning? Then you can decide if you want to continue or if you'd rather sleep…"

Dear God! The things he could do to her with that look! Any trace of tiredness was gone. All she could think about was the heat searing her body. Jethro's gaze was setting her nerve endings on fire, turning her insides into glowing embers.

"Show me what you've got." She lay back, noticing with pleasure Jethro's breathing was as labored as her own. It thrilled her to know she had this sort of power over him.

When Jethro began by tracking a teasing hand down her body, a soft moan of pleasure built in Vashti's throat. Her toes curled and her fingers gripped the sheets. Lowering his head, Jethro claimed her lips in an achingly slow kiss. Then his lips moved downward, to the neckline of her vest, and rational thought scattered. All that mattered was her desperate need for him and the fire consuming her body.

Jethro's lips traced her body through the thin vest, finding a nipple and sucking it through the fabric. Vashti's back arched off the bed and she cried out, gripping his hair as she was drawn into a swirling vortex of sensation. Jethro tugged the strap off her shoulder, pulling the vest down enough to bare one breast. His stubble scraped against her sensitive skin, adding to her arousal. His mouth was raw heat on her naked flesh and more cries of pleasure spilled from Vashti's lips as she writhed on the mattress. He reduced her to a bundle of nerve endings, each one thrumming for his touch.

Jethro slid a hand down, flicking open the button on her jeans and moving his fingers inside so he could stroke the cleft of her sex. Her hips pushed up off the bed as the warmth between her legs became an insistent ache.

"Still sleepy, Vashti?"

In answer, she helped him pull down her zipper, lifting her hips as he slid her jeans and underwear down her body. Jethro slipped one finger into her heat, stroking her, in and out, over and over. Vashti met every thrust of his finger with a tilt of her hips, moaning with each masterful caress. Waves of desire coiled through her, building and spiraling until she wanted to scream. Just when she thought she couldn't take any more, Jethro bent his head, trailing his lips lower, approaching the sweet spot that burned so wonderfully.

Finally his mouth was there, finding her clitoris and tormenting it with his tongue. Making love to it slowly and tenderly. He tasted her, his tongue flicking and swirling. Vashti's hips rose and fell in time with the commands of his mouth, her whole body shaking as she moaned, almost sobbing with pleasure. Jethro thrust his tongue right up inside her, then licked upward to her clitoris, circling and caressing, slowly alternating the movements until an orgasm stormed through her. He continued to lap as she came, increasing the sensations so the tremors ripped through her again, wave after wave. Vashti turned her head, muffling her screams with a pillow until Jethro finally raised his head and took her into his arms, kissing her and stilling her body into silence.

"My turn now," she murmured, using the heel of her hand to push him onto his back.

Copying the movements he had used, she inched her way down his body, undoing the buttons of his shirt, then the zipper of his jeans on the way. His stomach muscles tensed and trembled as she trailed her fingernails lightly over his skin. Impatiently, Jethro pushed his jeans and briefs down over his hips and legs before kicking them aside. The full, impressive length of his cock sprang free, straining toward her mouth. His crisp chest hair tickled her cheek as, with tantalizing slowness, Vashti moved her lips lower. She followed the line of hair down from his chest, across his defined abs, to the tip of his cock. Jethro's breathing became ragged. The musky aroma of his arousal filled her nostrils and she breathed it deep. Licking her lips, Vashti swirled her tongue around the head of his cock. Jethro quivered violently, a moan spilling from between his lips as he threaded his fingers through her hair.

Opening her mouth, she flexed her jaw, taking his full length, inch by inch. He was so hard, so big, so magnificent. His heady scent and spicy taste were glorious. Releasing him, she flicked her tongue along his length, then took him back in her mouth, following her instincts. Jethro's stomach muscles clenched and shuddered in time with the bobbing of her head. His groan reverberated around the room as he came, his body juddering and shaking wildly before coming to a standstill.

Vashti crawled back up the bed, curling into the security of his arms. She must have dozed because it seemed to be only minutes later that Jethro was easing away from her and righting his clothing.

"I get the feeling Maria will take no prisoners if we miss dinner," he explained.

Vashti sat up, stretching and yawning. She didn't want to do this. It wasn't just the overwhelming feeling of fatigue caused by days of traveling. An insistent, crawling feeling of dread was telling her she really did not want to go back down those stairs.

"Ready?" Jethro was watching her, a hint of concern dawning in his eyes.

She forced herself to smile. "Of course."

Dinner was delicious. The food simple and plentiful. Aydan introduced them to the group of resistance fighters around the table and one or two curious glances were sent Vashti's way. She couldn't blame them. These people dedicated their lives to fighting Moncoya. Now, all of a sudden, they found themselves sharing a meal with his daughter. It didn't make for an easy atmosphere.

The meal was almost over when Lisbet joined them. She slid silently into the empty seat next to Aydan, scarcely glancing at anyone else and keeping her eyes fixed on her plate of food. Fascinated by the woman's strange demeanor, Vashti kept one eye on Lisbet while listening to the conversation around her. For some reason she could tell Lisbet's behavior was out of character. *In the same way I know Aydan is honest and brave, I know Lisbet is not this shy, retiring wallflower. The change is a direct result of our arrival. Or rather, it is a result of Jethro's arrival.*

Because she was observing Lisbet so closely, Vashti noticed how often the other woman's curious, dark eyes were focused on Jethro's face. Each time she looked his way, Lisbet lowered her eyes swiftly, as though conscious she might give her thoughts away. Although she did her best to maintain a timid and downcast aspect, each time she looked at Jethro, Lisbet's face glowed.

"Have you met Lisbet before?" Vashti asked Jethro later as they cleared the plates and no one else was nearby.

"Which one is Lisbet?" His brow furrowed as he studied the group of three women and four men. Since his response was an answer in itself, Vashti didn't pursue the matter any further.

Once the meal had been cleared away, Maria produced bottles of beer and rich red wine before leaving them to talk. The group discussed the latest atrocities committed by Moncoya's followers. Although it no longer surprised Vashti to learn of her father's evil activities, it still stirred up a worm of discomfort whenever his malevolence was revealed.

"He is becoming bolder," Aydan said, filling glasses with the ruby wine. "It is said Moncoya knows there is no true opposition to his rule. Once the faeries are given the vote, he will be returned to power. And he will be stronger and more ruthless than ever."

"His destruction here in the mortal realm will be even more devastating." Lisbet spoke for the first time. Her voice was low, musical, and completely different to the way Vashti had imagined it would sound. "The trafficking and degradation we work so hard to wipe out now will be rampant once his own people have given him their seal of approval."

Vashti had learned from Tanzi much of the work of the resistance involved rescuing those beings Moncoya's followers trafficked between Otherworld and the mortal realm. The resistance faced a never-ending battle to shut down the brothels Moncoya's sidhes operated within the mortal realm. These loathsome establishments operated a personalized service for clients who could afford their extortionate prices. Moncoya had established a system whereby his henchmen would abduct a being from Otherworld, bring them to one of his brothels and force them to work there, obeying every whim of the client who had selected them.

"Moncoya's lackeys are no longer making any pretense at covering their tracks here in the mortal realm. And their terrorist activity in Otherworld is becoming more frequent. There were two attacks in wolf territory recently and Moncoya's followers were daring enough to stage a siege in the vampire domain. Prince Tibor was on it in an instant, but the fact they went there speaks volumes." Aydan shook his head. "Moncoya is making a statement. He's on his way back and he wants the world to know it."

As the conversation continued, Vashti's discomfort grew. Not because of the continued vitriol toward her father. That was bad enough. The greater source of her unease was Lisbet. Although her behavior continued to be discreet, there was no doubt about it. Lisbet was totally enthralled by Jethro. *I am not jealous. I have no right to be. He is not mine.* There was something deeper in the glances Lisbet cast Jethro's way, something that spoke of more than longing. Each time Lisbet looked at Jethro— and, as the night wore on, she looked at him increasingly more often—her eyes blazed with a combination of elation and triumph.

There was someone Vashti had to consult and there was no time like the present. Murmuring to Jethro she was tired, she left the kitchen and made her way up to their room. Sitting cross-legged in the middle of the bed, she tried to clear her mind of every thought except one.

Tanzi.

Vashti focused on her sister. Surely she should feel closer to Tanzi here than anywhere? It wasn't so very long ago Tanzi had fled to this place, seeking refuge with Lorcan when she tried to escape Moncoya's plans to force her into marriage with the devil. When they were growing up, Moncoya had encouraged their fiercely competitive natures, and as a result they had never been close. It was only in the last few months, since that whole wedding-to-Satan fiasco, that they had discovered a new bond. And with that relationship had come the realization they also had the most powerful psychic connection of all. They could communicate telepathically no matter how far apart they were. It was a gift unique to faerie twins and one they might never have discovered if it wasn't for their father's rabid, out-of-control ambition. *He did something good for us, after all. Unintentionally, it had to be said, but he brought us together. If he hadn't tried to sell Tanzi to the devil in that megalomaniac way of his, we might have spent the rest of our lives believing we hated each other.*

Tanzi, can you hear me?

The response was instant, almost as if Tanzi had been waiting for her. *Vashti, where are you?*

In Barcelona, at the safe house.

Have you murdered Jethro yet?

How long ago it seemed, that time when she hated Jethro! *No, he is here with me. We've found Aydan, and we're on our way to Avalon.*

Be careful.

I will. I need to ask you about someone. Aydan said when you were here you knew his girlfriend, Lisbet. Tell me about her.

Are they together now? That's a surprise. I always thought she had a thing for Lorcan. She's got the personality of a prodded wasp, but maybe that's because she suspected I had been sent by our father to destroy the resistance.

What do you know of her background?

Nothing at all. Why?

Vashti sighed. Maybe she was reading too much into this niggling feeling about Lisbet. Maybe—heaven forbid—she really was jealous because the other woman was showing an interest in Jethro. *No reason. She struck me as a little strange, that's all. How are you?*

By the time Vashti had listened to an enthusiastic account of Tanzi's marriage, her developing pregnancy and life on the Isle of Spae, she could hear the others making their way up the stairs. She said goodbye to her sister as Jethro entered the room. He looked weary, but also elated.

"I've spoken to Aydan about our mission. He's going to come to the palace with us to meet Cal before we set off for Avalon." He sat on the bed, stripping off his sweater.

"How did you persuade him to do that?"

"I used the story Lorcan suggested. Now Lorcan has stepped down, Cal is on the lookout for someone trustworthy to take his place. I said Lorcan had recommended Aydan. No self-respecting anti-Moncoya faerie is going to turn down the chance to work alongside the great Merlin Caledonius himself." He stretched and yawned. "Even better than that, Aydan is going to accompany us to Avalon."

Vashti had been slightly distracted by the rippling muscles that were revealed as Jethro stripped down to his underwear, but he gained her full attention at that. "Why would he do that?"

"Because he wants to help find the challenger. He doesn't know, of course, about Tanzi's theory he might actually be the person we are seeking. But, think about it. The Goddesses of Fate said the truth would be revealed on Avalon. If Aydan *is* the challenger, we need him with us to find out."

Personally, Vashti thought they were pinning too much on the slim possibility of Aydan being the lost heir. *Just because he's a faerie who doesn't look like a faerie and Lorcan knows him. We could be in danger of focusing our attention on Aydan and allowing the real challenger to pass us by.* She still felt unaccountably dispirited. "Sounds like a plan."

Vashti hoped her voice did not reveal the fact she was less than eager about this whole scheme. Since their arrival in Barcelona, it was as if a blanket, gossamer-light as a spider's web yet dark as the desert skies, had been wrapped around her heart. She couldn't shake the feeling something was very wrong. *No, not since our arrival in Barcelona. Since we met Lisbet.*

Hard on the heels of that thought, Jethro's next words destroyed any final trace of enthusiasm she might have felt about the journey to Avalon. Along with any hope it might end well. "Oh, and Lisbet is coming with us."

Chapter 13

La Casa Oscura. The Dark House. Only Moncoya could be arrogant enough to flaunt its function by naming his mortal dwelling place after its true purpose. There were many portals between the mortal realm and Otherworld. They were accessible only to those who knew of their existence. Most were innocuous. Dark houses were the flip side of those harmless entry points. Dark houses hid Otherworld's sleazy secrets, the portals used by Moncoya's followers to traffic beings between worlds and escape justice. Older than time, they were the gateway to an underbelly darker than the pit of hell itself.

All of it carefully orchestrated by my father, the maestro. The thought made Vashti grimace as she viewed the beautiful, quirky house clinging to the hillside high above the city. Bizarrely, she had never viewed La Casa Oscura from this angle. In the past, Moncoya had sent his daughters into the mortal realm with precise instructions about who they were to kill, attack or kidnap. They saw little of the mortal realm and were not permitted to interact with anyone other than their chosen target...for whom the outcome wasn't pretty.

"La Casa Oscura is unique," Aydan explained. "Unlike most portals, it serves several purposes. As well as being a dark house, it is also a direct link to the royal palace and it is the mortal headquarters of Moncoya Enterprises. Let's not forget that, until he was forced into hiding following the battle for control of Otherworld, Moncoya was able to maintain a mortal identity. As well as being King of the Faeries, he was also Ezra Moncoya, electronics billionaire."

"We never knew." Vashti shook her head in amazement. "Tanzi and I only learned of his double life after he went into hiding."

"So how do we get in?" Jethro scanned the terra-cotta rooftop that peeked out above the trees. They were standing across the street from the casa, slightly to one side of the main gates. "This side is the problem. Once we are in, and can get to Otherworld, Cal is in charge and entering the palace won't be a problem."

"Moncoya Enterprises's security systems are said to be the most sophisticated in the world. Ordinarily, there is no way we would get through those gates." Aydan gave them a mischievous grin. "But one of our resistance members works this shift, so we're in luck. He will have turned off the cameras on the rear wall. I hope you two are good at climbing."

Jethro groaned, flexing his injured arm. "It's not my favorite activity right now. By the way, where's Lisbet?"

"She had things to finish up back at the safe house. She said she'll meet us when we depart for Avalon. Ready?"

"As I'll ever be." Jethro caught hold of Vashti's hand, his eyes probing her face as if he sensed her mood. "You?"

She nodded, swallowing the tight feeling of apprehension that threatened to block her throat. What was wrong with her? Not so long ago she had dreaded entering the mortal realm, now she was dismayed at the prospect of leaving it.

Fear of the unknown. That is what you are experiencing. First of the mortal realm, now of Avalon. Get a grip, Vashti.

What had happened to the ferocious warrior princess? Had she ever existed or was she a figment of Moncoya's overactive imagination? In a way, it was comforting to know she was not an automaton.

Although, it has to be said, you do pick your moments to have these flashes of in-depth soul-searching.

They made their way along a path to the rear of the building. The tree-covered area of the hillside had been allowed to grow wild and lethal-looking shrubs scratched at Vashti's arms as they forced their way through to the rear of the casa. The section of wall Aydan indicated loomed over them. Made from rough, terra-cotta brick, it was at least ten feet high and topped with razor wire.

"We're supposed to climb that?" Vashti tilted her head back, regarding the obstruction before them with a daunted expression.

"It's not as bad as it looks." Aydan, ever the optimist, pointed to a length of rope hanging down from the coping stones at the top of the wall. "Our contact on the inside left that for us." Jethro and Vashti remained silent, their faces twin masks of doubt. "I'll go first, shall I?"

When no answer was forthcoming, Aydan rolled up his sleeves and spat on his hands. Grasping the rope, he commenced walking his feet up the wall while using his hands to haul himself up. In minutes he was at the top and navigating the razor wire. He gave them a grin and a thumbs-up before dropping down the other side.

"Will you be able to do this?" Vashti indicated the rope. "Your arm isn't fully healed."

"I guess there's only one way to find out." Jethro grimaced.

"You go next. I need to know you're okay."

Jethro paused, looking down at her. Something shifted in the depths of his eyes. Vashti knew it was because she'd told him she cared. Even though it was a tiny fraction of what she could have said, it tilted the balance of their relationship. *Not now. Not here.* Her eyes pleaded with him. *We don't do this.* Jethro gave an infinitesimal nod. The gesture was much more than agreement with her suggestion. It told her he knew what she was feeling. *Let's save this conversation for another time and place. Like when I'm not the daughter of the most hated man in either world and you know who you are and what you want.*

Unexpected, unaccustomed tears burned the back of her eyes. "Go. Aydan is waiting for us."

Jethro shook his head. His smile was irresistible. "Bad timing."

He caught hold of the rope, scaling the wall as Aydan had done. His progress was slower and Vashti could tell from the way he favored his left arm he was struggling. She bit her lip, willing him to reach the top safely, exhaling a long, relieved breath when he finally gripped the coping stones and pulled himself clear of the razor wire. Giving her a wave, he disappeared over the other side just as Vashti heard the bushes rustle with the unmistakable sound of someone approaching.

Dropping into a crouch, she shifted instantly and easily, transforming herself into a black cat and slinking into the cover of the surrounding shrubs. Faeries weren't shape-shifters and it had taken Vashti and Tanzi a long time to accept that and master the art of changing their form. Once they realized faeries did not change in the same way were-creatures did, and shifting for them was an illusion not a change in their bodies, they had become comfortable with the skill. Now, it was second nature. Vashti offered up a prayer to the ancient Celtic gods who watched over the fae that Jethro would not decide to look back over the wall to see what was keeping her.

Two mortals dressed in black uniforms emblazoned with the gold Moncoya Enterprises M came into view.

"Tell me again why we have to patrol the exterior of the casa?" One of them lit a cigarette and paused, looking back along the path in the direction they had come.

His companion walked over to the wall, tugging on the rope. "This looks like a pretty good reason."

"¡Dios!" The first man spat out his cigarette, grinding it into the dusty soil. "We'd better get back and sound the alarm."

Climbing the rope was too time-consuming. As soon as the men were out of sight, Vashti—still in her cat disguise—sprang up the wall. Reaching the top, she navigated the razor wire and leaped down the other side, landing in her own form, much to the surprise of Jethro and Aydan, who were hiding in the shadows.

"No time to explain. Security has found the rope. They will be here in minutes."

They took off at a run toward the terrace at the rear of the casa. This was the point at which the two worlds joined. The criteria for entry into Otherworld was easy. For centuries scholars had theorized about Otherworld's location and agonized over the magic involved in gaining entry. Some believed Otherworld consisted of a series of vast underground caverns. An opposing view held it was an archipelago of enchanted islands, visible only at dusk and dawn. Or could it have been set in some distant planetary dimension beyond the visible stars? Was it under water, guarded by that most powerful of all sorceresses, Niniane, the Lady of the Lake? Or was it a combination of all of these? Did Otherworld move from one location to another according to the mood and whim of the gods?

Those who resided in the land known to the ancient Celts as the "delightful plain" knew the truth of how to get there. Otherworld was all around, all the time. Anyone could go. All they had to do was know the location of the nearest portal. That, and their belief in Otherworld and desire to go there had to be strong enough to overcome any trace of skepticism.

Standing on the terrace, looking out over Barcelona, Vashti reached for Jethro's hand on one side and Aydan's on the other. Tactile gestures didn't come easily to her, but time was of the essence and she knew their conviction that they could do this would be strengthened if they made a physical connection. Together they closed their eyes. Vashti shut out the impending danger of discovery and forced herself to concentrate on her home. There was a shout as the security guards rounded the corner. She gripped Jethro's and Aydan's hands harder and then opened her eyes.

The sensation of floating lingered for a few seconds before her surroundings came fully into focus. She spared a moment for the Moncoya Enterprises guards who would forever tell the tale of the intruders who disappeared into thin air. Then the mortal realm was gone. They were standing on a cliff top. Far below them ocean waves tumbled in time with an Otherworld breeze. Behind them, soaring up as though hewn into the rock face itself, the white marble of the faerie palace—now the Alliance headquarters—sparkled in the noonday sun.

"It would have been easier if we'd found ourselves a tiger and stuck our heads in its mouth," Jethro commented as they made their way across perfectly manicured lawns toward the palace entrance.

Even in the short time she had been gone, the defenses around the Alliance headquarters had been ratcheted up the highest level. Ever since the battle for control of Otherworld, a peacekeeping force, led by the elves, had been in place. They took overall responsibility for ensuring the safety of the dignitaries who visited this palace. Elves were never warlike, but they took such duties seriously. For the first time ever, Vashti found her way barred by a lone guard as she tried to enter her childhood home.

"I am the Crown Princess Vashti of the faerie dynasty."

"I still need to see some identification." The elf guard was apologetic but determined.

"Send for Merlin Caledonius. He'll vouch for me."

The elf looked shocked. "I can't send for the Council leader."

"What's going on?" Stella's voice was a welcome interruption. "Vashti! Why are you waiting out here? Come inside at once." Stella appeared to have been on her way out to the garden, but she changed her mind and turned back into the palace, leading them with her.

Stella took them through the main entrance hall and into the sitting room she had claimed as a private space for her and Cal. The man himself was seated at a desk near the window, frowning over a sheaf of papers. When he saw who Stella's companions were he rose and came forward, a question in his eyes as he looked from Jethro to Aydan and back again.

Jethro gave a tiny shake of his head, then a slight shrug

of his shoulders. Vashti understood the silent communication between the two men. Cal was asking if Aydan was the challenger. Jethro was indicating he didn't know.

"This is Aydan." Jethro stated the obvious. "We're on our way to Avalon. We stopped off here so you can get that supercharged boat of yours ready for us."

"Igraine?" Cal smiled, but Vashti thought he looked tired. "She's a beauty. One of these days, I'm going to take Stella on a sailing holiday."

"Ahem." Stella patted her stomach. "I think we have to consider young Arthur may not like boats."

"Arthur?" Jethro raised his brows. Because Vashti was so in tune with his emotions, she sensed something more in his expression than the faintly mocking inquiry he directed at Cal. "You are going to name your baby after a medieval king?"

"Oh, come on." Cal laughed. "He was my best friend, besides being the bravest, truest man I ever knew. I can't think of a better name for our child." He frowned as Jethro shook his head. "What is it?"

"I don't know. Probably some sort of hangover from an encounter we had with Iago and the Sluagh. Take no notice of me." He forced a smile onto his face with what Vashti knew was a supreme effort. "What if the baby is a girl?"

"We haven't thought about that," Stella confessed. "Guinevere?"

"No!" Cal and Jethro spoke with one voice, then looked at each other in surprise.

"Calm down. It was just a suggestion." Stella raised her eyes heavenward. Linking her arm with Vashti's, she drew her to one side. "Let's leave them to it. How are you? I know the prospect of spending time with Jethro worried you. Has it been horrible?"

"Not as bad as I thought." Vashti flopped onto a sofa, patting the seat next to her.

Stella sat, her vivid green eyes scanning Vashti's face. Those eyes missed nothing. "You seem different."

"I haven't been gone that long." Vashti tried not to squirm under Stella's intense gaze.

"Not physically. You look exactly the same as always. I can't explain it. It's a feeling I'm getting from you. As though you've changed completely in the short time you've been away." Stella couldn't know how true those words were.

"Well, it was pretty hair-raising." Vashti proceeded to tell her about their encounters with Iago and the drama of Jethro's ordeal with the Sluagh.

"I, of all people, have no reason to love your father, after he tried to force me to marry him, but his villainy never ceases to amaze me. Moncoya must have known what Iago was up to. Yet he allowed Iago to go after Jethro even though he knew it would place you in danger."

Vashti had never known her mother and, although she and Stella were close in age, the knowledge the other woman cared for her in a maternal way caused a storm of new emotions. For a moment she was afraid that, if she tried to speak, she would disgrace herself and start crying. Only when she was sure she had mastered her emotions did she risk talking. "Nothing my father does surprises me anymore. Not after he escaped from me at knifepoint when we were on Spae. He would have used that knife on me if I'd tried to stop him. That was when I knew for sure how ruthless he is."

"Trying to get Tanzi to marry the devil was a bit of a clue," Stella pointed out.

"True. Murdering our mother wasn't exactly warm and fluffy." Vashti sighed. "Yet, if he walked into this room right now, he would light it up in his own unique, larger-than-life way and each of us would be unable to take our eyes away from him. He has that sort of charisma. He does the most outrageous things and yet people only notice his personal charisma. That's why it's so important to find this challenger before my father romps all over this election."

Stella regarded her in surprise. "I thought you didn't want this. That you would want to maintain the status quo."

"I want the truth. Even if it hurts." Vashti knew she sounded weary. "And Moncoya will make sure it hurts."

Stella glanced across to where the three men were deep in conversation. "What about Aydan? Do you think he is the challenger?"

Aydan looked fragile in comparison to Jethro and Cal with their muscular strength. Vashti shook her head. "I think not. Jethro is unsure."

"He seems nice." Stella's expression was way too innocent.

"Aydan? He is." Vashti choked back a laugh. "Hey, are you matchmaking?"

"Trying to. You need someone nice in your life."

Vashti's lips twitched in genuine amusement. If only Stella knew. *I don't need nice. Safe won't do for me. I need someone edgy and dangerous.* She looked up in time to catch the tail end of Jethro's paint-stripping gaze on her face. *I need to be in this state of permanent arousal, knowing he wants me, too. Life with Jethro is never comfortable, but it is always exciting.*

"I'm tired. Do you mind if I go up to my old room?"

"What am I thinking, keeping you talking like this when you must be exhausted?" Stella rose. "I'll show you all to your rooms. Cal, you can get things organized so the boat is ready for them to depart first thing in the morning."

"Yes, boss." Merlin Caledonius, the greatest sorcerer the world had ever known, the man about whom more legends had been written than any other, grinned at his wife and went away to follow her instructions.

"Separate rooms?" Jethro murmured to Vashti as they mounted the stairs in Stella's wake. His tone made the hairs on the back of her neck rise. "I'm not sure I like that idea."

She turned her head to look up at him and encountered a scorching light in those dark eyes. "We've a long journey ahead of us. You need to rest."

His smile was devilish. "I'll come to your room later, Princess…and show you how wrong you are."

"You are insatiable."

"With you I am." Jethro's voice was husky as he pinned Vashti's arms above her head and pushed deep inside her again. Dawn was tracing lighter fingers across the sky outside and they had slept only briefly. "Although I seem to remember you calling me a few other names not so long ago." He paused, drinking in her flushed face, her half-closed eyes, the soft sounds of her breathing. God, he loved watching her face as he tipped her over the edge. "What were they now? Ah, yes. I remember. Sanctimonious bastard. Second-rate soothsayer. Arrogant, money-grabbing mercenary." He punctuated each syllable with a powerful thrust of his hips, driving his cock farther into her. Each movement elicited a gasp from Vashti and her whole body jerked up to meet his, her muscles clenching hard around him.

"You forgot one." Somehow she managed to grind the words out. "Wannabe sorcerer."

With tormented groan, Jethro released her hands and reached beneath her to grip her buttocks, lifting her so he could open her wider. Vashti wrapped her legs around his waist. His thrusts became frantic in response, pushing them both further and harder. Vashti cried out incoherently as though trying to tell him it was too much but still not enough. Jethro silenced her cries with his lips. He led her, drove her, guided her to ecstasy and claimed her, carrying her until he felt her internal muscles spasm wildly around him before finally relaxing in submission.

Jethro cried out with his own endless release before pulling out of her and dropping heavily onto her, kissing her forehead. When he had recovered his breath, he moved his weight to her side. He raised himself on his elbow, scrutinizing her face. When had watching her become his obsession? It had sneaked up on him so quickly he had barely noticed it. Vashti's eyes were slightly unfocused, her breathing still ragged. After a few minutes she turned on her side to face him.

When she spoke, her voice was shy and strangely un-Vashti-like. "I will miss this."

"Hmm?" Absently he ran a finger down the curve of her neck.

"One way or another, this will soon be over. I will miss these times when it is just the two of us."

A frown pulled Jethro's brows together. The words jolted him out of the warmth and security he always felt after sex with her. It hadn't occurred to him the end of his mission would mean the end of this. Of them. The thought pierced something inside him. It felt like a reminder of the Sluagh slowly drawing his soul from his body. *No.* He gazed down into those endless blue eyes with their encircling ring of fire. *You don't know it yet, Princess, but it will never be over for us.*

Big words for a man who didn't believe in love. *Who said anything about love?* Two voices went to war inside his head. One seemed to be insisting he should listen to his heart. But when did hearts start talking sense? The other was putting forward a reasoned argument. Vashti wasn't the sort of woman who wanted flowers and promises. She would understand and accept him for what he was. She wouldn't want the whole white-wedding thing Tanzi had. They could be grown-ups.

"Are you okay?" Vashti was regarding him with concern in her eyes. "You look intense."

"I'm tired. You've worn me out."

"*I've* worn *you* out?" Her voice rose in protest. "It wasn't me who woke you up three times. And it certainly wasn't me who woke you with my tongue in your..."

Laughing, he drew her into his arms, stopping her protests with a kiss. No, he couldn't do without this—without her—in his life. As for the love thing, he could shut that voice up. He was fairly sure he could.

Chapter 14

The early morning was damp and gray with faint rays of sunlight poking through the clouds and tendrils of mist still clinging to the lower levels of the hillside. Vashti shivered and huddled into the thick sweater she wore. The sense of foreboding hadn't left her. If anything, it was growing stronger by the minute.

They stood at the edge of the cliff, looking out over the bay. Cal pointed to a sleek, white sailboat bobbing on the gunmetal waters. "You've sailed her before, right?"

Jethro nodded. "When we took Lorcan to Spae in search of Tanzi." He grinned. "I know my way around a boat, but I also know that's no ordinary vessel."

"You're right. That's *Igraine*." A faint smile touched his lips. "Named after King Arthur's mother. You won't need the sails. I've tinkered with her engines. She'll take you direct to Avalon and get you there in next to no time."

"Tinkered?" Jethro raised a brow.

Cal grinned and Vashti thought how young and handsome he looked when he smiled. So unlike the white-bearded sorcerer of legend. "I'm good at the old tinkering."

"Lorcan said Avalon is a magical isle. It only appears to those who are meant to see it." Vashti thought Jethro appeared more like an old-world adventurer than ever as he spoke. He stood straight and tall, turning his face to the ocean as the breeze ruffled his hair. She could imagine him as a corsair preparing to set sail on his pirate ship or a medieval knight riding out to do battle. *This is what lack of sleep can do to a girl. It makes your imagination run wild.*

Cal's face was grave. "From what we've learned, I think you, of all people, *are* meant to see it. The shape of the island looks like this." He traced an outline in the air with his finger. "Three pointed hills resembling cathedral spires, with the tallest in the center. You won't be able to miss it."

"No matter how much I may want to?" A corner of Jethro's mouth lifted in a smile. "Don't worry. If I can see it, I won't choose to miss it. I have a few scores to settle with Iago." He flexed his left arm and grimaced.

Aydan had been standing to one side looking back toward the palace. "Lisbet said she would meet us." His voice was fretful as he came to join them. "I don't know what could have happened to her."

"Perhaps something came up and she couldn't get word to you." Vashti did her best to hide her relief there was no sign of Lisbet. The task ahead was going to be difficult enough as it was. She was fairly sure having Lisbet along wouldn't have made her life any easier. "I'm sure she would be here if she could."

"Unfortunately we can't wait around for her." Jethro

joined in the conversation and Aydan nodded a glum acceptance.

Cal drew Vashti slightly to one side. "I have a feeling you, more than anyone, are going to need every ounce of your personal strength during this journey." His unusual light silver eyes probed her face. "Yet it was never meant to be your mission. Are you still sure you want to go ahead with it?"

Vashti couldn't help her gaze going to Jethro's tall, heroic-looking figure. "He needs me."

Cal raised his brows. "Does he know?"

She laughed. "Have you met him?"

He grinned appreciatively. "Then all I can do is wish you success." He seemed to sense her wariness of physical contact, probably because he knew of her strange, affection-starved childhood. So, instead of the requisite hug such occasions generally demanded, he took both her hands in his. "He is a lucky man, even if he doesn't know it. Or perhaps I should say, even if he will never accept it."

The words did something strange to her throat and, unable to answer, she nodded, withdrawing her hands. Stooping to pick up her bags, she raised a hand to Cal in a gesture of farewell before rejoining Jethro and Aydan. As they began to navigate the steps that were hewn into the cliff face, Cal turned and made his way back toward the palace. It seemed too final and Vashti experienced a sudden longing to run to him and beg him to—what? Turn back? Come with them? Shaking her head, she followed her companions down the precarious steps.

When they got to the beach, there was a serviceable dinghy waiting for them on the sand. Jethro tugged off his boots and rolled up his jeans before pulling the dinghy into the water. Vashti and Aydan clambered into the bobbing craft and Jethro joined them, starting the motor and

sending the dinghy skimming across the waves toward
the boat named after the woman who had given birth to
the legendary king of the Britons.

When they reached *Igraine*, Jethro tied the dinghy up
and sprang aboard, leaning down to assist Vashti. For
an instant he held her close and she was grateful for his
strength and warmth.

"Okay?" His dark eyes searched her face.

Before she could answer they were interrupted by a
bright voice. "What kept you?"

Aydan, in the act of stepping from the dinghy to the
boat was so surprised he almost lost his balance and toppled overboard. "Lisbet?"

"Were you expecting someone else?" She was standing on the deck, the weak sunlight turning her pale hair
silver. Her coal-black eyes were alight with secrets.

Jethro frowned. "How did you get here?"

Lisbet's laughter was musical. "I wanted to surprise
you. Now, are you all going to stand there like openmouthed statues or are we going to Avalon?"

No matter how sleek and swift *Igraine* might be, her
living quarters were cramped with four people on board
and Vashti soon found her nerves frayed by proximity to
Lisbet. The other woman seemed to be in determinedly
high spirits, a situation that was directly contrary to her
usual mood.

There was only one cabin, containing a large double
bed, and Jethro insisted the two women should share this.
He and Aydan could sleep on the cushioned bench seats
that ran on either side of the comfortable saloon. Vashti
greeted the suggestion with silent horror. Share a room—
and a bed—with Lisbet? Iago's leering propositions were
beginning to sound preferable.

She went on deck and came to stand beside Jethro as he expertly skimmed the dainty boat across the open seas. "I suppose you have a dozen luxury yachts moored at various locations throughout the mortal realm?" Her teasing reference to his wealth reminded her of their time together on de Loix Island. It seemed so long ago. She experienced a sudden, fierce longing to be back in that beautiful, lonely setting, just the two of them, shut away from the rest of either world.

He smiled down at her and her heart flipped over with love. "Funnily enough, I don't. But *Igraine* here is such a pleasure to manage, I might have to reconsider. Since her engines are supercharged by Cal's magic, I might be disappointed by any boat I come across in the mortal realm."

Her eyes scanned the vast expanse of empty ocean. "How long will it take us to reach Avalon?"

"By rights it should be weeks. At this rate, I reckon we'll be there in a couple of days."

"When Tanzi and Lorcan undertook this journey to get to Valhalla, they had to pass through Prince Tibor's territory." Vashti raised worried eyes to his face. "That would be dangerous for you."

Jethro grinned. "Let's not mince our words. That would be certain death for me. Tibor would love to get his hands on me—or rather his teeth into me—on his own land."

His ability to talk about what Tibor would like to do to him with such cheerfulness did nothing for Vashti's mood. "Can we avoid the Vampire Archipelago?"

"It's done. Until Tanzi and Lorcan made the journey, no one knew what the route looked like. It was all supposition and legend. But Lorcan was able to fill in the blanks on the ancient maps. Cal has plotted a route that takes us wide of any potential conflict areas. We won't encounter another soul, alive or dead, until we reach the Isles of the Aesir where Avalon is situated." Letting go of the wheel with one hand, he drew her to him, holding her close against his side. How was it her whole "no physical contact thing" didn't apply to Jethro? *Oh, that'll be because I'm madly, hopelessly, in love with him.* Vashti snuggled close, rubbing her cheek against the hard muscles of his chest, taking comfort from his warmth. "Stop being such a worrywart."

She looked up at him with dawning incredulity. "Because there is nothing to worry about? Is that what you are trying to tell me? We are not heading for the most dangerous island in Otherworld? There is no mad trickster and his evil sorceress grandmother waiting for us? You didn't nearly get your soul ripped from your body by the Sluagh a few days ago? They are not responsible for killing your parents? Iago didn't almost kill you in a fireball while you were at your weakest?"

He laughed, dropping a kiss on the top of her head. "When you put it like that…"

Her eyes narrowed. "Jethro de Loix, you are the most infuriating man I have ever met. To think I once believed it was all about money with you! You just love the danger, don't you? You'd go and stick your head in a lion's mouth if there was one available. I'm surprised you haven't decided to sail into vampire waters and thumb your nose at Tibor just for the fun of it."

"Vashti, what the hell is this all about?" He was regarding her in astonishment. "Why are you so angry with me all of a sudden?"

"Because I…" She was so wound up, she'd have said it. If Lisbet hadn't appeared on the deck at that precise moment, she'd have blurted out, "Because I love you, you big, brave idiot." She was glad of Lisbet's appearance, for once. Vashti didn't want to see the bemused light in Jethro's eyes change to one of pity. She didn't want to see how fast his passion for her could fade and become excuses. Jethro didn't do love. She was fairly sure that also meant he didn't want love from her. She'd gotten that message. She could have as much of that amazing body as she wanted. As long as she never asked for anything more. Could she live with that?

As Lisbet determinedly drew Jethro's attention to a barely discernible point on the horizon, Vashti moved away from his side.

She had told Cal the truth when she'd said she was here because Jethro needed her. On one level he recognized and was grateful for that. It was a physical level. She healed him. On another level, they had a sexual connection like nothing he had experienced before. She knew without him having to tell her. He could never have experienced what they shared with anyone else. It wasn't vanity that told her that. It was a fact. Just thinking about it sent a jolt of pure, molten heat searing through her. It was the reason she would never be jealous of Lisbet or any of the other women who looked at him with such blatant longing. Gratitude didn't come into that need. It was raw longing. There was another level. One Vashti understood but Jethro remained unaware of. Would Jethro ever realize his need for Vashti went deeper than that intense physical craving? *Will we live long enough to find out?* This was not the time for chasing answers. The time to deal with questions about the future would be when they knew if there was a future.

Vashti looked up, smoothing away the frown from between her brows. Jethro was still suffering the barrage of Lisbet's discourse. He caught Vashti's gaze and rolled his eyes at her. She smiled sweetly in return. It was strange how Lisbet seemed to have quickly overcome her awe of Jethro. But Lisbet *was* strange.

"Help me." He mouthed the words silently over Lisbet's head.

In reply, she went down into the saloon, leaving him staring after her in silent frustration. Sometime later, Jethro appeared, filling the small space with his large frame. Hauling her up from the bench seat, he backed Vashti up against the paneled bulkhead.

"What the fuck do you mean by leaving me alone to listen to that drivel for another half an hour?" His voice was low as he ground the words into her ear. "I was so bored, I had to shout for Aydan to come and take the wheel."

"I thought you liked living dangerously. Lisbet is the conversational equivalent of sticking your head in a lion's mouth."

"I am going to enjoy making you pay for that, Princess." His thigh was pressed up hard between her legs, his hand snaking under her sweater, already moving the cup of her bra aside.

"How?" She was panting as his finger and thumb found her nipple and tweaked it hard.

"You'll find out." His breathing was ragged. "The hard way." He caught hold of her hand, moving it down so she could feel his erection straining at the cloth of his jeans.

"You decided I should share the cabin with Lisbet, remember?"

Vashti thought she had never heard anyone curse so long or so fluently as Jethro did then. "I owe you."

She locked her eyes on his, making sure he felt the erotic shudder rippling through her. "When the time is right, I'll remind you of it."

With a groan that reverberated around the small saloon, Jethro flung away from her, kicking the table on his way up onto the deck. With shaking hands, Vashti fixed her clothing and waited for her breathing to return to something approaching normality before following him.

Sleeping on *Igraine*'s deck for the last two nights had not been conducive to either Vashti's physical well-being or her mood. Lisbet, on the other hand, seemed to grow more cheerful by the minute.

"The cabin is really comfortable," she told Vashti, pouring herself a cup of coffee. "I can't understand why you don't want to sleep in there."

"I get seasick." Vashti stuck to the excuse she'd used on the first day. "It's not as bad if I'm in the open air."

Lisbet shrugged and went to sit next to Jethro, helping herself to a piece of toast from his plate. Her glaring crush on him had increased as the journey progressed. Vashti didn't like Lisbet. She wouldn't have liked her even if the other woman didn't blatantly throw herself at Jethro. Perhaps he gave off some sort of vibe that he was still available, though he made no secret of the fact he was with Vashti. *With me, but not with me.* That said it all, but it wasn't the point.

What annoyed Vashti most about Lisbet was that she was supposed to be Aydan's girlfriend. Sweet, kind, honest Aydan, who looked on with hurt in his pale green eyes as his girlfriend flirted and cooed at Jethro. Vashti wanted to tell him to fight for her. Actually, she wanted to tell him to dump Lisbet and find someone worth having. She had never met such a mismatched couple. Hadn't Tanzi been surprised they were together? She remembered her sister saying Lisbet had been infatuated with Lorcan. What was it with this woman? Should she tell her to leave Jethro alone? With everything else going on, it felt wrong to do so. As if she was allowing her personal dislike of Lisbet to intrude on the more momentous events surrounding the reason for this journey.

She waited until Aydan and Lisbet had gone up on deck and then fixed Jethro with a speculative look. "Necromancer groupies. Is that a thing?"

He choked slightly on his coffee. "Pardon?"

"You heard me. Are there women who follow necromancers around hoping to have sex with them?"

"Where is this going?"

"Tanzi said Lisbet had a thing for Lorcan when they were in Barcelona. She definitely has a thing for you."

"Jealous, Vashti?"

She kept her voice light. "You can think that if you want. I happen to like Aydan and I don't enjoy seeing him humiliated."

A faint flush tinged Jethro's high cheekbones. "I haven't encouraged her."

"I didn't say you had."

He was silent for a few minutes. "If she had a thing about necromancers, she'd have moved heaven and earth to meet Cal and Stella—the two greatest living necromancers. But she didn't come to the palace with us."

"True." Vashti smiled at him. "It must be your personal magnetism, after all."

"Thank God for that. The idea there might be women out there who want me to drag them off and do unspeakable things to them over a tombstone doesn't bear thinking about."

"Oh, I don't know." Vashti teased him with her eyes. "I quite like the idea of doing unspeakable things with you. Tombstone optional."

They were still laughing when Lisbet appeared. Her

eyes narrowed as she took in their shared hilarity. "What's funny?"

"We've discovered Vashti here is a necromancer groupie." Jethro stood, holding his hand out to Vashti. "I'm going to take the wheel from Aydan. Come and keep me company."

"Just so we're clear, I'm a picky groupie." Vashti slid her hand into his. "I won't follow any necromancer."

"I should think not." Jethro's eyes were still alight with laughter as he gazed down at her. "You're not the only one who can get jealous."

She trailed behind him onto the deck, her heart pounding. Did he know what he'd just said? Or was he still teasing? If he could feel jealousy, that meant he must care about her. *Stop it. Stop right there.* She kept lecturing herself but it didn't work. As she reached the deck, her grin was as wide as the gates of Valhalla itself.

Her euphoria lasted about as long as it took her to follow the direction of Aydan's shaking finger. The island he pointed to was large enough to fill the horizon. Its outline had three distinct peaks, like cathedral spires, with the tallest in the center. The hills wore an encircling skirt of mist, giving the effect the island was floating just above the water.

"Avalon." Aydan's voice trembled more than his finger as he infused the single word with a mixture of excitement and dread.

"I heard a story once." Lisbet's voice had a soft, faraway note as if she were recapturing a childhood memory or a pleasurable dream. They were all standing on the deck beside Jethro as he steered the boat. None of them took their eyes off the island as it loomed closer. "It was a folk story about the hills of Avalon. It tells of two

springs, one on each of the outer slopes. The water from
the spring on the right is the purest in all Otherworld, as
sweet and as clean as the morning dew. It is said to have
healing properties. The water on the left hill comes from
a different fountain. The liquid that bubbles up between
its rocks is foul and stagnant. Where it touches the veg-
etation, it scorches it brown as if acid has been poured
over the grass. No birds fly nearby, no living creatures
drink or bathe in its waters."

"There are many stories of Avalon. No one really
knows which are true." Jethro kept his eyes fixed on the
island.

Lisbet continued as if he had not spoken. "It is said if
the two spring waters ever flow all the way to the foot of
the hills, they will meet at the base of the central mount.
There they will merge to form an elixir more powerful
than any magic that has existed since time began."

"I heard the same story." Where Lisbet's voice had
been dreamy, Aydan's was fearful. "In the version I was
told, the waters on the right contain the tears of angels
while those on the left carry the blood of demons."

The fog clinging to the lower slopes of the hills had a
faint incandescent glow. What lurked in its depths? Jethro
wondered. Mystery? Madness? His hand automatically
groped for Vashti's. Seeking the security of her touch had
become second nature to him now. Her fingers were cold
as ice. When he glanced down at her, her face gave away
nothing of her emotions, but he knew how much she was
dreading this. She was here for him. Their unique sym-
biosis was her only reason for placing her life in danger.
The thought strengthened his resolve. Jethro had never
lacked courage, but couldn't courage and foolhardiness
sometimes be confused for the same thing? Vashti's pres-

ence reminded him of the difference. She reassured him of more than that.

Somewhere, over the course of this mission, finding the challenger had started to matter to Jethro for reasons other than money. He had always known Moncoya was an evil bastard, but that knowledge had never touched him personally. Until now. He believed his feelings had changed because Moncoya had sent Iago after him. It surprised him to realize that was not the case. He wanted to find the challenger and topple Moncoya from his throne forever because of the way the faerie king had treated Vashti. Because of the untold hurt he saw in those glorious blue eyes whenever she heard her father's name. Because of all the things she never said. He wanted to hurt Moncoya in return for all the times the faerie king had made his own daughter suffer.

They were close enough now to see houses huddled on the central hillside within the drifting, ever-shifting fog. Higher again, rising out of the remnants of clinging mist, there was a vast castle. It was perched precariously on a ridge, perfectly positioned so it gave a three-hundred-and-sixty-degree view of the surrounding ocean.

"We are being watched." Jethro's voice was grim.

"Did you think we would not be?" Vashti looked up at him. "Iago knew we were coming. If he's here, and I sense he is, he will have been expecting us."

"Will he kill us as soon as we step foot onto the island?" Aydan asked.

"That won't be nearly enough fun for Iago. He'll have some game in mind first." Jethro tried to sound confident. "We have to make sure we emerge as the winners." He glanced down at Vashti. "Right?"

There was a flicker of a smile in the depths of her eyes. "You've met my father. He taught me winning is the only way. Being a good loser was never an option for Moncoya's daughters."

"You have never been to Avalon before." Lisbet's voice was cold as she issued the warning.

"And on that cheering note, I think our welcome party awaits." Jethro steered *Igraine* into a harbor. From what he could see through the mist, it was a pretty place, dotted with tiny fishing craft. His comment about a welcome party was a reference to the murky figures his sharp eyes had picked out. A group of three men stood on the harbor wall, observing their arrival. With a sinking heart, Jethro recognized Iago in their center. A confrontation on his arrival after a long journey would not have been Jethro's choice. But would anything about this have been his choice?

I chose you. The words were spoken inside his head. The voice—a woman's—was soft and insidious, mildly amused and vaguely familiar. *My God, I need to stop listening to Lisbet and Aydan and their folk tales. I'll be spouting my own stories of woodcutters and wolves before we leave this place.* That did it. By focusing on the time when he—*they*—had accomplished what they had come here to do and could leave Avalon, he was able to look up and face the mocking smile of his nemesis.

"Welcome to my home." Jethro didn't like the way Iago's eyes lingered on Vashti's face and wandered over her body. There was a promise of ownership within the action. Jethro wanted to challenge it. Actually, he wanted to rip the smile off the other man's face so he never dared look her way again. On balance, he decided it might be better to let it pass. Sooner or later, Iago was going to pay for every trick, every insult, every mocking remark... including each lecherous thought he had directed at

Vashti. Iago would pay in blood. And Jethro was going to enjoy wringing every drop from him.

With that thought in his mind, he pinned a smile on his lips and brought *Igraine* into place alongside the harbor wall, shutting off her engines. Leaping onto the wall, he deftly secured the boat, gesturing for the others to remain on board. "I am here at your invitation," he reminded Iago.

"That's not quite true." Iago appeared more restless than ever. His green eyes glowed, he could barely stand still and there was a triumphant light in his eyes Jethro didn't like. *Let's face it, you wouldn't like any light in this guy's eyes.* "You are here at the invitation of one far greater than I."

"Can we skip the riddles? It's been a long journey... and some dick set the Sluagh on me before we set off."

Iago's smile shifted and became nasty. "I love riddles, but I see you are not blessed with a similar sense of humor. As I'm sure you have surmised, you are here at the invitation of my grandmother, the greatest sorceress ever known." He looked at each of them in turn, speaking the next words with a dramatic flourish. "Morgan le Fay."

Jethro remained unimpressed. "No doubt she will explain the reason for her invitation when you take me to meet her."

"I expect she will. She is not here at present, however."

Jethro's brows drew together in annoyance. More games? "We've been summoned here by someone we've never met, for an unspecified reason. And she can't make the effort to be here to meet us?"

"You should be groveling in delight at the prospect of meeting her, no matter how long you must wait."

"You'll excuse me if I manage to contain my delight."

Iago's eyes narrowed and Jethro sensed him battling to get his temper under control. For a moment the outcome hung in the balance. Then Iago burst out laughing. Clapping Jethro on the back—*do that again and you'll lose that hand, you trickster bastard*—Iago became the genial host once more. "My instructions are to make you welcome. You are my honored guests until my grandmother's return. Rest assured, you are safe here on Avalon...until she decrees otherwise."

Chapter 15

It was like stepping back in time, Jethro couldn't help thinking. As if the centuries between King Arthur's rule and the modern day had never passed. Avalon remained suspended in another era. Iago's two companions were servants clad in doublet and hose. They led them to a group of horses and helped them to mount.

"We lead a simpler life here," Iago explained as they rode through cobbled lanes and past quaint, thatched cottages. "The earth-born would scoff and try to tell you their life today is preferable. They would cite modern medicine and advances in technology. But such arguments ignore the truth. Times were happier when magic was accepted as reality. When the barrier between Otherworld and the mortal realm was nonexistent and the cure for illness and unhappiness rested in the hands of the fae. The Seelie and Unseelie courts decided the fate of the earth-born, even in the time of Camelot."

The road they followed wound up above the fishing village and toward the castle they had seen from the ocean. Aydan's voice was low as he spoke to Jethro. "I don't know enough about Morgan le Fay. Was she faerie or witch?"

"I don't think anyone knows for sure if she was either or both. Morgan was the daughter of Gorlois, Duke of Cornwall and his wife, Igraine. Her sister was Niniane, the infamous Lady of the Lake. When Uther Pendragon fell in love with Igraine, Merlin—as Cal was known in those days—used his magic powers to disguise Uther as Gorlois. In his disguise, Uther seduced Igraine and Arthur was conceived. Uther went on to kill Gorlois, marry Igraine and hand Arthur over to Merlin to be raised as the future king of the Britons and founder of Camelot."

Aydan gave him a sidelong glance. "Is it just me, or does Cal not come out of that story well?"

Jethro laughed. "It was another time, another place. The mortal realm needed a strong leader. Cal was given the task of ensuring it got him. Cal doesn't speak of it, but I think he did what he had to do to make sure King Arthur was born and, more importantly, that he had the right parents."

"The right parents?" Aydan looked surprised. "If King Arthur was to be brought up by Merlin, did it matter who his parents were?"

"Unless Cal decides to reveal all, I'm just guessing, but I believe Igraine must have had some strong magical powers of her own. Both her daughters were incredibly powerful sorceresses. There has never been any suggestion Arthur had magical powers, but his ability to draw others to him was legendary. Who knows whether that was something more than mortal charisma? On his father's side, he inherited Uther's strength. Uther was a king, a brave and noble warrior, a man who was prepared to fight for what he held to be right. No, I think Cal chose Arthur's parents carefully."

"You know a lot about the story of King Arthur." Aydan lowered his voice again. They were approaching the castle itself now and Iago glanced over his shoulder as though inviting their admiration.

Jethro grinned, feeling somewhat sheepish as he disclosed the truth. "I've always been fascinated by the legends surrounding Camelot. I have to confess I was starstruck when I first met Cal. Dare I admit that, even though I know him so well now, I'm in awe of the great Merlin Caledonius? And, although I've heard all the warnings about Avalon, a tiny part of me, the part that was a boy reading the stories of Arthur's life under my bedclothes by flashlight, is thrilled to be here."

"This is not what I expected." Vashti, who had been riding behind them in silence, listening to their conversation, spoke up suddenly. Jethro shifted slightly in the saddle so he could look at her. Vashti's eyes were fixed on the vast walls of the castle.

"What did you expect?" Jethro moved his horse closer to hers.

"I don't know. Darkness and danger, I suppose. Not beauty and light. Everything I have ever heard about Avalon led me to believe it would be a hateful, evil place." Vashti indicated the beautiful, whitewashed castle. "It's not."

"It's almost as if the noble court of Camelot has been recreated here on Avalon." Aydan's words resonated deep inside Jethro, striking a new note, something he didn't recognize but that was achingly familiar. Like a memory of the unknown or homesickness for a place he had never been.

"Perhaps that's true." Their little cavalcade was pausing now at the castle gates. "Although Morgan spent many years fighting against Arthur, there had been a fondness between them once. They weren't raised together. When they met as adults, they fell deeply in love. They had a relationship and a son together. Some stories say Morgan knew of their relationship while Arthur, who was much younger, did not. When he discovered the truth, he was devastated and refused to have anything more to do with her. They became sworn enemies from then on and Morgan was banished from Camelot."

Jethro looked up at the iron portcullis that was being slowly raised so they could enter. A cold finger of dread tracked its way down his spine and he would have given anything in that moment to have been able to grab Vashti's hand and walk away from that place. Forget walking. If he could, he'd have run as though the hounds of hell were snapping at his heels. Yet that eagerness he'd spoken of was still there, drawing him onward. He'd never felt so conflicted. It was as if he was being pulled apart by opposing forces and neither of which was what he wanted. "Tintagel, the Cornish castle that was Gorlois's stronghold, later became the court of Camelot. It was the place where Morgan and Niniane were raised. I suppose she has tried to recreate her childhood home here on Avalon."

Lisbet, who had been trailing behind the group, urged her horse forward now so she could ride alongside Jethro. It meant they rode into the courtyard first with Vashti and Aydan bringing up the rear. Jethro recalled Vashti's comments about Lisbet's obsession with him. He wondered if Vashti would see Lisbet's action as deliberate, as though it had some sort of symbolism. Might Vashti be annoyed at being relegated into second place? She was a princess, after all, although she never flaunted her royal status.

"You look almost exultant," Lisbet commented. "Is your interest in King Arthur really so strong?"

Jethro looked around him as they entered the castle courtyard, sensing Morgan le Fay would have left nothing to chance. This is how Camelot would have looked and felt. Down to the last detail. He knew it was true. Exultant? It wasn't the first word that came into his mind, but maybe a tiny part of him felt it. "I suppose it must be."

"Yet this is where he died. It is the home of the evil sorceress who did her best to destroy him." Her eyes, those strange, dark eyes, challenged him and he wondered, not for the first time, what Aydan saw in her. Lisbet was high-maintenance, while Aydan was pleasant and easygoing. They were an oddly matched couple. Her words seemed to have a hidden meaning and he couldn't fathom what response she was trying to elicit from him. Was it her version of flirting?

"She also tried to save him. He was brought here to Avalon because, if anyone could heal him, it was Morgan. By all the accounts that were written, she was distraught and really did try, but the blow Mordred dealt him during the battle proved fatal." Was he defending Morgan le Fay?

"So King Arthur died in the arms of his half sister, the only woman who ever truly loved him."

"I think I've read just about everything there is on the subject, but I never read that he died in her arms."

"Ah, you are not the only one who knows your Arthurian legends." Lisbet's smile was teasing. "Admit it. It makes for an almost happy ending. A remorseful Morgan, unable to save King Arthur's life, cradles her dying brother to her breast as his life slips away. Desperate to preserve him, she casts a spell that keeps him suspended in an enchanted sleep until she is able to find a cure. Then she buries him here on the Isle of Avalon, swearing she will one day discover a way to bring him back to life."

"You are being somewhat creative with the truth. Legend states only that Arthur *may* lie here, ready to rise again when the world needs him. No one knows for sure."

"Nevertheless, I prefer my version," Lisbet teased, her eyes twinkling mischievously. "So much more romantic, don't you think?"

In the style of all great medieval dwellings, this was a castle within a castle. Inside the outer walls there was a luxurious, fortified keep, the home of the most noble family. Iago was dismounting in front of the entrance to this residence. Gesturing for his guests to do the same, he waited, a little smile dancing on his lips. Jethro was glad to move away from Lisbet. He always got the feeling he was missing some double meaning to her conversation, as if she was having a private joke at his expense. Or had Vashti made him paranoid with her comments about necromancer groupies?

"It is my pleasure to escort you into my home." Iago bowed low. "Welcome to Camelot."

Vashti faced Iago sometime later, unable to hide her belligerence. "What if I don't wish to follow your decree?"

Iago had sent a maid to wait on her and, out of the corner of her eye, Vashti saw the young woman wince and make an attempt to sidle away from the forthcoming confrontation.

Iago smiled. It was a pleasant enough expression, but his eyes remained hard. "It is not *my* decree. These are the orders of Morgan le Fay, ruler of this island. If they are not to your liking, you may leave now."

Jethro, who could clearly sense the storm of defiance building in Vashti, placed a hand on her arm and answered for her. "We will wear what you wish." Vashti muttered a furious protest. Pulling her closer to him, Jethro turned her away from the others so he could whisper to her and not be heard. "We need to choose our battles wisely while we are here."

"I intend to." She raised solemn eyes to his face. "I haven't forgotten what Iago did to you. I remember what we owe him."

"So do I. He has told us we are safe until Morgan returns. I still don't trust him, but let's see where this leads us."

His eyes reassured her he wasn't backing down from the fight. Their expression calmed her outrage at Iago's determination to control her, even down to the details of her wardrobe. Taking a deep breath, she nodded. "Very well." She raised her voice enough to ensure the words carried across to Iago.

The trickster allowed himself a genuine smile this time. "I am so glad you have agreed. I chose your dresses myself with your perfect coloring in mind." He indicated the gowns the maidservant held draped over her arm.

Resisting the impulse to shudder, Vashti pinned a smile on her face. "Let's get on with it."

They were standing in the grand hall of the castle. It was a vast chamber, dominated by the inevitable, symbolic round table. The walls were hung with bright silks embroidered in the colors of different knights, presumably those of King Arthur's court. A huge number of people had congregated in the space. Although they all seemed interested in the new arrivals, a curious hush hung over the crowded room as though no one dared speak.

As she turned to follow the maidservant up a wide, central staircase, Vashti was conscious of dozens of pairs of eyes upon her. It wasn't exactly a new sensation. She was the daughter of the most notorious and attention-seeking man in Otherworld. She wasn't exactly an unknown herself. Yet this felt different. She instinctively knew she wasn't being watched for any reason that was about her. These people were observing her because someone else had plans for her. The thought unnerved her. Had Iago and Morgan shared their intentions with every other person on Avalon? *If we tried to escape, would each of these dumbstruck serfs carry out their masters' instructions and prevent us?* The weight of those silent gazes bored into her back as she reached the top and turned onto the gallery. Trusting Jethro's instincts, she continued along an unknown passage.

The maidservant, whose name was Ilsa, led her to a small but comfortable bedchamber. She placed a number of rich gowns on the bed. They were all in shades of blue ranging from deepest indigo through brilliant sapphire to palest powder. Their slippery silks and velvets were trimmed with brocade and lace and, in spite of her annoyance, Vashti ran her hand over the rich cloth in admiration.

"Why are there so many people in the hall?" She asked the words diffidently, pretending not to watch the girl's face closely as Ilsa hung the dresses in a huge oak closet that occupied most of one wall.

"They are here for the banquet, my lady."

"What banquet would that be?"

"The banquet to celebrate your arrival." Ilsa finished her task and turned to Vashti with a shy smile. "There has not been so much excitement here on Avalon for—" she frowned as if in an effort to remember, then she laughed "—I do not think there has ever been this much excitement here!"

"Why is that?"

Ilsa had a pleasant, open face and her smile was without guile. "We lead very simple lives."

"No, I mean why should *our* arrival be the cause of such excitement?"

"Because you are such honored guests." It had the rhythm of a rehearsed speech.

Vashti sighed. She had a feeling interrogating Ilsa would prove frustrating and fruitless. "I'd better get into one of those dresses." She regarded the rich array of gowns with dislike. "Which one do you think I should wear for this banquet?"

Ilsa's eyes shone with pleasure. "I know exactly the one."

Some considerable time later, having submitted to Ilsa's ministrations, Vashti descended the staircase once more. She was clad in a full-length velvet tunic in a brilliant shade of turquoise blue. The low-cut, square neckline and long, tight sleeves were edged with jewels and the waist was clinched with a matching jeweled belt. The wide skirts swept the floor as she walked.

Ilsa had pursed her lips over Vashti's hair. "It is the fashion to wear waist-length plaits."

"I can't wait up here until it grows."

Ilsa had laughed. "No, indeed, but no one will know." Her cryptic comment had been explained as she hid Vashti's short locks beneath a simple white veil, securing it in place with a circular tiara.

Dainty silk slippers completed the outfit. There was no mirror in her room, but Ilsa had clasped her hands together in delight at the finished product. "My lady, you look beautiful."

Jethro's eyes, when he moved forward to greet her as she reached the foot of the stairs, told her the same thing.

Vashti decided she was more interested in his opinion than that of the maid.

"My God, Vashti." His smile warmed her heart. "Those clothes really do suit you."

"You wouldn't believe how many layers there are," she grumbled. "Yet, curiously, there is no underwear involved."

His eyes glittered. "I'll bear that information in mind for another time." He leaned closer. "When I can use it to my own advantage…and yours."

She gave a little gasp, her nerve endings instantly firing up at the prospect. "Don't say things like that to me. Not here."

"Why not? Since we have to be in this god-awful place, we may as well enjoy ourselves. And, believe me, the thought of you with no underwear is probably the only thing that will get me through the next few hours."

Vashti took a moment to study his garments. Jethro was clad in breeches, hose, boots and a velvet doublet with a short cloak flung back over one shoulder. The outfit suited his devil-may-care looks. "You look…" She paused, seeking the right words to explain. "As though you were born to wear those clothes."

He grimaced. "The sooner we get back to civilization the better. I don't like the feeling of being powerless, of waiting for something to happen." He glanced around the crowded room. "Is it just me or do you get the feeling we're the main attraction?"

He was right. Surreptitious glances were being constantly cast in their direction. "I suppose it's because people don't come here," Vashti said. "Even Cal is afraid of Avalon. And remember how Lorcan and Tanzi described the way it fades in and out of view as if it is only intended to be reached by a select few? We are probably the first visitors this castle has seen for centuries."

"Hmm." Jethro looked unconvinced. "Either that or we're wearing these clothes all wrong."

They were joined by Aydan and Lisbet, both suitably attired in their medieval clothing. "So what's the plan?" Aydan asked. "We can't go around asking every man in the room if he is the real heir to the faerie crown."

The look Lisbet gave him was faintly annoyed. It wasn't the first time Vashti had observed her intolerance toward him. She was his girlfriend, how could she fail to see his good qualities? "Can't we just enjoy the atmosphere?"

"No, we came here for one reason only," Jethro reminded her. "Two in my case," he added as Iago appeared at the head of the staircase. "I have a few scores to settle."

Ever the showman, Iago halted, drawing all eyes to him. "It is my great pleasure to welcome our guests to my home and to invite you all to join me in this banquet in their honor." There was a ripple of applause. "They have been summoned here by our great leader—my beloved grandmother—Morgan le Fay, who, sadly, cannot join us in person."

Was it Vashti's imagination or was there a ripple of nervous laughter at those words? She definitely didn't imagine Iago's frown or the instant silence that followed it. Maybe the laughter was relief. She couldn't believe Morgan's presence would be conducive to a pleasant occasion.

"So, my friends—" Iago clapped his hands together "—let us eat, drink and be merry!"

Vashti supposed she should have predicted she would be seated next to Iago. Jethro, at the opposite side of the vast round table, between Lisbet and Aydan, sent a helpless, sympathetic glance in her direction. The food, served on wooden platters, was delicious. Iago was determined to be attentive. If that meant leaning a little too close and watching her with a proprietorial look in his eye, Vashti did her best to ignore it.

When his hand dropped to her thigh, she decided enough was enough. Gripping his wrist with all her strength—which was not insignificant—she looked him in the eye. "Touch me again and I'll cut off the part of you that is closest to me."

"You don't mean that. Not here in my own castle, in front of all these people."

"Try me." She kept her eyes fixed on his.

With a slight, nervous laugh, Iago withdrew his hand, rubbing his wrist. "When my grandmother returns, she has promised me I can have you."

"I'm not a toy in a shop window."

He lifted one shoulder. "You may as well be. If I want you, you are mine."

Vashti tilted her knife onto its hilt, watching as the candlelight caught the blade. "Remember what I said. The part that is closest to me." As Iago shuddered slightly and crossed his legs, she smiled. "So, where is Morgan? We are expected to dance to her tune, yet we have no idea of when, or even if, she will return."

"It is wise not to question the ways of the fae one." Some of the sulkiness left his tone and he sounded pompous once more.

The fae one. Vashti frowned as she chased an elusive memory. Where had she heard those words recently? *The fae one will seek me out.* That was what Bertha had said when she realized Jethro was finally sending her to Otherworld. When Vashti had asked Jethro what his mother meant, he'd replied it was impossible to tell because her mind was full of holes and she probably didn't know herself. What if Bertha had known exactly what she meant? Could she have been referring to Morgan le Fay? Why would Jethro's mother think the legendary sorceress would seek her out? Bertha had been afraid when she'd said it. There was no question about that.

"So we must remain here until Morgan decides to honor us with her presence?"

Iago inclined his head. "I see you understand the ways of the fae one."

Vashti made a small, strangled sound of impatience and, rising from her seat, stomped away.

Chapter 16

Because everyone was inside the great hall, the court-yard was empty. Vashti, glad of a few moments away from Iago's claustrophobic—and infuriating—presence, leaned against the wall and dragged in a welcome breath of fresh air. While there was no doubt about his amorous intentions toward her, Iago was obviously taking greater pleasure from annoying her. *And I keep rising to it.* If she was going to get through her time on Avalon with her sanity intact, she would have to learn to ignore his taunts. *Yes, I will simply change my personality. Become serene and swanlike. That should be easy.*

She was distracted from her thoughts by footsteps crossing the stone flags of the courtyard. She didn't want anyone to see her and question her presence here. Unless it was Jethro, of course. The sidhe woman who walked across the courtyard didn't glance in her direction. She was an unremarkable figure. Small and slender, with nothing to make her stand out in a crowd. Except Vashti would have known her anywhere. She was the woman who had raised her. The only person to show her and Tanzi love during their formative years. The reason they knew right from wrong, despite Moncoya's efforts to the contrary.

"Rina!" Hitching up her skirts and breaking into a run, Vashti dashed across the cobblestones almost scaring the other woman half to death.

Rina paused, clearly wondering whether to stop or run away. When she saw who it was, her face lit up. Her delicate features broke into the smile she had always reserved for her royal charges.

"My dearest Princess Vashti." She uttered the words fondly as Vashti hurtled to a standstill in front of her. Rina was one of the few people who had been able to tell them apart as they were growing up. As adults they made a concerted effort to look different and Tanzi wore her hair long while Vashti kept hers short. As children they'd both had waist-length blond hair that Rina had brushed and plaited every night.

Forgetting her dislike of physical contact—that was reserved for people she didn't love—Vashti threw her arms around Rina, drawing her into an embrace that washed away all the irritation caused by Iago's barbs. When they drew apart, Rina's face was shining and Vashti's cheeks were wet with tears.

Rina led her to a stone bench set in a shadowy corner of the courtyard. "How are you? The last time I saw you, you were recovering from the injuries you sustained during the battle." Rina bit her lip. "You were very ill. I was afraid you might not live."

"Tanzi nursed me. Without her care I might have died."

Vashti clasped Rina's hands in her own. "But what are you doing here?"

"Avalon is my home. I am one of Morgan le Fay's maidservants."

Vashti tried to contain her shock at the words. So many questions rose to her lips. They never knew what had happened to Rina after her father dismissed her. Vashti and Tanzi had been the equivalent of twelve mortal years on that fateful day when Moncoya had decided they were too close to their nurse. So, one fine morning, they had come down to breakfast to be given the news that Rina was gone.

"We missed you so much, Tanzi and I. We tried everything we could think of to get you back."

Rina returned the clasp of her hands. "The years we had together were the happiest of my life."

"If you are Morgan's maidservant, how did you manage to get away from Avalon so you could come to see me when I was injured?"

Rina became flustered. "My mistress was very generous—"

"Morgan le Fay?" Vashti interrupted. "Generous?"

Rina cast a quick glance around her. "Very well." She lowered her voice. "She allowed me to visit you at the faerie palace because she wanted information about the outcome of the battle for Otherworld, particularly about the death of her sister, Niniane."

"So she sent you to spy on us."

Rina hung her head. "Please do not blame me. It meant I could see you and make sure you were well, my princess."

Vashti thought back to that time. She had sustained a broken pelvis during the battle and had been left for dead by her father when he made his escape. It was only through Tanzi's insistence the battlefield should be searched for her body that she had been found in time to be saved. Then, despite Vashti's determination to be the worst patient in history, Tanzi had nursed her back to health. Vashti had been healing when her sister had disappeared. Later it had emerged that Tanzi had fled to the mortal realm in search of Lorcan when Moncoya had announced his plans for her marriage to the devil. Alone, hurt, angry at her sister's apparent desertion, Vashti remembered the day Rina had walked through her door. It had been like a ray of sunshine in the gloom.

"I don't blame you. I know exactly who I blame." Vashti knew her voice must be cold by the way Rina raised scared eyes to her face. "Morgan le Fay."

Once again Rina cast that scared look around. "Listen to me. You must get away from here. You don't know what is going on."

"So tell me."

"I cannot." Rina's eyes filled with tears and Vashti realized she was witnessing genuine terror.

"Vashti!" Jethro's voice rang out across the empty courtyard. "I've been looking everywhere for you."

Vashti turned to face him. Even through her anger at Morgan, he had the power to take her breath away. As he reached them, he glanced at her hands clasping Rina's and raised a curious brow. "Jethro, this is my old nurse, Rina. Rina, this is..."

"I know who you are." Rina was gazing at Jethro with the strangest expression on her face. It was a combination of wonder and—Vashti paused to consider if she had the right word—yes, it really was adoration.

Jethro gave a slight head jerk in Rina's direction while keeping his eyes on Vashti's. One of those all-encompassing "is she okay?" gestures. "Nice to meet you, Rina." He paused, looking down into the older woman's face. "Rina. I know that name. Have we met before?"

Rina seemed to collect herself. Shaking her head vehemently, she rose. "No, never. Please remember what I said, my princess. This is not a good place. You should leave here at once. Both of you." On those words, she scurried away.

"Well, she seems nice. Well-balanced. Levelheaded. Just the type of person you'd want for a child's nurse." Jethro stared after Rina's departing figure.

"She wasn't like that when we were children."

Jethro didn't answer, his eyes held a faraway, unfocused look as he stared around the courtyard. "Something isn't right here."

"You can say that again." Vashti laughed.

"No, I mean here, in this courtyard. That tower shouldn't be as tall as that. And it was never at that angle in the original castle of Camelot."

"Is that something you read in your Arthurian legends?" Vashti asked. "Did they contain that much detail?"

"Pardon?" Jethro shook himself as though coming out of a trance. "I suppose we should go back inside," he said with a lack of enthusiasm that matched Vashti's own.

Reaching out a hand, he pulled her up from her seat. Together, they entered the castle. The sounds of merriment from the great hall reached them and Vashti grimaced, steeling herself for a return to Iago's side. Instead she was surprised when Jethro took a turn down a different corridor, leading her away from the noise and light, into a darker, narrower passageway.

"Where are we going?"

He glanced down at her, his eyes sparkling with that flash of devilment unique to him. "Wait and see."

"Jethro, we can't..."

Rounding a corner Jethro glanced quickly around before tugging her behind a tapestry screen and into a dark alcove. "What can't we do?" His lips were on her neck as he pushed her up against the wall.

Vashti melted instantly, everything except the pleasure of being in his arms instantly forgotten. Jethro's kiss was urgent, his tongue seeking hers and she gave herself up to the demands of his mouth, squirming with pleasure as he tugged her dress down from her shoulders so his lips could move lower and claim her breasts.

"I love it when your nipples harden in anticipation before my lips close over them." His voice was husky and Vashti groaned as he bent his head, matching actions to his words. His tongue flicked back and forth over one stiff nub then the other, driving her to a point just short of delirium. She tangled her hands in his hair, holding him to her, wanting the moment to last forever yet craving more.

Jethro raised his head, his eyes glinting pure passion in the gloom. His hands moved over her buttocks, holding her tight against his body as he lifted her skirts. Helpless, Vashti rested her forehead against his chest as his fingers probed and separated her buttocks before probing the flesh between them. He bent his head, touching his lips to the side of her neck before nipping the tender skin. They stood pressed together in the shadows as distant sounds of revelry reached them. Vashti opened her legs wider, allowing him to reach her core.

"I love how you feel." Jethro pressed one long finger deep inside her. Withdrawing it, he held her gaze. Raising the finger to his mouth, he slowly sucked on it. "And how you taste."

His mouth descended on hers, hot and demanding. His kiss stifled her moans as his fingers stroked and teased. Pressure built inside her as Jethro found her clitoris and rubbed. His tongue delved into her mouth and, in a mirror movement, he pressed that long finger deep inside her. Her muscles tightened around him and her breasts ached as they pressed against the muscled hardness of his chest. His erection was rock-hard as he ground himself against her, stimulating himself while he pleasured her.

"I love those sounds you make when you come." His breathing was ragged in her ear. "Make them for me now, Vashti."

Vashti cried out into his mouth as Jethro finally tipped her over the edge. Their kisses grew more desperate as he rocked his fingers against her a few more times, then swung her around so she could support herself with her hands against the wall.

Freeing his cock from the restraining breeches, he drove into her from behind. So fast and hard she cried out. "But most of all, I love this." He was panting now as he plunged in and out of her. "I love being inside you, feeling you hot and tight around me. You feel like heaven."

Lost to anything but the sensation of his iron-hard erection pistoning into her with increasing ferocity, Vashti pushed back against him, matching his furious rhythm, feeling the tension rising within her once more. She was already coming a second time when she felt Jethro's cock swell and jerk inside her as, unable to hold back, his release overwhelmed him.

When the frenzy subsided and Jethro withdrew from her, turning her so he could hold her, Vashti rested her head against his chest, listening to his heart as it gradually returned to a normal beat.

"Was I too rough? Too fast?" His voice was filled with concern. Unable to speak, she shook her head. "I wanted you so badly. Needed you. You are the only thing that makes this place bearable."

Vashti lifted her head. Standing on the tips of her toes, she pressed her lips to his. "Just so you know, I liked it rough and fast. So anytime you need me…"

He groaned. "Stop it, you minx, or you'll find yourself up against that wall again. I think we really should get back to that damn banquet, don't you?"

Sighing as she adjusted her clothes, Vashti nodded. "I suppose it's the only way we'll find the challenger." She looked up at him, surprised to see him watching her with an arrested expression on his face. "What is it?"

"The challenger. I'd forgotten all about him."

Jethro found their way back to the great hall through the maze of corridors with unerring ease. "How did you know that place was there?" Vashti asked. He'd managed to find a private place, yet there hadn't been time for him to check it out in advance.

"I don't know." He frowned as though trying to remember. "I just did."

Vashti didn't have any opportunity to question him further as they arrived at the great hall and Iago hurried forward to greet them. His expression was sullen. "We were about to start the toasts. It would look a bit odd without the guests of honor."

Jethro flashed his wicked grin in Vashti's direction as he explained the reason for their lengthy absence. "We lost our way in the castle corridors."

The next morning Jethro and Vashti met at the base of the highest hill. Iago had granted them the freedom to treat Avalon as their home while they were there. He had no idea, of course, that they were seeking the challenger as well as awaiting Morgan's arrival.

"I still think we would know the challenger if we saw him," Vashti insisted.

"How? Ailie said he doesn't look like a faerie," Jethro reminded her. "That's why Tanzi thought it could be Aydan."

"What could be me?" Aydan came up behind them, his footsteps muffled by the long grass.

Jethro glanced at Vashti and she nodded. It was time to discover the truth about Aydan. One way or another. "Tanzi thought you might be the challenger to the faerie crown," Jethro explained. "Because you are a faerie who doesn't look like a faerie."

"Me?" Aydan started to laugh. "I'm flattered, but I'm not the man you're looking for. I know my background and who my parents are. My father was half satyr. I can prove it, although I'm not about to show you." He blushed as he spoke. Since satyrs were known for their enormous, horselike penis, it seemed safe to say they could rule Aydan out.

Jethro sighed. "I made some furtive inquiries during the banquet. How about you?" Vashti and Aydan nodded. "Nothing. Either no one knew what I was talking about or they are all sworn to secrecy."

"The only thing I did discover was when I asked about prisoners," Vashti said. "It occurred to me the challenger might be imprisoned in the castle."

"Good thinking. Did you find anything out?"

"Only that there is no such thing as a prisoner here on Avalon. If you cross Morgan le Fay you don't stay alive."

"Good morning." They turned at the sound of Lisbet's cheery greeting. "Did you all have the same idea as me?" When they regarded her blankly, she pointed to the summit of the hill. "King Arthur's tomb is at the top."

With one accord, they followed as Lisbet started to climb. The hill was almost conical, ringed around its base with tall pine trees. They accomplished the climb in silence, aware of the solemnity of the occasion. Could this be the place of so much speculation? The legendary resting place of King Arthur? The morning was bright but cold, and Vashti's breath plumed in front of her as she walked in silence, her long skirts swishing around her ankles. At the top, the whole island of Avalon was spread below them in a tapestry of green and gold.

An eerie quiet hung over the hilltop as though the creatures who frequented the surrounding hills and fields had reached a consensus to avoid this one. The summit was flat and, in the center, there was a marble tomb guarded at each corner by a dragon carved in stone. Aydan placed his hand on the head of one of the stone beasts and a deep rumbling sound came from within the ground itself. He withdrew his hand in surprise and the sound ceased.

"What do you think would happen if I tried to touch the casket itself?" His voice was little more than a whisper.

"I don't recommend you find out," Vashti replied.

Jethro and Lisbet were both curiously quiet. Jethro's eyes were fixed on the tomb. Lisbet's gaze was fastened hungrily on Jethro's face. To Vashti it seemed the other woman was trying to drink in his every flicker of emotion as he viewed this place. She had become used to Lisbet's near obsession with Jethro, but the gloating expression on her face as she watched him was unsettling. Vashti turned away from the raw emotion on Lisbet's face and focused her attention on the tomb.

"To think King Arthur lies here." Aydan's voice was hushed with awe. "Waiting for the time when the world needs him once more."

"No, that isn't true." Vashti spoke automatically, unaware of what she was going to say until the words had left her lips.

"What do you mean?" Aydan looked at her in surprise.

Vashti shook herself, but the feeling persisted. She knew she was right. Her fae intuition was stronger than ever here. "King Arthur's body was placed here, that much of the legend is true, but his spirit is long gone from this place." She pointed to the casket. "All that lies within that tomb are the mortal remains of the man he once was."

"So is he a ghost? Does he walk the mortal realm?" Aydan clasped his hands to his head as though trying to contain the questions that were forming there. "Or does he reside in Otherworld? If that was the case, surely he would have made himself known to Cal, the man who was his friend and mentor in life?"

Vashti didn't answer. Her concentration was all on Jethro. He was a necromancer. If she could sense so much from King Arthur's resting place, how much stronger must it be for him? Her answer was clear in his physical reaction. His face was pale, his eyes wide and his limbs trembling. His dark gaze seemed fixed on a point just beyond the casket. Vashti moved toward him but before she could reach him he fell to his knees. She knelt beside him, throwing her arms around him. Gratefully, he returned her embrace, his whole body juddering violently.

"What is it? Tell me."

He shook his head. His teeth were chattering so hard he could barely speak. "I can't explain it. I've never felt a connection so strong before. Yet you're right. There is no soul left here." Gradually the tremors running through him stilled. "How can I relate to something that doesn't exist?"

Lisbet, in that strange way she had, seemed to be lost in her own thoughts. A tiny smile played around her lips as she looked at the tomb. After casting a wary glance in her direction, Aydan came closer to Jethro and Vashti.

"Could your extreme reaction have been caused by the emotion of who he was? Let's face it, this is no ordinary grave. He was no ordinary man."

Shakily, Jethro rose. "I suppose that's one explanation." He looked out across the landscape. Beyond the rolling fields of Avalon, the seas of Otherworld were visible. "If his spirit is gone from Avalon, it raises an important question."

Aydan spoke the thought that was in all their minds. "Where is Arthur now?"

They all fell silent as they contemplated the words.

"We may never find out." Vashti decided someone needed to be the practical one. "And that is not our quest."

Jethro laughed. "You're right. We have a challenger to find before we can go in search of the ancient king of the Britons." Linking his arm through Vashti's, he called over his shoulder to Lisbet. "Shall we go?"

Her face had a dreamy, faraway quality, and she didn't look away from the tomb when she finally spoke. "I'll stay here a while longer."

"I'll keep you company," Aydan offered.

"No." A flicker of impatience penetrated her reverie. "I want to be alone here."

Jethro's face softened with a touch of sympathy for the younger man. "Only those truly fascinated with the Arthurian legends would get it," he explained. "Let's leave her to her obsession."

"The proposal I have been told to make is a simple one. You are to remain here. In exchange for your cooperation, your companions will be permitted to leave Avalon." Iago's wolfish smile gleamed. "Unharmed."

Jethro regarded him thoughtfully across the wide, oak

desk. Iago had summoned him to this meeting and insisted they speak alone. "Why am I to stay here?"

"That information has not been shared with me."

"Can you find out?" Jethro felt his temper begin to boil.

"I can ask, but it is not always wise to question the ways of Morgan le Fay."

Jethro stood in an explosive movement. "If it was your fucking future we were talking about, you might have a few questions."

Iago inclined his head. "I will see what I can do."

Jethro's mind was racing. Should he agree to this bizarre offer? It meant Vashti would be safe—and Aydan and Lisbet, of course—then he could make his own escape without having to worry about them. But what did Morgan want with him? It seemed the challenger wasn't on Avalon. Could he string this out long enough to make certain of that and also deal with Iago?

"How long would I be expected to stay here?"

"Forever." Iago's smile deepened. "You, my friend, are the chosen consort of Morgan le Fay."

Jethro muttered a curse. "Consort? You mean her partner?"

"Partner. Lover. Husband. These are just words. The outcome is the same."

Of the dozens of thoughts whirling around in Jethro's mind, one insistently forced its way to the top and onto his lips. "How can Morgan make such a proposition to me? We have never met." He hated the slight croak to his voice. It made him sound fearful instead of plain incredulous. "Don't tell me. It is wise not to question?"

Iago grinned in genuine amusement. "You learn fast."

"You're willing to let Vashti go as part of this deal? I thought you had other plans for her."

Iago's lips thinned so much they almost disappeared. "I did. Let's just say, I have been informed my desires are unimportant in this matter. Morgan wants you. She feels Vashti would be an unnecessary complication if she remained on Avalon."

So Morgan—a woman he'd never met—knew of his relationship with Vashti? Knew enough of it to be jealous. How? The thought of Morgan le Fay watching him without his knowledge made his flesh crawl. *You think I'm going to stick around and be your consort...your lapdog? Think again.*

"I need time to consider this."

Iago inclined his head. "I cannot give you long. Shall we say you will give me your reply tomorrow?"

"If I say no?"

"Former hostilities will resume." The wolfish smile dawned.

Former hostilities will resume. It was tempting to give Iago his answer there and then. *Bring it on.*

When he left Iago, Jethro went in search of Vashti. He found her on the castle's high battlements, gazing out across the landscape. She looked up at his face in astonishment as he drew her into his arms and held her without speaking. As always, her presence soothed and strengthened him.

"What is it?"

Briefly he outlined his conversation with Iago. "You are to leave and I am to stay. Forever. As Morgan's consort."

Her smooth brow furrowed. "This is madness."

He gave a harsh laugh. "The sort of madness that exists only on Avalon. We have to leave this place before we succumb to it, as well."

Vashti leaned back in his arms. "Jethro, can she see

us *all the time*? Is Morgan le Fay watching us right now, listening in on our conversation?"

"Can she have those sorts of powers? Surely she operates through Iago?"

"Think about it. Haven't you noticed how people here look over their shoulder when they talk about her? How else has she seen enough of you to know she wants you at her side for all time? How does she know enough about us to decide she needs to get rid of me?"

"It doesn't make sense. If she's been observing me, she must know I'm not the sort of person who's going to bow down and obey her commands. Why would she want *me*, after all these centuries of being on her own?"

"I don't think it will do us any good to try to get inside the mind of Morgan le Fay."

He drew Vashti closer. "Well, if she is watching us right now, she can fucking watch this." He lowered his head, searing her lips with a kiss.

Vashti responded instantly, wrapping her arms around his neck and fitting her body tightly to his.

When they moved apart, Jethro stood against the battlement wall, looking onto the green field below. "In Camelot, that was where the jousts were held." He could almost see the colors and hear the shouts as the knights lined up for the tournament.

"How do you know these things?" Vashti came to stand at his side.

"I wish I knew. It's the oddest feeling. Like a distant memory that grows stronger all the time." He ran a hand through his hair. "Perhaps I'm becoming infected with the madness of Avalon."

"Rina!" Vashti's eyes sparkled suddenly. "Although she was scared, she definitely knew something. Maybe she can tell me how Morgan gets to know everything without physically being here."

"Shall I come with you?"

She shook her head. "You caused the strangest reaction when she saw you, remember? Like you were a movie star she'd had a crush on from way back."

Jethro pulled a wry face. "Good luck getting any sense out of her. I think she might be mad."

"You probably would have fit right in at Camelot," Vashti told him sternly. "Political correctness isn't your strong point."

"If I'd been born in medieval times I'd know that young ladies wouldn't lift their skirts up to their knees or run like an Olympic sprinter out of the starting block," he called after her as she set off. "And they certainly wouldn't make those sorts of rude gestures at their gentleman friends."

Chapter 17

As she searched for Rina, Vashti also tried to contact her sister. She felt an overwhelming need to hear her sister's voice.

Tanzi, can you hear me? No matter how hard she tried, there was no response to her psychic cries for help.

After searching the castle for almost an hour, Vashti found Rina near the kitchens. Although the little sidhe protested she was busy, she eventually allowed herself to be dragged off to Vashti's room.

"Can anyone overhear our conversation?" Vashti asked as she closed the door behind them.

Rina appeared genuinely confused. "I don't think so."

"Rina, how does Morgan le Fay know so much about what goes on here when she is away?"

"She is a powerful sorceress." Rina sounded like a child reciting lines from a poem she had learned by heart.

"Does she have some kind of magical closed-circuit television?"

Rina was starting to look a little scared. "I don't know what you mean."

"Can Morgan watch anyone on Avalon, any time she wants?"

"No. She confides in me. She wishes she had that sort of power. Her magic is illusory and, of course, it can be extremely destructive. But, although she has a psychic link with Iago, she does not have a second sight of the sort that has been granted to the Spae."

So much for the theory Morgan was here, maintaining an all-seeing, invisible presence. Vashti sat on the bed, patting the space next to her. Warily, Rina joined her. "I need to confide in you about why we are here on Avalon, because you may be able to help me."

"I don't think…"

"Rina, please hear me out. Other than the friends I came here with, you are the only person I can trust." Rina gave a single, nervous nod. "Everyone here on Avalon believes we are here at the invitation of Morgan le Fay and, in a way, that is true. But we are also here in search of someone. You know the story of how my father came to the faerie throne?"

Rina swallowed hard. "I know your father has threatened death to any who speaks of it."

"My father is in exile. And I want you to speak of it."

Even with that permission, Rina's voice was hesitant. "Your father was a sidhe general in King Ivo's army. He had no claim to the throne, only great ambition and, it was said, a ruthlessness that knew no bounds. One night, the royal family was gathered together at the faerie palace for a celebration. Your father and his followers massacred them all and staged a coup in which Moncoya claimed the throne. His rule from then on has been bloody and absolute. No one has dared to oppose him."

"There is one other story about the night of the massacre. That a child—a royal baby—escaped."

Rina's hands twisted in the folds of her gown. "I have heard that story."

"That child will be a man now, of course. Soon, each Otherworld dynasty will be offered the chance to choose their own leader in a democratic election. There is a strong chance that, even though he has been in exile after the battle to depose him, the fae will choose Moncoya. That is because there is no real opposition for them to choose. If we can find King Ivo's heir, the faeries will have an alternative to the harshness of my father's regime. That is why we are here on Avalon. We have come in search of that child."

"He is not here." Rina spoke quickly. Too quickly.

This was where the old Vashti and the new Vashti differed. The old Vashti would have grasped Rina by her shoulders and shaken her, dragging the truth from her by force. The new Vashti, the one who had discovered her fae intuition, took a breath. Sometimes she wished the new Vashti would go to hell, but maybe—just maybe—she had her uses. Even though her heart was pounding wildly, Vashti kept her voice even and gentle. "How do you know that?"

Rina raised a shaking hand to her lips. Any color she might have had drained from her face, leaving it ashen. Realizing she had said too much, she shook her head. "I can't…"

Vashti moved closer to her. "Rina, do you know something more about that child? If you do, I'm begging you to tell me." She reached for Rina's hand and was encouraged when the other woman didn't pull away. "No one will ever know it was you who told me."

Slowly, Rina nodded. "It has been my burden ever since that night."

Vashti resisted the inclination to gasp dramatically. "You were there?"

Rina's eyes filled with tears. "I was his nurse. I smuggled him out of the castle minutes before the killing began."

Aydan's jaw dropped in a comical expression when Jethro told him of Morgan's proposition. "She actually said she wanted you to stay here and be her..." He glanced over his shoulder and Jethro wanted to yell at him not to do that. *Don't fall for it. She can't hear you.* "Her lover?"

"The message came via Iago but, yes, that was it exactly. If you can believe it. I'm not sure I can."

Lisbet was standing between them. Her dark, unfathomable eyes raked Jethro's face. "And will you stay?"

Rage boiled up instantly inside him and overflowed like molten lava. How the hell could she ask him something like that? The longer he spent in her company, the greater his unease around Lisbet grew. Although he knew his anger was directed at Morgan, Jethro's reply came out more harshly than he'd intended it to. "Are you out of your fucking mind? What do you take me for? You seriously think I'd consider staying here, living in the past so some demented old witch can keep me as her toy boy? In the next twenty-four hours I intend to choke the life out of that trickster bastard Iago before I leave this hellhole behind me forever."

With a sob, Lisbet whirled around and ran inside the castle. Jethro stared after her, his anger turning in on himself. "Damn it all to hell." He turned to Aydan. "I'm

sorry. Will you go after her? The mood I'm in, I'm likely
to say the wrong thing and make it worse."

Aydan nodded. "For what it's worth, I don't blame you
for losing your temper. It was a stupid question."

Jethro gave him a shaky half smile of thanks. Left
alone, he climbed the steps onto the battlements where
he had met Vashti earlier. Where was she? Surely she
must have finished talking to Rina by now? Vashti was
the only person who could restore his mood.

Even so, as he stood surveying the scene, he felt he
could be losing his mind. He hadn't begun to confide the
strangeness of his thoughts even to Vashti. Were they
thoughts or could they actually be the memories they
appeared? Since he'd arrived on Avalon, Jethro seemed
to be viewing the world through someone else's eyes.
Things were coming back to him he never knew he'd
experienced. *No, that's wrong. I* can't *have experienced.*
Yet the things he was recalling were too real to have happened to someone else.

Was it something in the atmosphere of Avalon? If that
was the case why weren't Vashti, Aydan and Lisbet experiencing the same illusions? Was someone—Iago or Morgan—forcing these experiences on him? Was he being
given hallucinogenic drugs or was some sort of subtle
hypnosis at work?

*Or am I simply caught up in the atmosphere? So sus-
ceptible to what this place means I have convinced myself I am an Arthurian knight, one of the legendary king's
faithful followers? Because that's the only reason I can
think of for these strange imaginings in which I picture
Camelot—the true Camelot—and my own place within it.*

A footstep behind him made him swing around, a
smile on his face as he anticipated Vashti's return. "Well,
what did you discover?"

"I discovered you have no intention of taking my grandmother's proposal seriously." Iago's usual smile was missing.

"I don't know what you mean." *Play for time. Stall. Deny everything.* Jethro wasn't good at lying, but he was prepared to give it a damn good try.

"Let me remind you. I think the words you used were... 'demented old witch...trickster bastard'—who you plan to choke the life out of—and 'hellhole.' Do any of those things sound familiar?"

Clearly, Vashti had been right all along. He should have been looking over his shoulder. Morgan had some sort of omnipotent presence whereby she could see and hear what was going on all the time. With his little outburst, he had effectively announced his intentions. *So what?*

He shrugged. "You didn't seriously think I *would* stay, did you? Or that, after the stunt you pulled with the Slu-agh, there was any way I wasn't going to rip your fuck-ing throat out?"

The smile did appear then but it was a façade. Behind it, Iago's eyes glittered pure evil. "So sad. But good news for me. This way, I get to keep your little princess."

Jethro lunged at him. Or rather, he tried to. Nothing happened. It was as if an invisible force pinned him to the spot.

"Keep your filthy hands off her." That was what he wanted to say. No words came out of his lips.

The edges of his vision began to darken. His limbs felt like lead. The last thing he saw was Iago's smile. The last word he tried to say was "Vashti."

By the time night fell, Vashti was frantic with worry. There was no sign of Jethro anywhere and she had scoured every inch of the castle twice over, enlisting help from Aydan.

She told him of her conversation with Rina. "She was adamant the challenger is not here on Avalon. I suppose she should know."

"Did she say what happened to him after he left King Ivo's castle?"

"She was vague about that," Vashti admitted. "Just that she took him to a place of safety. Then she became tearful and incoherent. She was scared she'd said too much and Morgan would learn of it and punish her. I wanted to find Jethro and tell him what I knew. I intend to question her more tomorrow."

They were close to Vashti's room when Ilsa appeared. She looked surprised to see Vashti there. "My lady, the hour of the banquet approaches."

Vashti's lips opened but Aydan—perhaps sensing where she was about to confine Ilsa, the banquet and the whole of Avalon—stepped in diplomatically before she could speak. "Princess Vashti will join you now."

Ilsa nodded and went along to Vashti's room. "Look, wherever Jethro is, I'm sure he'll turn up at the banquet. We can talk to him there."

"You're right. It's this place. It makes you fear the worst." Giving him a grateful smile, she made her way along to her room.

Ilsa was full of important news. "The largest guest suite has been prepared for a new arrival. I have been told an important visitor arrives tonight."

"Is it Morgan le Fay?"

Ilsa cast that familiar, furtive glance over her shoulder. "She is not a visitor."

"Who is it, then?"

"I don't know. I think it is a man."

"It must be hell living in a place where everything is a secret," Vashti remarked as Ilsa poured water into a very un-medieval-looking bubble bath.

"What do you mean?"

Shaking her head, Vashti waved Ilsa away. They had engaged in a lengthy dispute about whether it was proper for Vashti to dispense with the services of a maid during her bath. Eventually, it had been decided that—proper or not—Vashti was going to bathe on her own. "Decided" was probably the wrong word. It implied a democratic process that had been conspicuously absent. *Morgan is not the only one who can go around decreeing things*, Vashti thought as she sank back into the scented water. *In spite of recent events, I can still remember how to be regal when I want to.* She had pulled rank and insisted on being left alone. Ilsa had clearly regarded this desire for privacy as bizarre and left the room muttering under her breath. Sighing with relief, Vashti sank further down under the mass of bubbles, closing her eyes with a sigh. It would have been too much to say she was enjoying its scented warmth—how could she possibly enjoy anything when she was on *Avalon*?—but a few minutes' quiet reflection would be welcome.

It didn't happen.

"What have you been doing to make that girl regard you as an eccentric?" The voice was cool, amused and unmistakable.

Vashti opened one eye. *An important guest. A man.* Since this place was a nightmare that only got worse by the hour, she should have already guessed his identity. Thank goodness for the bubbles. "You may be my father, but you never paid any attention to my bath time when I was a child. Why would you imagine I might feel comfortable with the arrangement now?"

Moncoya waved a dismissive hand. "I may be depraved, but you can acquit me of any unnatural designs upon you, my daughter."

"I do. I would feel a whole lot more comfortable if you pulled that screen over here and stayed on the other side of it."

Moncoya sighed but did as she asked. "You must have inherited these puritanical tendencies from your mother," he remarked from the other side of the dressing screen as Vashti hurriedly finished her bath. "I certainly did not raise you to be prudish."

Tying a full-length robe tightly around her body, Vashti emerged from behind the screen. Her father had elevated his already stunning good looks into an art form. His shoulder-length, signature mane of tousled, morning-after hair, was highlighted in shades ranging from honey-gold to caramel. The diamond studs in his ears reflected the firelight. His expertly manicured nails were painted with black polish. His eyes—so like Vashti's own—were bluer than a summer evening, the irises edged with gold as if encircled by fire. Moncoya, not content with perfection, drew further attention to his eyes by encircling them with blue eyeliner.

Vashti had heard Cal and Lorcan joke about her father's fixation with his wardrobe and makeup, yet Moncoya in the flesh was devastating. She knew, of course, that his sexual prowess was legendary. It was impossible to live in the same palace—the same world—as him and avoid the rumors. The nail polish and eyeliner clearly did nothing to detract from his potency.

On this occasion Moncoya was clad in a peacock-blue doublet, with a jeweled coronet resting in his hair. He regarded Vashti with his head tilted to one side. "You look tired, my Vashti."

For a brief moment she almost allowed herself to hear a fatherly note of concern in his voice. Almost dreamed this was not the man who had kidnapped Enja, her mother, because he'd had sexual fantasies about Valkyrie women. In that instant she nearly believed he had not murdered Enja when she'd tried to leave him and take her infant daughters with her. Even that this was not the father who had tried to sell Tanzi to Satan in a bizarre marriage pact. It was only when her memory took her back to the last time she'd seen Moncoya and reminded her that he had tricked her into releasing him from his constraints at knifepoint that Vashti's mind finally rebelled.

"I could almost believe you cared." She felt her lips curl back in a sneer reminiscent of his own.

Moncoya placed a hand over his heart. "You wound me."

"I'd like to. What are you doing here?"

He took a seat in a chair by the fire, striking a graceful pose with his shapely, hosed and booted legs crossed in front of him. "I was invited."

Vashti sat on the end of the bed. "I haven't got time for riddles. A friend of mine is missing, possibly in grave danger." As she spoke the words aloud, she knew they were true. Jethro would not be at the banquet tonight. "I thought you couldn't leave your hiding place?"

His smile contained mischief and menace in equal measure. "Who will pursue me here? That half-blood mongrel who dares call himself my brother?"

"Merlin Caledonius *is* your brother, although he doesn't care to admit it any more than you do. I suppose you are right about one thing. No one is going to follow you to Avalon. Not unless they have a death wish."

"You see. We think alike, you and I. Who is this friend? The one you said is in grave danger."

Vashti paused. She didn't trust his motives for being here, but she didn't see how telling him could harm Jethro. If her fae instincts were right, Jethro was in enough trouble already. "You already know him. It is Jethro de Loix."

"What is it about these necromancers?" As always, Moncoya's voice was caressing, slightly teasing and decidedly hypnotic. Even after everything he had done, his magnetism was such that it would be easy to be fooled by him. She had a feeling she wasn't telling him anything he didn't already know. "Your sister was prepared to throw away the brilliant future I offered her in order to go and live on the very edge of civilization with her Irish sorcerer. Now I find you—the sensible one—have fallen under the spell of another necromancer. And not any necromancer. No, you had to choose the only one you cannot have. The one who has been claimed by none other than Morgan le Fay herself."

Vashti regarded him speculatively. There was an outside chance she might get some answers here. Not because her father would take pity on her. On the contrary. Pity was an alien concept to Moncoya—along with so many other mortal emotions. But he loved gossip and he had a vindictive tongue. If he knew of any scandal, Moncoya would be unable to resist sharing it. "Why is that? Why has Morgan decided she wants an unknown American mercenary to be her mate?"

Moncoya's laughter rang out and, in Vashti's opinion, went on far too long. "Oh, my dear child, you really do not know?"

"If I did, I wouldn't have asked." She tried, and failed, to keep the caustic note out of her voice.

He studied her face, his head to one side. "Can it be true? You do not know who Jethro de Loix is?"

Vashti felt her temper rise at the same time as her

heart sank. Moncoya was toying with her, but she was sure now he knew something. And that secretive smile was telling her it was something huge. "Don't start being cryptic. I know as much about Jethro's background as he does himself."

Moncoya whistled. "Really? I wonder why Morgan hasn't told him. She'll play a deep game, that's for sure."

"She isn't here, so she hasn't been able to tell him anything."

His eyes narrowed and Vashti thought he was about to say more. Instead he gave an elegant shrug. "I daresay Morgan will reveal all in her own good time."

Vashti resisted the urge to stamp her foot. "Reveal what? For God's sake, just tell me!"

Moncoya shook his head. "I'm not going to risk getting on the wrong side of Morgan at any time. If you think I'm going to do it here on Avalon, you can think again. Not even for you, my Vashti."

"Then get the hell out of my room." Vashti bounced up from the bed, her whole body trembling with suppressed rage.

With that feline grace that was his alone, Moncoya rose. His features were schooled into an expression of sadness that might have fooled anyone who didn't know him. "I had hoped for a more pleasurable reunion."

"Fuck off."

"Have you been learning this interesting new vocabulary from that coarse necromancer? You did not glean it in our royal home."

Vashti padded to the door in her bare feet and held it open. When Moncoya drew level with her, he halted, any pretense at paternal concern gone. "Don't fight me, Vashti. You have enough problems."

"Is that a threat?"

"Strangely, it is not. Call it a warning. You may not believe me, but I mean you no harm."

Despite his huge personality, Moncoya wasn't tall. Vashti only had to tilt her head back slightly to look him fully in the face. "I don't believe you. You never think of anyone but yourself."

"I never said that wasn't the case." With his customary swagger, he bowed slightly before walking away from her along the corridor.

Vashti waited until he was out of sight before closing her bedchamber door and leaning against it. Now he was gone, she found her limbs were shaking violently in the aftermath of the encounter.

Tanzi, please answer me! Why did it have to be here, on Avalon of all places, that their psychic bond was broken?

When Ilsa returned to help her, she was outraged to find Vashti was already dressed and only needed her assistance to lace the back of her gown. Ignoring the girl's protests, she hurried down to the great hall, where the guests were already gathered for the banquet to welcome Moncoya. There was great excitement. From being an island that no one visited, Avalon had seen two such celebrations in a matter of days.

Vashti's heart sank. There was no sign of Jethro. Lisbet arrived late, sidling into her chair, her eyes downcast and her manner subdued. Aydan explained in a whisper she was probably still upset after Jethro had lost his temper with her earlier. By the time the food arrived, Vashti's nerves were stretched to the point where she wanted to do someone—probably Iago, though Moncoya would make a good substitute—a serious injury.

"If Iago is a trickster, why can't he make himself look

better?" Aydan speculated. In response, Vashti turned impatient eyes on him. He subsided into his chair. "Sorry."

She regarded her father from beneath lowered brows. "Jethro disappears and my father arrives. I can't believe this is a coincidence."

"You think he knows something?"

"I asked him, but he wriggled his way out of giving me a straight answer. As always." Vashti pushed her plate of uneaten food away. Where was Jethro? What was happening to him right now? The thought of the empty dungeons plagued her. *There are no prisoners on Avalon. Displease Morgan and there is only one option...*

"What did your father say?" Aydan asked. He, too, had eaten very little.

"He made a few cryptic comments about why Morgan brought Jethro here, but he didn't actually say anything useful. He likes being mysterious." She rose from her seat. "I'm going to ask Iago."

When Vashti crossed the room and halted in front of Iago, he ceased his conversation, regarding her across the table with speculation in his eyes. "Your beautiful daughter." The words were addressed to Moncoya, although his gaze remained on Vashti. Moncoya remained silent.

"Where is Jethro de Loix?"

"Somewhere neither you nor I can help him." Iago gave an exaggerated sigh. "He should have accepted the offer that was made to him." He turned to Moncoya. "These necromancers. They seem to feel they can solve every problem with brute strength. I prefer a little finesse."

Vashti placed her hands on the table, leaning close. "I will find him, and when I do, you and Morgan will discover brute strength works."

"That's the point—" Iago's teeth gleamed as he smiled

"—you won't find him. Now, as you will observe, the musicians are beginning to play. Would you care to dance?"

Vashti launched herself at him across the table, her fingers curling into claws in preparation to gouge his eyes.

Moncoya rose in a fluid movement, but Aydan was faster. Catching Vashti around the waist, he hauled her away from Iago.

"If you get yourself in trouble here, you'll be no use to Jethro. And there are no prisoners on Avalon, remember?"

Taking a deep breath, she nodded, allowing Aydan to lead her out of the hall. As she passed Lisbet, the other woman looked up and Vashti caught a glimpse of her expression. She frowned. Lisbet didn't look upset. Far from it. The smile that played around her lips was radiant and curiously triumphant.

Chapter 18

Jethro lay in complete darkness. Sometimes he drifted in and out of consciousness as though his mind was suspended in a different place to his body. On those occasions when he regained lucidity, he knew he was in a confined space. He was lying on his back with his arms at his sides. His hands and ankles were unbound, but if he stretched out his fingertips or feet they immediately encountered a solid obstacle.

I am not hurt. There was no pain anywhere on his body. Even his injured left arm no longer pained him. Whatever spell he was under, or drug he had been given, the effects were mildly euphoric. Apart from the fact that he was imprisoned and unable to think clearly, of course. Those were definite inconveniences.

He didn't know how long he'd been there. He thought it wasn't minutes. It could have been hours. His disordered awareness told him it was longer. *Let it not be weeks or months.* Yet, why not? It wasn't unpleasant. When the memories came, he lost all sense of self, all appreciation of Jethro de Loix, and drifted into another time, another place and another man's life.

And there was the voice. *Her* voice. It soothed him, enticed him and wooed him all at the same time. He knew that voice. Now and from the past. He wanted to reach out and touch her, hold her still so he could slide his fingers over her face, rediscover his connection to her. He also wanted to run from her.

"You are all mine once more, my love." Even in his cramped enclosure, he felt her breath touch his face.

He wanted to protest. That couldn't be right. How could he be hers? Being hers was unnatural and wrong. But it was easier not to fight her. The blackness was warm and welcoming. She was so compelling, waiting within that darkness for him to come to her. Why try to resist the inevitable?

When he closed his eyes again he could see the great hall and the round table. The same but different. He was there, presiding over the order of things. As it should be. Everyone present bowed down to him. At first he had been confused. Gradually, realization began to dawn on him. Now he knew the truth. Although the memories were disjointed, they were as real as his recollections of life with Bertha and Gillespie. He knew who he was.

Or do I? Is this part of her plan? A sudden return to clarity brought with it a moment of panic. Was she planting false memories as a way of confusing him? Was this a form of mental torture? Would he emerge from this confinement a gibbering wreck who believed he was someone else? Not just anyone, either. *No, if I'm going to go mad and have an alter ego, I'm going to do it in style.*

"Why must you fight me?" Her voice was soft in his

ear, soothing away his fears. "Let it come. Let the past return so the future can be ours."

His body relaxed. She was right. As the tension oozed away, he was no longer there within that restricted space. Instead he was on top of a cliff, seated astride a huge black stallion. He wore armor and his cloak was blown behind him like a pennant by the breeze. The pain in his chest was worse than anything he had ever felt. He wanted to hurl himself from the horse and into the churning waves below. *How can I when the future of my whole nation depends on me?*

The man who approached him was barefoot and clad in the robes of a druid. His handsome face showed only concern for a friend. Even in his dreaming state, Jethro felt comforted as the other man reached up and placed his hand lightly on Jethro's.

"Did you know?" He heard the anguish in his words as they reverberated through his body.

Merlin Caledonius shook his head. "I would have told you."

"How could she?" Jethro—this Jethro who was not Jethro—almost choked on the words. "How could she be unfaithful to me with Mordred? My own son. The son born of the relationship I have tried so hard to forget…"

"If you let this defeat you, Morgan will have won."

Morgan! His eyes flew open in the darkness as he returned to the present. Of course he knew that voice. It was the voice of the woman who had seduced him when he was an eighteen-year-old virgin. The woman who had borne him a child, a boy called Mordred who grew up to hate his father. The woman who had not thought to tell him she was his older sister. The woman who, when he discovered their relationship, had tried to persuade him they could still be lovers. The woman who had haunted him throughout his life. *That* life. Who wanted him still in this one, it seemed.

"You." His voice was a hoarse croak in the darkness.

"Yes, my love, it is I. I was always here. Always waiting. Always true. Always faithful. Unlike her, the one you took to be your wife."

He tried to move, but there was no space. "Guinevere was unfaithful because of you. Because of Mordred and his desire for revenge. Between you, you took the woman I loved from me."

"No." The voice was still soft and coaxing. He had to fight hard not to lose himself in it. "I am the woman you love."

The woman I love. Forget the others. Think of her. Forcing himself to concentrate, Jethro conjured up her image, focusing on the way her eyes looked when they smiled into his. Those lips when they parted in a mischievous smile, or better still when they opened beneath his. The sound of her laughter, the feel of her hand in his...

"Come back to me." There was a touch of impatience in Morgan's voice.

"Never." He felt her power tugging at him and forced his mind back to the image of a slender body twining itself around his.

"You will. You cannot escape. I will be back."

He sensed Morgan's presence leaving him and heaved a sigh of relief. *You cannot escape.* Morgan thought she had the man he once was imprisoned. She believed she had her brother Arthur trapped here in this dark, confined space. And, of course, she did. He knew that beyond a doubt. This was not a mind game. As incredible as it seemed, Jethro was Arthur, King of the Britons. But Morgan had also imprisoned the man he was now. She had Jethro de Loix locked up in this tiny space. And she didn't know what she was dealing with. *I have skills now I did not have then.* Jethro permitted himself a little smile. *What would the Romans have thought of my necromancing powers? Those long campaigns away from home would have been so much easier if I could have summoned an army of corpses to our aid...*

Morgan thought she had him where she wanted him. *We'll see about that. Locking up a necromancer isn't as easy as you might think.* He relaxed, flexing his fingers. Okay, it wasn't an ideal position, but Jethro had been in worse situations in his time.

He lifted his arms as far as they would go. "*Hidercyme.* Come here. Come to me." He spoke in commanding tones. The same ones he had used to lead his armies into battle all those centuries ago.

At first there was nothing and he wondered if it had worked. Then he heard the faintest rumble within the earth itself. It grew louder, and he lay back with a satisfied smile. They were on their way.

It was early morning, before the bustle of the day had begun, and Vashti waited until there was no one around before she approached Rina in the courtyard.

"Jethro de Loix has gone missing." She blurted the words right out. "I need to try to unravel some of the secrets around this place."

Rina regarded her with wide, frightened eyes. "I am not the person to ask."

"Rina, no one else will tell me. Please, if I am to find him and save him, I have to find out why Jethro is so important to Morgan le Fay. If you know anything that can help me—even the tiniest piece of information—I'm begging you to help me."

Rina cast a swift look around her, checking no one

was near. "Meet me by the old well at the far side of the garden."

The old well Rina referred to was situated in an overgrown and disused part of the castle grounds. The minutes Vashti spent waiting for her nurse to arrive were among the longest of her life. Just when she had decided Rina was not going to come, she heard a rustling in the foliage. Looking furtive and troubled, Rina appeared.

"I'm sorry. One of the court ladies stopped me and wanted to talk. I thought I'd never get away. Follow me."

She led Vashti to an empty potting shed that leaned precariously against one of the castle's outer walls. Inside, it smelled of dank earth and mildew. There was a rickety wooden bench inside and Rina sat, gesturing for Vashti to sit next to her. To Vashti's surprise, Rina's eyes were filled with tears.

"What is it?" She took both Rina's hands in her own and was amazed to feel they were cold as ice.

"I would do anything to spare you pain, my princess."

"I know that."

Rina's tears spilled over. "What I must tell you now will cause you great misery."

A dreadful sense of foreboding settled over Vashti. "This is about Jethro." Rina nodded. "Tell me. I need to know."

"It concerns the child. The one you call the challenger. He was not just any child. Even before his birth, he was destined for greatness."

Vashti wrinkled her brow. "How could that be? I thought he was not an immediate successor to King Ivo. He only became the heir to the faerie crown because he was the sole survivor of the massacre. Everyone else in line to the throne was murdered on that terrible night... by my father."

Rina swallowed hard. "That is true. But this child was already special. He was the great King Arthur of the Britons...born again."

Vashti heard the words but her mind refused to process what Rina was saying. For long, silent moments she simply stared, openmouthed, at the other woman. When she was finally able to speak, her voice was little more than a croak. "Explain."

"I will start at the beginning. When I was a young girl, I was a maidservant here at the castle. The great Morgan le Fay took a liking to me and introduced me into her entourage as her personal maid. I knew of her love for her half brother and her devastation she had been unable to save him when he was fatally wounded. She would spend long hours poring over her spell books, trying to find ways of bringing him out of the enchanted sleep she had placed him in. Her dilemma was that, if she did so, she knew he would die of his injuries. Then, one day, she became very excited. She believed she had found a way. If she could use her powers to extract his spirit and transfer it into the body of an unborn baby, that child would grow up to be Arthur. 'Don't you see, Rina?' she said to me in great excitement. 'He will no longer be my brother. I will wait for him and we can be together at last.'"

"You are not going to tell me she went through with this plan?" Vashti felt a tight knot of nausea forming in her stomach.

Rina hung her head. "I couldn't stop her."

Vashti squeezed her hands. "I know that. From what I've heard of Morgan, no one can stop her."

"A few days after she hatched this plan, a contingent of faeries arrived here on Avalon. Their boat had been blown off course. One of the women, a noble princess who was a niece to King Ivo, was in the later stages of pregnancy.

I saw a plan forming in Morgan's eyes. That very night she drugged the princess and performed the magic ceremony. The woman didn't know what had happened. She never knew that after that night her unborn child carried the soul of King Arthur within him. When the faeries left here, Morgan insisted the princess should take me with her as a gift. I was a skilled nursemaid. It was her way of ensuring I would be there to care for the child."

"Did anyone suspect anything after the child was born?" Vashti asked.

Rina shook her head. "No. The birth was a normal one. He was a beautiful child." She smiled reminiscently. "When he was a few months old, I received a message from Morgan. Moncoya was planning to overthrow King Ivo. There were no other details. Just that I was to take the baby and leave the faerie palace at midnight on the specified date." Tears filled her eyes again. "I had become fond of my faerie mistress. If I had known…"

"You could not have known my father's plan was to kill them all. No one could have predicted how ruthless he would be in his quest to become the King of the Faeries."

Rina drew a breath, steadying herself so she could continue her tale. "I received no further instructions from Morgan. I was terrified. I knew if Moncoya discovered the whereabouts of the child, he would have him killed. Jethro was the only surviving relative of King Ivo, the new heir to the faerie crown. I went into hiding with him, but I had to think of a long-term plan to ensure his safety. I thought if I tried to get back to Avalon there was a good chance I would encounter Moncoya or some of his followers. The only place where I believed I might be safe from the new faerie king was the mortal realm. Moncoya's hatred of the earth-born was legendary. And I knew a mortal woman who I thought might help." She looked embarrassed. "I had become friends with her in the days before your father's rule. When it was still acceptable to cross over into the mortal realm to do kind deeds or bring good fortune to those who deserved it. This woman was one whose goodness shone out of her. Her name was—"

"Bertha de Loix." Vashti said it for her. Her heart was racing as the pieces of the puzzle began to fall into place. Could it be true? Surely the scenario her mind was conjuring up was too fanciful to be true.

"She was Bertha Toussaint when I first knew her. The sweetest, kindest mortal who ever walked the earthly realm. As a girl, she was always sickly. Back then, before your father banned such practices, those of us who followed the ways of the Seelie Court had an obligation to bestow vitality upon deserving mortals. I did my best to restore Bertha to good health. Later, when she married and it became obvious she couldn't have the child she so desperately craved, I tried to help her. My efforts were to no avail. When I brought the faerie heir to the mortal realm and sought refuge with Bertha, it seemed we had found a solution to both our problems."

"You gave the child to Bertha to raise as her own." Vashti spoke with certainty. She recalled that strange scene in the old de Loix house. When Jethro had asked Bertha if the challenger had been taken to Avalon, his mother had remained silent, avoiding his eyes. When he'd suggested he had been taken elsewhere in Otherworld, she had started to rock back and forth, still refusing to answer. But when he'd asked if the challenger's nurse had taken him to the mortal realm, Bertha had become so distressed Gillespie had told Jethro to leave her alone. Of course she had become distressed! She didn't want to be forced into telling Jethro the truth about his own origins.

Because the irony—the incredible, impossible irony—of the situation they were in was that the challenger they were seeking was Jethro himself. If it wasn't so maddening, Vashti could almost have laughed out loud. *I have wasted all this time, and faced all this danger, looking for someone who was at my side all along!*

"Why doesn't he look like a faerie?" She blurted out the first question that came into her head. She knew her voice must have sounded fierce by the way Rina shrank away from her. Forcing herself to soften her tone, she tried to explain. "You gave the child to Bertha. She raised him as a mortal and yet he did not look different or stand out. He looked like a mortal. He still looks like a mortal. Jethro believes he *is* mortal, yet he is faerie royalty."

Rina gave her a sidelong glance. "You have heard of a changeling?"

Vashti frowned. "A changeling is a faerie substitute for a mortal baby. There was no exchange, there was no mortal child to be replaced."

"The magic was the same. I used the same spell to enchant him. He was a changeling. He didn't take a mortal child's place. He stayed himself. I simply made him look like a mortal baby."

"A changeling is a spiteful, hateful thing, bringing chaos and destruction into a mortal family's lives." Vashti thought of the man she loved. The man who used his power and money to care for deprived children. A good man. "Jethro is none of those things."

Rina shook her head. "A changeling is only evil if the faerie who makes the substitution wills it. I had no reason to wish that. Why would I? I wanted only happiness for the child in my care and for Bertha and her husband."

"Bertha never told Gillespie how she came by the child."

Rina hung her head. "We concocted the plan between us. Bertha knew if her husband discovered the truth about the child's background he would never agree. She told him the baby had been left on the doorstep of her orphanage. He knew the adoption was not strictly legal, but he never learned the full extent of our deception."

"How did Jethro come by his necromancing powers?"

"Is he a necromancer? I don't know when those powers were bestowed." Rina considered the matter. "Maybe at birth as a result of Morgan's spells or perhaps when I be-spelled him to make him a changeling?"

"Why did you take a job with my father?"

Rina's little face became sad. "I left Bertha and the child. If he was to survive, they had to be a normal mortal family. But I wanted to be close to Moncoya, to see if any suspicion ever leaked out about the child who survived and his whereabouts. My time at the faerie palace wasn't all subterfuge. I loved you and Tanzi, my princess. You became like my own family. Over the years the rumors about the lost heir persisted, but no one ever knew if they were truth or legend. Moncoya was secure on his throne. He wasn't interested in the challenger. There was only one person I feared."

"Morgan le Fay."

Rina cast a fearful glance over her shoulder as though expecting the powerful sorceress to appear. "Morgan had commanded me to take the child to safety. She knew the rumors a baby had survived the massacre, but, of course, she didn't know where the child was or what had become of me. Over the centuries, Morgan's powers have waned. Here on Avalon, she is still incredibly forceful. Elsewhere in Otherworld, she is less potent. In the mortal realm, her magic skills no longer have any effect." Rina's face was white, her hands trembling. "Of course, she found me. She dragged the truth from me. Part of it, at least. I told her the child was alive and being reared as a mortal. Her fury was boundless. She hurt me—" her lip trembled "—but I didn't tell her his identity. She made the connection with Bertha, but, because of the orphanage, the child could have been one of hundreds. As long as Bertha remained in the mortal realm, Morgan couldn't pry the truth from her. She even had Bertha and Gillespie killed, in an attempt to force them to come to Otherworld as ghosts."

"So *that* was why Bertha wanted to remain in the mortal realm after her death. That was why she was afraid of the fae one. And that was why everything changed on Halloween!" Vashti exclaimed. "That was the night when Jethro sent Bertha to Otherworld. Morgan must have had her spies looking out for Bertha. That was the night Morgan discovered who Jethro really was and sent her psychic message to Iago, telling him not to kill him." She turned concerned eyes to Rina. "Tell me she didn't harm Bertha."

"No. Morgan had no further use for Bertha once she had forced the truth from her. As soon as she revealed the identity of the lost heir—Morgan's beloved Arthur—Bertha was safe. Morgan may be vindictive, but she wouldn't waste her energy when she could be searching for Arthur. Besides, she left Otherworld immediately and went straight to the mortal realm."

Vashti's brow wrinkled. "That seems an odd thing to do if her powers don't work in the mortal realm."

Rina seemed to be trying to convey an important message with her eyes. "Morgan le Fay never does anything without a reason."

Vashti shook her head as though trying to clear it. She thought of Cal laughingly telling Jethro he was as stubborn as King Arthur. Of Jethro, who drew people to him like a magnet, as that long-ago King of the Britons had done. "It's almost unbelievable and yet it makes a strange kind of sense. What I don't understand is, if the man she loves and has waited for all these years is finally here on Avalon, why has Morgan stayed away?"

Again, Rina cast that fearful glance around. When she answered, her voice was a whisper. "But she hasn't stayed away. Don't you see? Morgan has been here all along."

Vashti's brow furrowed in an effort to understand. "You mean she's invisible?"

Rina didn't answer. Vashti got the impression the little maid was willing her—trying to force her—to grasp an elusive truth. Something that was just out of reach. Vashti didn't have time for riddles. Impatiently she leaped to her feet. "I have to find Aydan."

Rina's voice followed her as she dashed out of the shed. "Be careful, my princess."

Chapter 19

"No." Aydan's expression was stubborn. "It isn't possible. Cal was King Arthur's best friend, his mentor, the person who knew him best. The first time he met Jethro, he'd have known him."

Vashti was so hyped up she couldn't keep still. She paced the length of Aydan's small bedroom, forcing him to turn his head from side to side so he could follow her movements. "Jethro is not King Arthur brought back to life." She tried to keep her voice patient. "Morgan's original spell preserved Arthur in some sort of enchanted sleep. When she was able to, she transferred his spirit into the body of the unborn faerie child. Then, of course, he became a changeling. Jethro himself doesn't know he's Arthur. It's hardly surprising Cal has no idea."

"So what's the point? Why would Morgan do this if Jethro doesn't know who he is? Surely she would want him to be aware of his past? Otherwise the whole scheme becomes meaningless."

It was a good question. Vashti paused in her pacing while she considered it. "There has to be some symbolism about his return to Avalon. She got Iago to challenge him to come here. Getting him to stay here must be important. Look what happened when he threatened to leave. Morgan has him incarcerated somewhere."

"You think his past life memories will return if he remains here?"

"Who knows? He was already beginning to have unexplained flashbacks. He thought they were Avalon-induced mania, but it's possible they were actually memories of his former life." Vashti threw herself down into a chair next to the window. "Or was he right and this is all madness?"

"I can see why Iago and Morgan would want to mess with our heads, but Rina? What's her motive?"

"Rina would never do anything to harm me." Vashti was adamant. "But she's no match for Morgan or Iago when it comes to deviousness. Who knows what sort of pressure they could have put on her to get her to tell this tale?"

Aydan's expression was a combination of earnestness and trepidation. "There is someone else we could ask."

"Who?"

His nervousness increased. "You said your father made cryptic comments about Morgan's reason for bringing Jethro here."

Vashti was about to refuse point-blank to ask her father for help, even in so mild a form as confirmation of Rina's story. Then she thought of what was at stake. Of Jethro who had been through so much already. Who was who knew where, suffering at Morgan's hands. She had to do whatever it took to free him. Her mind began to race through the possibilities.

"My father has known Jethro for a long time. Before the battle for Otherworld, Jethro used to work for my father now and then. For money, of course." Everything had changed with the great battle. Jethro had joined what became known as "Team Stella," placing himself on the side of the other necromancers and fighting against the formidable triumvirate of Moncoya, Prince Tibor and Niniane. It had marked the end of his days as a loner. Cal and Lorcan might frown on the fact that Jethro was a mercenary, but friendships had been forged on that battlefield. Vashti had heard the stories of how Jethro had joined forces with Cal and Stella against Niniane and gone on—with his friend Dimitar, who had once been Prince Tibor's human slave—to save Lorcan's life.

"My father would never have tolerated Jethro's presence, let alone allowed him to live if the slightest rumor about his true identity had filtered through to him. Believe me, Jethro would have had one of my father's daggers between his shoulder blades the first time he stepped foot inside the faerie palace."

"So why would Morgan tell your father anything about Jethro's identity now? And why would Moncoya be okay with it?"

Vashti covered her face with her hands in an effort to concentrate. When she looked up again, she spoke slowly, trying to express her thoughts clearly. "Because Morgan needs Jethro to stay here on Avalon. It must be only here that he will recall his true identity and become King Arthur once more. We are a problem because we are the ones who will take him away. We'll take him back to the palace so he can occupy his rightful place as the king of the faeries. Morgan's most powerful ally, the person who will stand beside her and support her in keeping him here and preventing us from taking him away…"

"Is Moncoya," Aydan finished for her. "Because he is the person who has the most to lose if Jethro ever leaves Avalon."

"My father wasn't happy when Niniane died and he lost her support. She was one of his closest allies. If he can replace her with Morgan, he will gain another powerful friend to stand by him if he returns to his place as the King of the Faeries. Which he will do if there is no one to oppose him. Morgan seems to know everyone's weaknesses. Moncoya didn't come here on a whim. She brought him here to help her get rid of us. She must believe he can exert some sort of fatherly pressure over me."

Vashti's whole body slumped. It felt so hopeless. They were fighting the most powerful sorceress in Otherworld on her home turf and she wasn't even prepared to show herself to them. They had no idea where Jethro was being held or how to release him. Now she had her father—the most ruthless man in Otherworld—to contend with, as well. She needed Tanzi more than she ever had in her life, but her psychic link to her sister had failed her since she had come to this cursed island.

Tanzi, why the hell can't you hear me?

"What I don't understand is why Morgan thinks it will all be different this time." Aydan's voice interrupted her thoughts.

"Pardon?" Vashti stopped trying to contact Tanzi and forced herself to focus on what Aydan was saying.

"Arthur didn't love Morgan. They had a relationship, they had a child together, but that was when he didn't know she was his sister. Arthur was eaten up with guilt about it. From then on he hated her. What makes her think things will have changed?"

"Because he will no longer be her brother. Morgan believes they will be able to rekindle the passion they once felt for each other and now there will be nothing to stand in their way."

Aydan sent a sidelong glance her way. "What about you? Jethro cares about you."

Vashti shook her head, swallowing the sudden obstruction in her throat. She wasn't having this conversation. But if they were talking about relationships... "Where's Lisbet?" She seemed to come up against some sort of mental block when she tried to think about the other woman, as though there was a barrier to her fae senses where Lisbet was concerned. *Maybe I just don't like thinking about her.*

Aydan looked embarrassed. "I don't know. Since we arrived here, I've barely seen her." He sighed heavily. "She's been caught up in the whole Arthurian legend thing. I don't think she was ever interested in me, to be honest."

Vashti leaned over and patted his hand. She probably wasn't the best person to offer advice, but she had a feeling something might be required of her. "You're too good for her." Surely there should be something more she could say to comfort him? She searched around wildly and came up with nothing. Aware that Aydan was regarding her in wary fascination, she returned to the subject in hand. "Anyway, being with a hornet like Lisbet has probably been a good preparation for what you are about to encounter next."

"What's that?"

"Brace yourself, my friend. I am taking you to make the closer acquaintance of the one and only Moncoya."

Aydan looked more than a little worried as he followed her along the maze of corridors that led to the grandest of the guest chambers. "Are you sure this is a good idea?"

"No, but do you have any better ones?" There was no response, but that might have been because she didn't give him time to reply before bursting through the door of the largest guest suite. "I want the truth and I want it now. Why did you come here?"

"You know I have the greatest dislike of raised voices," Moncoya said in a tone of mild complaint. He was lounging full-length on a sofa. Clad in impeccable doublet and hose, only Moncoya could make medieval clothing into a fashion statement. He had his booted ankles crossed and his hands behind his head. He glanced up in feigned surprise at Vashti's turbulent entrance. "I thought I taught you manners, including how to knock before entering?"

"Don't try to evade me. Answer the question."

Moncoya raised his eyes heavenward. "Always so demanding. You were the same as a child. It gets exhausting after a while. Aren't you going to introduce me?" He rose gracefully to his feet, regarding her companion with interest. Her father's eyes, their sidhe ring of fire blazing brightly, scanned Aydan's face. Vashti wished Aydan wouldn't look so nervous. Moncoya could sense weakness the way a cat could scent a mouse. It was a good analogy. He played with his prey in the same feline way before going in for the kill.

Despite his nerves, Aydan surprised her by stepping forward bravely. It wasn't the way most people behaved when faced with Moncoya's huge personality and that mocking expression. "My name is Aydan. I'm a friend of Jethro de Loix."

"Really?" Moncoya elongated the word. "I suppose it had to happen one day. That he would manage to find himself an ally, I mean. Not even a mercenary loner can remain on the outskirts of society forever."

Vashti ground out her question again. "Why are you here?"

"Until you disturbed me, I was trying to rest." When she muttered an expletive, he raised his finely arched brows in mock horror. "Dear me, your language really has deteriorated. Since we are hurling questions at each other...when did I become answerable to you?"

"When you might have been summoned here by Morgan le Fay to force me to leave without Jethro."

His eyes narrowed. "Since you are my daughter, I suppose I should not be surprised at your quick wits."

"So it is true."

As Moncoya moved closer, attempting to drape a fatherly arm around her shoulders, Vashti evaded his touch. "My child, you do not know what you are dealing with. Morgan has made up her mind about Jethro. You cannot fight her."

"If she shows herself to me, I not only can... I will look forward to the opportunity."

He frowned. "She would crush you like a bug under her heel. Jethro's fate is sealed. Come away with me. Let us leave this place before it is too late."

"You are saying this because he is the challenger."

He laughed, and the sound was an unpleasant reminder of those times in her childhood when she had displeased him. "Of course I am. Did you think I would bow down and allow him to take my throne?"

"It is *his* throne." Aydan spoke up bravely.

Moncoya's eyes glittered briefly with the threat of future retribution. Ignoring the interruption, he turned back to Vashti, shutting Aydan out. His voice was low and hypnotic, his eyes mesmerizing. "I have already lost one daughter to these necromancers. Do not desert me as Tanzi has done. You must see the futility of fighting Morgan."

Vashti was overwhelmed by a sense of weariness and failure. He was right. What was she fighting for? A man who had told her all along he could never love her? A challenger who would plunge the fae people into a bloody civil war? A chance to be torn apart by Morgan le Fay?

She raised her head, glancing out the window at the sunlit mountaintop. It was a perfect day. Avalon really was a beautiful place. King Arthur's tomb was visible at the summit of the hill. Her heart began to beat faster.

A slight smile touched Vashti's lips as she moved purposefully toward the door. "Aydan, come with me. We've got work to do."

"Where are we going?" Aydan followed her down the corridor, glancing over his shoulder as if expecting to see Moncoya pursuing them.

"I know where she has imprisoned him. First, I need to get out of these clothes."

"What about the decree?" Aydan stared at her as if she had gone mad. Perhaps she finally had.

"I'm about to desecrate King Arthur's grave. I'd say Morgan will be more annoyed about that than she will about my refusal to wear a long skirt, wouldn't you?" His jaw dropped and he nodded slowly. "See if you can find something to pry open that casket and meet me back here in ten minutes."

Running to her room, Vashti was already half out of her dress by the time she hurtled through the door. She was finally going to take action and that felt better than anything that had happened since they'd stepped foot on Avalon's beautiful, cursed shores. She might die trying, but she was determined to release Jethro. Her fae sense,

always strongest where he was concerned, told her he
was in King Arthur's casket. She just had to get past four
dragons and probably Morgan le Fay at her angriest to
prove it. *Bring it on.*

Clad in her own jeans, boots and tight-fitting black
sweater, she ran out of the room, back down the stairs
and across the courtyard to where Aydan was waiting. He
carried a spiked pike, an ax and a sword that was nearly
as long as he was tall. His expression was anxious but
determined. Taking in all of these factors, Vashti over-
came her aversion to physical contact and slid her arms
around his waist, carefully avoiding the weaponry, so
she could hug him.

Aydan blushed. "It might be worth getting disembow-
eled by Morgan just for that."

"We don't have time for stand-up comedy." *God help
me, I'm starting to sound like Jethro.* "We have a grave
to defile."

"About that…" His face became serious.

"Remember what Jethro said? King Arthur's spirit
isn't there. But right now that tomb is being used as Jethro's prison."

The uncertainty left his features and he nodded. "I'm
in."

Vashti was so fast as she made her way up the hill that
Aydan struggled to keep up with her. To be fair, she decided as she glanced impatiently back over her shoulder,
he was weighed down by a number of large, unwieldy
medieval weapons. When she reached the summit, she
halted so abruptly that Aydan almost cannoned into her.
They both stared at the woman who knelt in silence beside the tomb. At least they had finally discovered where
Lisbet was.

"Is she okay?" Aydan whispered when Lisbet remained trancelike and unaware of their presence.

"No, but you must have figured that out by now." Vashti held up her hands. "I'm sorry. That was uncalled for. How long do you think she's been here?"

"I haven't seen her since the banquet for Moncoya. But she can't have been here this whole time." Aydan turned troubled eyes to Vashti. "Can she?"

Looking at Lisbet's intent expression, Vashti had her doubts, but she decided to keep them to herself. It looked like Lisbet was talking to the marble casket, but that was taking obsession too far. Surely?

"We were wondering where you'd got to," she said brightly, stepping forward and making her presence known.

The venom in Lisbet's voice as she swung around to face them made Vashti recoil. "Get away from here."

Deciding to ignore the hint of lunacy in the other woman's eyes, Vashti carried relentlessly on. "Long story, but we need to get the lid off that casket." That speech had sounded so much better in her head.

Lisbet rose, moving closer to the tomb. Standing with her back to the casket, she spread her arms wide. "Take a step closer and I will kill you both."

Looking into her eyes, Vashti had no doubt she meant it. What the hell was going on here?

"It looks like the cavalry has arrived just in time." Vashti frowned in confusion at Aydan's words. He nodded at the two tall figures coming toward them up the hill.

Vashti gave a little cry of delight as she recognized Cal and Lorcan. "How did you know I needed you?" she asked as they reached the summit.

"Sure, didn't you keep sending out cries for help to

Tanzi and not replying whenever she tried to answer you?" Lorcan frowned as he took in the scene.

"You mean she could hear me all the time?"

"Hear you? You nearly deafened her." He grinned. "Me and the big feller here decided we'd better come and check things out for ourselves." He clapped Aydan on the back so hard the smaller man nearly toppled to his knees. "Good to see you." His greeting for Lisbet was less enthusiastic, and he nodded curtly at her. No doubt he was remembering Lisbet's harsh treatment of Tanzi.

Lorcan's coolness was nothing in comparison to his friend's expression as he looked at Lisbet. Cal was regarding her in much the same way he would stare at a coiled snake. Vashti turned to look at Lisbet and the uncomfortable feeling inside her began to spiral out of control. Could her fae senses have been so hopelessly wrong where the other woman was concerned? Yes, she had felt something out of whack about Lisbet all along, but Cal's expression told her it was much more than that.

Lisbet's earlier anger was gone and she was now gazing back at Cal, a slight, victorious smile playing around her lips.

"Merlin." There was a hint of laughter in her tone as she called Cal by the name he hadn't used for centuries. The name everyone knew he hated. "It's been too long."

"Never wouldn't be long enough for me." Cal's unusual silver-gray eyes were like slivers of ice.

Lisbet placed a hand over her heart in a gesture of mock hurt. "You always were harsh. As my sister found at the cost of her life."

"Oh, my God." Vashti shook her head as realization hit her like a kick in the gut. "No wonder you didn't come to the palace with us before we came to Avalon. It was because Cal would have recognized you. You scheming bitch."

The other woman laughed. "How unoriginal of you. Do you know how many times that's been said about me? Scheming implies there is intelligence in my opposition. Yet I did nothing to outwit you. It was boring in its simplicity. *He* figured it out, of course. Just as it was too late." Her eyes flickered to the casket, confirming Vashti's suspicions.

Jethro was in there.

Aydan stared from one to the other in confusion. "What's going on? Who figured what out?"

Even though it would hurt him, Vashti decided to put an end to the taunts. "Jethro figured out that the woman we have been calling Lisbet is actually Morgan le Fay."

"No." His face blanched as he faced Morgan. "You told me you cared about me."

"Get over it, you sad little faerie."

Of all the things Morgan le Fay was going to pay for, the look on Aydan's face when she said those words went close to the top of Vashti's list. She moved toward Cal. "This is likely to be the strangest summary you have ever heard."

"Try me." A hint of humor lightened his expression. "I've heard some stories in my time."

"Not like this one." Vashti spoke with confidence. "When she—" she pointed a finger at Morgan, who was still watching them with that superior smile on her face "—found she couldn't save King Arthur, she placed him in an enchanted sleep until she was able to discover a way to restore him. She hatched a scheme to place his spirit in the body of an unborn child. A fae child who just happened to be the same child who is the challenger we have been seeking."

While Cal assimilated the implications of what she was saying, Lorcan whistled. "What are the chances?"

Cal's expression became urgent, his eyes fixed on her face. "Who is he?"

"Jethro." Her voice broke.

"*Jethro?* What the fuck...?" For a moment Cal looked dumbfounded. Then he turned to Lorcan. "And yet, strange as it seems, I can see it. Can you?"

Lorcan's face was a mirror image of Cal's shocked expression, but he nodded slowly. "Now you mention it... the swagger, the stubbornness, the sarcasm, the arrogant refusal to listen to anyone else's opinion. Yes, he's Arthur, all right. No doubt about it. I'm only surprised we didn't notice it before."

While they were talking, Vashti was able to regain control of her emotions. "Jethro has no idea. But memories of his past life were beginning to return. I think it was something to do with being here on Avalon. Then he became impatient and threatened to leave, so Morgan imprisoned him. I'm sure—I'm almost positive—that he is in this tomb. It's King Arthur's grave."

"So what are we waiting for?" Rolling up the sleeves of his chambray work shirt, Lorcan strode toward the casket.

"Wait." Cal's voice halted his friend in his tracks. After centuries of being in charge, issuing commands was second nature to the great sorcerer.

Morgan raised a brow. "Scared?"

The look he gave her was scathing. "No. Wise. I know you, remember? I've seen what you can do. I was there when you tried your best to ruin the life of the finest man I ever knew. Arthur. Your own brother. And you did it over and over."

She flew at him then, the action so fast that it took everyone by surprise. Morgan's hands curled into claws and aimed for Cal's eyes, but he caught hold of her wrists, bearing down on them with his superior strength until she fell to her knees. Vashti supposed Morgan knew her magic wouldn't work on one whose own powers were so much stronger, even here on the island she had made her own. Despite that, Morgan's eyes flashed pure evil up at Cal as she panted and writhed in his grasp.

"Don't you dare speak his name!"

"Not speak the name of one of my best friends? Who are you to forbid me to say the name Arthur out loud?"

His voice took on a commanding, mountain-moving tone that reminded everyone who he really was. Vashti shivered. She could almost have believed she felt the earth beneath her feet move when he very deliberately pronounced each syllable of Arthur's name.

"*Galdre. Deófolwítga.*" Morgan spat the words at Cal. Vashti recognized the demeaning old English words for a wizard. Her father had often used the same insults when talking of his half brother. "You will pay for that."

"Quite the family gathering." Iago's voice made Vashti's flesh crawl and she turned slowly to face him as he reached the top of the hill. He was accompanied by Moncoya. Iago grinned cheerfully at her father. "My grandmother. Your daughter and your half brother. Not to mention your new son-in-law. While we're all gathered here together, we should throw a party."

Lorcan cracked his knuckles suggestively. Moncoya nodded, his expression one of weary distaste as he looked at Iago. "I never thought I'd find myself in agreement with you, necromancer, but he's starting to get on my nerves, as well."

"Can we all stop talking and get Jethro out of there?" Vashti pleaded.

"You can try. I will enjoy breaking you in two when you do." Morgan, still in Cal's grip, spat the words at her.

"I'm not sure we need to do anything." Cal's eyes were fixed on a point midway down the slope. "I think Jethro might have already found his own way out of the tomb."

Chapter 20

Jethro led his troops up the hillside toward the tomb from which he had escaped a few hours before. Some of the soldiers were on horseback, some followed on foot. When he lay in that casket and summoned them, he hadn't known what to expect. After all these centuries of lying dormant since the battle of Camlan, in which Mordred had dealt Arthur that fatal blow, would they still know him? Would they recognize their beloved Arthur in the features of Jethro de Loix? They would follow him as the necromancer who had raised them, but he wanted more from them than that. Would they follow him as their king?

He needed not have worried. Every man had gazed at him with reverence before bending his knee in an obsequious gesture. There had been laughter, reminiscences and tears. They had insisted he, their sovereign, must take the finest steed. He rode it proudly now as he advanced toward his age-old enemy. Morgan. She was at the top of that hill. He hated her, yet she still had the power to mesmerize him. If he was ever to leave this island and move on from this day, he had to destroy the woman who had darkened his past life and wanted to control his future. And there was still Iago. He had summoned his army for a different reason, but he might need them for the coming fight.

As he approached the summit, Jethro could see a number of people gathered around the casket. His eyes were drawn to only one. Vashti looked so delicate standing between the powerful figures of Cal and Lorcan, but Jethro knew different. She was the strongest of them all. As he approached, she turned her head to gaze up at him, her expression half relief and half surprise. Her love for him shone out of her face in that instant, and all he wanted to do was to forget what was going on around them, leap off his horse, crush her against his chest and kiss her until she begged him for mercy. Next time he was able to do that, he wasn't letting her go for a very long time.

Jethro dismounted, handing the reins to one of his soldiers. Releasing his hold on Morgan, Cal came forward, the light in his eyes affectionate and laughing. "How did I not know? You even look like him now."

"If I didn't know, how the fuck was anyone else supposed to guess?"

"Sure, don't you owe me a silver shilling? We had ourselves a bet back in old Camelot I'd not be able to drink three flagons of mead and then walk a straight line. You never did pay up." Lorcan clapped Jethro on the back.

"That's because Gawain told me two of those flagons contained water not mead, my cheating friend."

"Gawain was always a goody-goody. Is he here?"

Iago turned to Moncoya. "It's like a Knights of the Round Table reunion. You and I are automatically excluded for not being heroic or prepared to lay down our lives in the cause of the mighty King Arthur."

"Shut up." Moncoya spoke through clenched teeth. The faerie king looked like a man who was watching his hopes and dreams disappearing before his eyes. He turned to where Morgan was still kneeling on the ground. She was gazing up at Jethro, her eyes shining. "You promised me you would keep him here. Do something. Make it happen."

Moncoya's voice seemed to rouse Morgan from her trance. Rising, she came to Jethro with her hands held out. "You came back to me, my love. Just as I knew you would."

Jethro was vaguely aware of Cal placing an arm around Vashti's shoulders and felt a flicker of gratitude toward his friend. He faced Morgan, looking down into the eyes that had claimed his soul so many times in the past. "Why the pretense of being someone else? That whole Lisbet thing was cruel."

"She was a useful disguise. A way of getting close to Merlin. I thought if anyone knew your identity it would be him." She laughed. "I should have known they were all too stupid to figure it out."

"Aydan is a good person. He didn't deserve to be caught up in your tricks."

"Nothing matters except us." Her eyes were hungry, her hands reaching eagerly for him. He allowed her to grasp the front of his doublet. "When I saw you again, the centuries melted away. All the pain of being without you was worth waiting to have one more glimpse of your face."

Morgan pressed her body tight up against his. "Look closely at it, because this is the last glimpse you'll ever get." Gripping her throat with one hand, Jethro produced a small earthenware bottle from his pocket with the other. He sensed Lorcan moving to assist him. "Stand back."

Morgan's hands came up to clasp his wrist. Her eyes grew wild and frightened. "What are you doing?"

Jethro forced the neck of the bottle between her lips. "What I should have done centuries ago. Drink it, you evil witch." Tipping her throat back further, he pushed her teeth apart, emptying the contents of the bottle into Morgan's mouth.

When he had finished, he released her. Morgan flung herself away from him. Dashing the liquid dripping from her mouth away with her sleeve, she regarded him with horrified eyes. "Don't you know no poison can harm me?"

"It's not poison. After my men released me from your prison, we undertook a little landscaping task. It was quite a job, but we managed it." Jethro swept an arm wide to encompass the hills on either side of them. "We created two channels. You will find the spring on the right hill and the spring on the left hill now flow all the way to the bottom of each. They come together at the base of this hill."

Morgan stared at him in growing horror. "The two springs meet in the center now?"

"That's right. It was you who told me that story, remember? They form an elixir that is more powerful than any magic ever known. Even that of Merlin Caledonius himself." He flashed a quick grin at his friend. "Sorry, Cal." Jethro held up the bottle and tilted it to show it was empty. "Guess what you have just swallowed?"

"No." Morgan's hands came up to her throat. Her eyes were frenzied. "What have I ever done except love you?"

"What have you done? You cast a spell on me and seduced me when I was eighteen, forgetting to mention you were my sister. You kept me in ignorance of that fact even after you bore my child. When I refused to continue the relationship, you turned our son, Mordred, into my worst enemy. With him, you raised armies against me. When I was away fighting the Romans, you conspired with Mordred so he seduced Guinevere, my wife. It was only after Mordred struck me that fatal blow at Camlan you decided you wanted to keep me in the world." As he was speaking, Morgan fell to the ground, curling into a fetal position. "Maybe I should thank you for this new life you gave me. But I'm sure as hell not going to hand you my future so you can screw with it the way you did with my past."

"Your grandmother is dying. Go to her." As she spoke to Iago, Jethro was amazed at how strong Vashti's fae sense had become. She could feel sympathy for her worst enemy.

Iago recoiled from the suggestion. "I might get some of the elixir on my skin."

Jethro glanced over his shoulder at the trickster. "I wouldn't worry about that. When we get to the base of this hill, you're going to bathe in it."

He gave a signal and several soldiers came forward to seize Iago by the arms. Casting a look of disgust at Iago, who slumped sobbing in the grip of his captors, Vashti knelt beside Morgan.

Lorcan joined her, placing a hand on Vashti's shoulder. He looked up at Jethro, shaking his head. "Morgan le Fay is dead."

There was a minute of complete silence as each of them thought of what the dead woman had done to their lives. The sun broke through the clouds and a light breeze blew Jethro's hair back from his face as he thought of all the emotions Morgan had aroused in him throughout the centuries. None of them had been quiet. Passion, love, hatred, fury. Now there was only peace and an overwhelming sense of relief.

The quiet was broken by an almighty wail as Iago began to beg and plead for his own life.

Cal glanced around. "Where the fuck is Moncoya?"

Night was falling when the three necromancers and Aydan returned to the castle. "No sign of the slippery little fucker," Lorcan announced, throwing himself down into one of the seats at the round table.

"He means your father," Cal explained to Vashti. "As far as we know, he is still alive. Jethro's soldiers have scoured the island and found no sign of him."

"And Iago?"

"Dead." Jethro's voice was grim. "I decided the elixir pool was a lot kinder than ripping his throat out." He looked down at her face. "There was no prison that could hold him, and none of us—especially you—would ever be safe again with him alive."

Vashti nodded, swallowing the obstruction in her throat. "I did not help my father to escape."

Jethro's eyes burned into hers. "I never thought you did."

"You thought it last time."

"And you will never forgive me for it. I get it." He sounded weary. They were all weary.

"I hate to be the one to break up the party, but our mission here is over. I, for one, don't want to spend any more time than I have to on Avalon." Cal glanced around and they all nodded in agreement. "The most important thing is to get Jethro back to the palace so he can be introduced to his people. *Igraine* won't carry us all, but we also have the boat that Lorcan and I came on."

"You and Jethro should take *Igraine*. She's the fastest. The rest of us can follow at a slower pace," Lorcan suggested.

Jethro's eyes were fixed on Vashti's face. He seemed about to protest, but she forestalled him by agreeing with Lorcan. "That suits me. When can we leave?"

"How soon can you pack?" Cal asked.

"Give me ten minutes to say goodbye to an old friend and five more to pack my things."

Saying goodbye to Rina was emotional. When Jethro thanked her for saving his life, Rina became incoherent with tears. At least now that Morgan was gone, Vashti could extract a promise from her old nurse to come and visit her regularly. *Visit me where? I have no idea where my home will be now I am no longer a royal princess.* The idea was scary and exciting at the same time.

When they left Rina, Vashti darted away, purposely avoiding Jethro's stare. He was trying to convey something to her with his eyes. Probably that he wanted to talk to her. She didn't want to hear what he had to say. *It's been nice, but...?* He'd done the whole "I don't do love" speech right at the start; she didn't need any reminders. She knew he cared about her, even if love might not be the right word. But Jethro's whole life had just been turned upside down. Not only was he the new King of the Faeries, he had to cope with a centuries-old past he never knew he had. The last thing he needed was the complication of dealing with a relationship with the daughter of the man who would seek to destroy him. *I walked into this with my eyes open. I wanted you as much as you wanted me. Okay, I didn't mean to fall in love. But don't feel sorry for me. I'll deal with it.*

When Vashti had packed her belongings and returned to the great hall, Cal and Aydan were deep in conversation. "Aydan is going to remain here as my ambassador," Cal explained. "He will bring Avalon into the Alliance and ensure its people get a vote." He grimaced. "You might also want to do something about bringing the place up to date."

"President Aydan of Avalon. It has a ring to it." Vashti grinned at her friend.

Aydan blushed. "Will you come and visit me?"

Vashti nodded, hugging him. "I only do this to people I love."

Jethro walked in at that moment with his backpack over his shoulder. As he took in the scene, his expression instantly resembled a lowering thundercloud. "What's going on? Why are you hugging Aydan and telling him you love him?" When Cal explained, Jethro's face lightened instantly. "If Aydan is staying here, Vashti can return on *Igraine* with us."

"I'll keep Lorcan company on the other boat," Vashti said quickly. The thundercloud promptly returned to Jethro's brow.

Cal glanced from Vashti to Jethro. "I think Lorcan went to the kitchens in search of a snack. He could be gone a while. Vashti, let's see if we can find him."

Vashti followed him out of the banquet hall and along the corridor. Before they reached the kitchen, Cal turned to her. "You did a good job of keeping Jethro safe. I can see he means a lot to you."

She felt the blush rise in her cheeks as his eyes probed her face. "He does."

Cal sighed. "I don't want to hurt you, Vashti, but I think you should know the truth. Jethro told me the only thing that gave him the strength to get out of that tomb was focusing on the woman he loved. After all this time, that must mean he still loves Guinevere."

Vashti bit her lip so hard it hurt. She knew Cal wasn't trying to be hurtful. He was attempting to be honest with her. "I know he doesn't love me. He told me he never could."

Cal nodded. "I'm sorry."

"Don't be. We found the challenger."

"And I found pie. We all got our happy ending." Lorcan appeared and placed an arm around each of their shoulders.

After returning to the great hall to collect Jethro and Aydan, they made their way down through the village to the quayside. After a flurry of goodbyes to Aydan, Cal leaped down onto *Igraine*'s deck. He raised his brows at Jethro, waiting for his friend to join him.

"A moment." Jethro drew Vashti to one side. "I need to speak to you."

"Not here." She kept her eyes lowered.

He muttered an expletive. "No, I suppose you're right. I don't think doing this in front of an audience is such a good idea. I'll see you back at the palace." He ducked his head, trying to get a look at her face, but she resolutely fixed her gaze on the cobbles.

When he had gone, Vashti drew in the breath she'd been holding. "Ready, shipmate?" Lorcan called.

Fixing a bright smile to her lips, she jumped onto the deck of the small sailboat. "Aye, captain."

It was sometime later, when they were at sea, Vashti decided to ask Lorcan the question that had been forming in her mind. "Do we have to go to the palace?"

He regarded her in surprise. "Not if you don't want to. Where would you like to go?"

She smiled. "Take me to my sister. Let's go to Spae."

Chapter 21

Vashti hadn't seen Jethro since her arrival at the palace for the coronation. She had toyed with the idea of staying away, but she knew how that would have looked. Moncoya's daughter stays away? A rift with the new king already? She could picture the headlines, hear the speculation. No, she wouldn't do that to him.

In the few weeks since he had left Avalon, Jethro had won the election by a landslide. Of course. How could it have been otherwise? He was King Ivo's rightful heir. Handsome, incredibly charismatic and with an air of mystery about him. Okay, he didn't look like a faerie. That was a drawback. But he had the endorsement of Merlin Caledonius as well as the other Alliance leaders. And the biggest thing in his favor...he wasn't Moncoya. The fae race was enchanted with him. At last they had a leader they could be proud of, one who had also been the greatest king the world had ever known.

Getting ready for the coronation ceremony in her old suite of rooms was a bittersweet experience for Vashti. "I can't stay here," she had protested when Stella had escorted her up the stairs on her arrival. "Some visiting dignitary should be in these rooms."

Stella had kissed her cheek. "This is where you belong. Besides, did you get a chance to buy a new dress on Spae?" They both laughed at the idea. "All your clothes are still here."

What to wear when the man you love is taking part in the most important ceremony of his life, but you don't want to draw his attention to you? Vashti ran her hand through the dresses in her closet, settling on a full-length, sleeveless, silver sheath. Tightly fitted to the curves of her upper body, it flared from her hips, falling in shimmering waves as she walked. Her jewels were still locked away in their cases and she selected a pearl-and-diamond tiara with matching necklace and bracelet.

She had just finished her makeup when there was a knock on the door. Her heart gave a lurch. Telling herself not to be foolish—Jethro would be too busy to spare a thought for her—she went to answer it.

Cal and Stella were there. "Can you come to Tanzi's room with us, please?" Stella took Vashti's arm.

When they reached Tanzi's room, Lorcan was seated with her sister on a sofa near the window. Cal's face was grave. "There's no easy way to say this. A body was found in the sea close to the Vampire Archipelago a few days ago. It's been identified as Moncoya."

Vashti went to kneel beside Tanzi. "He killed himself?"

"We think he was murdered. He had been gathering an army together in preparation for an attack on Jethro. Reports are sketchy, but it seems he may have been killed by his own men."

"Does Jethro know?" Lorcan asked.

Cal shook his head. "I thought Moncoya's daughters should be the first to hear about it." He glanced at the clock over the fire. "The ceremony starts in half an hour."

Vashti glanced at Tanzi, who nodded. "We'll be there."

When Cal and Stella had left them, Lorcan vacated his seat so the sisters could sit together. "I know he was a bastard..." Tanzi's voice trailed away on a sound halfway between a laugh and a sob.

Vashti nodded. "But he was *our* bastard." She started to laugh. "Killed by his own men. It seems fitting somehow."

Lorcan eyed them in surprise as they clung to each other and laughed then cried. Sometime later they dried their eyes and fixed each other's makeup before making their way to the banquet hall for the coronation ceremony.

It was a solemn occasion and all eyes were on one figure. Tall and straight, clad in a somber dark suit and crisp white shirt, Jethro wore the scarlet sash of the faerie king with pride. Looking neither left nor right, he made his way down the center of the room to the podium and knelt before Cal. For once the great sorcerer complied with convention. He wore a full-length white robe—a garment reminiscent of the druid's clothing he favored back in the days when he was known as Merlin—and held the faerie crown aloft.

"Is Your Majesty willing to take the sacred oath?" Cal's commanding tones easily reached the farthest corner of the vast room.

Vashti only realized she was holding her breath when Jethro spoke. His voice was confident and steady. "I am willing."

"Do you solemnly swear to govern the people of the faerie dynasty, according to their wishes, laws and customs?"

"I solemnly promise and swear to do so."

"And, so swearing, will you nevertheless uphold the Otherworld Alliance's fundamental principle of respect for all species?"

"I will." Jethro stood and turned to face the company. Vashti's heart gave a thud. *I can't help it. I love him so much it actually hurts to look at him.* "The things I have this day promised, I will perform and keep. I call upon those here assembled as my witnesses, as guides, as I restore the Seelie Court to its former glory."

Jethro took his seat on the throne and Cal stepped behind him to place the ornate crown on his head. There was a spontaneous cheer as everyone rose to applaud the new King of the Faeries. In the front row Bertha and Gillespie de Loix held hands and beamed with pride. Next to them, Rina wiped away tears with a handkerchief handed to her by Aydan.

"And, of course, the speculation will now begin about who will occupy that empty throne on his left. The handsome new faerie king needs to get himself a queen as soon as he can to silence the gossips," Stella commented, watching as her husband broke with convention and embraced his friend.

Stella was right, of course, but Vashti didn't want to listen to any more of that sort of conjecture. Waiting until the formality had subsided and groups were forming to sip champagne and chat prior to the celebration dinner, she attempted to slip quietly away. She almost made it as far as the door.

"Where are you going?" The voice made her heart race. The face, although it was the one that tormented her dreams, was expressionless. No one could do enigmatic quite like King Jethro.

"Your guests are waiting to talk to you." Conscious of

several pairs of eyes upon them, she made another attempt to sidle toward the door.

"So?" He leaned one shoulder against the wall, blocking her exit. "I'm the king. I get to choose who I talk to. It's in the job description. I'm sorry about your father." Jethro's voice was a caress. "I know that, no matter how he behaved, there were still feelings there."

"Thank you." She risked a brief glance at his face. How did he do that? How did those brown eyes manage to scorch her flesh?

"Ah, there you are." Prince Tibor's cultured tones made Jethro blink, and Vashti managed to start breathing again.

"Stay right where you are," Jethro murmured before turning to the prince. "Your Highness?"

"Princess." Tibor's lips were cool as he kissed Vashti first on one cheek then on the other. She marveled at his restraint, knowing he longed to sink his fangs into her flesh. "Can I still call you that?" He glanced from Vashti's downcast face to Jethro's expressionless one. "So, Your Majesty, I think perhaps the time has come for me to stop trying to kill you."

"That would be nice." Jethro's sarcasm appeared lost on the vampire overlord.

"At last I understand why Dimitar abandoned me in favor of you. He recognized your majesty."

Jethro, who had been watching Vashti's face intently, turned back to the prince with a frown. "He did what?"

"Yes, it is a rare gift, one granted only to a fortunate few. Dimitar had it. He knew you had the divine right to rule. I am a prince, you are a king. He had no choice. He was obliged to leave me to serve you." Tibor's aristocratic features expressed confusion as Jethro started to laugh. "Something amuses you?"

Jethro shook his head, sadness replacing the laughter.

"Dimitar told me I was *maiestuos*. It was a Romanian word and he tried to explain it, saying it meant 'imposing' or 'stately.' I laughed and refused to listen to him. Don't you see? He knew the truth all along."

Vashti looked from one man to the other. "You mean Dimitar could have told us you were the challenger?"

Jethro nodded. "So it seems. If the prince here hadn't killed him before he had a chance to explain."

Tibor's smile held an unaccustomed trace of nervousness. "I think it's time to bury the past." He held out his hand.

After a brief hesitation Jethro clasped Tibor's hand in his. Vashti could see from the tension in his jaw the effort it took him. "To the future."

Cal and Lorcan were approaching and, while Jethro was distracted by his friends, Vashti managed to slip away. The new King of the Faeries was focusing on the future… it was time for her to do the same.

As the faerie representative to the Alliance, Vashti had occupied her own office. She glanced around the familiar room now. It would be needed for someone else. Jethro would take her place at the Alliance table. Clearing this room would give her something to do. She went to her desk and started sorting papers into piles. Almost immediately the door opened then closed again with a distinct slam.

"I told you to stay where you were." It was definitely the voice of a king. "Stop running away from me."

"I had things to do. I spoke to Stella earlier and she has found me a small bedroom until I've sorted out where I am going to stay." She glanced up. Once again, he was doing that whole enigmatic thing he did so well. His expression was unreadable to the point of coldness. "I hope that's okay? It's your palace now, after all."

He didn't reply. "I have a proposition for you."

Vashti swallowed hard. She supposed she should have anticipated this. It would be a good move diplomatically for Jethro if he could secure Vashti's support by getting her on his team. The fae race would appreciate seeing Moncoya's daughter working at their new king's side. It would mean he was listening to the sidhes and not simply dismissing the past. But Vashti knew she couldn't work alongside him each day and pretend she didn't care. Her heart wouldn't stand it.

"I don't want political office or a job in your new team." She carried on sorting papers, not looking at him. "I'm going to continue doing my best for my people, but I intend to take a step back from the public eye."

"Vashti—" Jethro stepped closer, grasping her hands in his and pulling her away from the desk "—look at me." She risked a glance at his face. What she saw took her breath away. There was no mistaking the blaze of love in his eyes. "I'm not offering you a job. I'm trying to ask you to marry me, but—as has been the case since the first moment we met—you are making things fucking difficult for me!"

"Oh!"

"Is that all you can say?" A smile lit the depths of his eyes as he scanned her face. "Just 'oh'?"

"Cal said the only way you got out of that tomb was by remembering your true love. He said it was Guinevere. I know I could never come close to what you had with her."

She tried to hang her head but Jethro slid his fingertips under her chin and forced her to look up. "Cal said that, did he? I must remember to thank him later. So the legend still persists that Guinevere was my true love? Yes, I loved her. Once. She loved me, too…for a while. Up until the point when she was unfaithful to me with Mordred and then Lancelot. I could never understand why, in this life, I believed love wasn't for me. Now I know I was scarred by my experiences during my marriage.

"When I told Cal I fought my way out of that tomb because I remembered my true love, I wasn't thinking of Guinevere. I was thinking of you. I kept your face in my mind the whole time. I got out of there because I knew I wanted to be with you."

"Me?" Vashti's voice was an undignified high-pitched squeak.

Jethro's smile deepened. "You and only you. There has only ever been one woman for me. In any life. I don't want to recapture the past, Vashti. I want the future and I do want love…with you. Since you first fought and growled your way into my life, I've loved you." He laughed. "I just didn't know it. God knows, I tried hard enough to fight it."

That did make her look up, her brows pulling together. "I know you did. You say I made things difficult for you, but you did the same. Every time I tried to get close to you, you put barriers up between us."

"I'd say that means we were made for each other, wouldn't you? I don't know if you were meant to be with me on that mad quest so you could save me or so you could show me how to love. Maybe it's the same thing. I do know we'll make a formidable team as king and queen of the faerie race…and the Seelie Court."

Vashti tried to answer him but all that came out was a strangled sound somewhere between a sob and a laugh.

"Can I take that as a yes?"

Frantically she nodded her head against the restraint of his hand. Needing no further encouragement, Jethro lifted her against him, crushing her lips beneath his in a kiss that left her in little doubt about his feelings. There was also very little doubt about his next plans for her as he backed her up against the desk so she could feel his erection pressing insistently into her stomach.

"Is this a good time to remind you that you once said you'd make me pay? The hard way?" Her voice was husky as she exulted in the blaze of passion in those dark eyes. "Or do you need to get back to your guests?"

"There's only one guest I'm interested in, and what I have in mind for you, my love, cannot take place in public." His hand slid down over the curve of her hip as he started to lift her dress.

Quick footsteps sounded on the tiled corridor outside and Stella's voice calling Vashti's name made them spring apart just before the door opened. "Vashti? I came to see if…" Stella stepped into the room. Her bright eyes narrowed as she took in the scene before her. "Oh, I'm sorry. I'll go."

Jethro smiled. He raised a questioning brow at Vashti. Blushing, she nodded. Taking Vashti by the hand, he led her forward. "Stella, you can be the first to congratulate us. Meet the future Queen of the Faeries."

Stella's surprise was almost comical but she recovered quickly. "I told Cal there was something between you two, but he wouldn't listen. Can we go back now and make an announcement?"

Vashti made a move to accompany her but Jethro kept hold of her hand, pulling her back to his side. "We have a few things to do here first. Can you give us half an hour?" He glanced down at Vashti, his wicked smile glinting. "Or maybe forty minutes?"

* * * * *

MILLS & BOON®

n o c t u r n e™

AN EXHILARATING UNDERWORLD OF DARK DESIRES

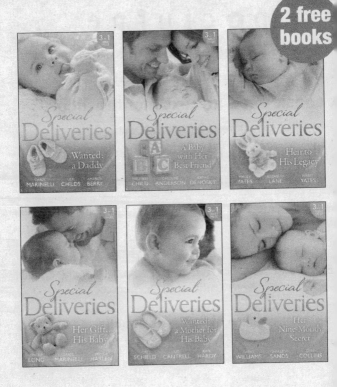